OATH SWORN

JACKY LEON BOOK ONE

K.N. BANET

Copyright © 2019 by K.N. Banet

All rights reserved.

No part of this book may be reproduced in any form or by any electronic or mechanical means, including information storage and retrieval systems, without written permission from the author, except for the use of brief quotations in a book review.

This is a work of fiction. Names, characters, businesses, places, events, locales, and incidents are either the products of the author's imagination or used in a fictitious manner. Any resemblance to actual persons, living or dead, or actual events is purely coincidental.

CHAPTER ONE
AUGUST 23, 2018

Summer in East Texas was never easy. When it wasn't over ninety degrees, it was humid and sticky, where sweat just made life miserable, even if it was cooling down a little. The pine trees that covered the area and the shade they provided weren't all that amazing. Normally, the pine needles had a tendency to get in places they shouldn't when someone tried to use the shade that was offered.

The heat was all I could think about as I stood behind the bar, closing my eyes and trying to ignore the pounding in my head. I could hear the news, which was the source of my growing headache, from the television in the corner of the room. I didn't want to think about what was being said, so I focused on the heat and wondering if it would ever end, like I did every summer just outside the small town of Jacksonville. It was ninety-five degrees and well past dusk. It didn't have the right to be this hot after the sun went down. Only Hell had the right to be this fucking hot, and East Texas wasn't Hell, no matter how hard it tried to be sometimes.

"For those who are just tuning in, we've got breaking news. Earlier today, the Dallas-Fort Worth Pack experienced a hostile takeover, unsanctioned by the Werewolf Council of North America. The Council is telling people to stay in their homes and not approach any werewolves that they may see, stating that during events like this one, a werewolf can be prone to lashing out at any perceived threats. Our Governor here in Texas is also asking people of the Metroplex to use caution and lock their doors tonight."

And the werewolves in DFW didn't have the right to be so stupid, but they were wolves. I kind of figured they were always that stupid, whether they had right to be or not. My head throbbed in annoyance. *Do they not understand that just because humans know about them, they can't run off and start small wars in the middle of big cities?*

"Jacky! Can I get another beer?" a rough voice called across the dimly-lit room.

With a sigh, I stopped staring out of the window and looked back over my patrons, wondering how long I had until I could toss everyone out. Because Joey, the man across the bar, was calling for me. Jacky Leon. Sometimes I loved when Joey, my most wonderful and consistent regular, called out for me, and sometimes I hated it.

Tonight, I hated it. I wasn't in the mood, and it was mostly because of the werewolves running around just about two hours away from me. Sadly, I had a job to do.

"Yeah. I got you, Joey," I said back, sighing heavily. I didn't need to ask what he was drinking or what he could possibly want. I already knew. See, Kick Shot was my bar and had been for six years. Joey was the most regular of the regulars. He never changed. He always wanted Blue Moon—ironic, really. I held it up. "I'm not coming to you. Get off your ass and come get your own damn beer."

"Ah, Jacky, don't you love me anymore? My knee hurts, and—"

"No. Six years now, Joey, and still you're asking me to play waitress. It's never going to happen. Get up, come get your beer, go sit back down." I shook the beer just a little, hoping he would just get up and do it without another comment. There were five other people in the bar tonight, slow for a Thursday, but that didn't mean I was suddenly also the waitress.

He groaned and pushed away from his buddies. It wasn't that I didn't like Joey, but I wasn't a waitress. I was the owner of the damn bar and I didn't run around and give people drinks. Not that there's anything wrong with waitressing, but I had tried that when I first opened the place and it hadn't gone well. I'd caught people grabbing their own drinks for free while I was running around. Now, I could have fixed the problem by hiring servers—or really, anyone—to help out, but I didn't. I was stubborn like that. I had wanted to own a bar by myself and work in it alone, so I did. If that meant my patrons had to walk twenty feet to get their drink, then so be it.

His friends were laughing at him as he walked to me, like always. Joey's friends were all locals like him and I knew all their names. Sometimes it felt like I knew everyone's name. John grew up in Jacksonville, the son of a couple of teachers at the high school. He'd gone to college and followed in their footsteps, becoming a teacher himself. Mark was new, at least by Jacksonville's standards. He'd lived there for five years and still was considered the new face. Adam was another local, and like Joey, once played football at the high school, dreaming of the pros. He married his high school sweetheart and just never left.

But Joey's special. I liked him more than most of my patrons, which was why I took a second beer out and put it next to the first.

"So you don't need to make the walk again any time soon. On the house," I explained, smiling kindly. He gave me a worried expression, looking over the two bottles. He picked up one, cracked it open, and took a swig before continuing to examine me.

"You okay, Jacky? Seems like something's bothering you."

"Why do you say that?" This was why Joey was special. He cared a bit more than most. I didn't know why and I probably never would, but he noticed things. He noticed when I was having an off day or needed some space. He sometimes stayed to help me close up, shooing people out when they wouldn't leave at closing. He was just too good of a guy, and sometimes I wanted to strangle him for it. Tonight was one of those nights.

"You seem distant, Jacky. Is this about the

werewolves in the city? I mean, DFW is just down the road..."

"It's nearly two hours away," I countered. "And why would the werewolves in Dallas have anything to do with me?"

"Oh come on, Jacky! Admit it already! You're a werewolf! We've known for years!" Adam called out from across the bar.

It started right there. Every voice in the bar rose, all asking or demanding for me to admit to something that I couldn't.

"I'm not a werewolf," I said politely, for probably the fifth time in the last twenty-four hours. Whenever the werewolves had drama that hit the news, I ran into the same question, the same accusation. "I'm not even sure where you keep getting this idea, Joey, but I'm not a werewolf." I had to fight the deadly urge to go over the bar and smack the closest human to me, poor Joey, though I couldn't shake the feeling he deserved it for starting this up *again*. If I've told them once, I've told them a thousand times. I wasn't a werewolf. I would never be a werewolf. They just refused to drop it, much to my annoyance.

Sadly, I couldn't hit Joey over the head. It would probably kill him.

"You're always closed on a full moon. Let's just be honest here." He had a point. He had a very good point, but lots of places were now closed on full moons. No one, human or otherwise, wanted to go out when the werewolves were running.

"Lots of places are closed on full moons, including

half of town. It's the only thing that interrupts Friday night football at the Tomato Bowl. Speaking of, why aren't you down there tonight? You never miss a game, even the odd Thursday game." I grabbed a rag and began wiping down my bar, hoping the physical work would help me ignore the fools. Hoping.

It didn't. It never did.

"It's an away game tonight, Jacky. You would know that if you kept up with the schedule. I bring you one every year, and you never do. You should, if you ever want anyone in town to think you belong." He gave me one of those mock glares that was supposed to make me think he was mad, but all I could do was laugh. There was nothing scary about Joey and there never would be.

"I'm not a werewolf, so trying to belong and fit in with the local community isn't on my political agenda, so...I have the right not to care about the local high school football team and their ridiculously-named stadium in the middle of town," I retorted, shaking my head. They called the thing the Tomato Bowl. How was I ever supposed to take that seriously, or be remotely interested in it past making fun of it? "At least I remembered there was a game today...on a Thursday. Be proud of me." It was one of the reasons my bar was so empty when normally I could get ten or so people in on a weeknight, more the closer the weekend got. "Go drink your beer, Joey, and-" I looked over to my clock on the wall above the window I had previously been staring out of, "-I close in an hour."

"Fine, fine." He waved a dismissive hand at me, then

grabbed both his drinks and sauntered off. In another life, I would have found a saunter like that attractive, but Joey was absolutely not my type. Physically, he was fine, except the beginning of a beer gut. He was an average five foot nine, only an inch taller than myself, with a decent build. He had clean brown hair and nice brown eyes. He kept a perpetual scruff that didn't turn me off.

Like always, though, there were some problems. Off the top of my head, I could think of three. One, he was a blazing alcoholic, and that had always been a turn off for me. Two, I didn't fix men, and Joey was the type who needed a woman to come in and fix him. Desperately. I didn't have it in me. So, while he might have been attractive, I wouldn't overstep friendly bartender, no matter how kind he was. He could be attractive and kind might work with other women, but I was never going to fall for it. I couldn't.

Three? My kind didn't date humans. Never. Not even for a fling. Not even for a one night stand. It was completely out of the question.

An hour later, and the news was still talking about the werewolves in the Dallas-Fort Worth area. I still had a throbbing headache, which wasn't normal since I almost never got headaches, and Joey was long gone, earlier than normal.

"All right, everyone! Time to get the fuck up and get the fuck out!" I yelled over the news and the quiet country music that I naturally blocked out. I hated country, but the regulars didn't and it paid to keep them happy. "Move!" It was what I said every night, and like a good little herd of sheep, everyone, all of the three people left in my bar, stood up.

"G'night, Jacky!" one called, followed by the other two.

I waved towards the door, continuing to try and usher them out. I still had to clean up before I could leave and they were taking their sweet-ass time. "Goodbye, boys! Drive home safe or call Ubers!" If they even knew what Uber was, I'd be amazed. *Does Uber even get to this area? I have no idea.*

When I could finally lock the door behind them, I sighed. It was a normal Thursday night, really. I let my head fall against the door thinking about it. Another Thursday night in a tiny dive bar named Kick Shot off US-175. It was the life I had wanted six years ago when I opened it.

It was still the life I wanted, but it was lonely, and I wasn't afraid to admit that. It was lonely and tiring. I was open five nights a week, Tuesday through Saturday. Five to one. No one helping out, no one to go home to.

I was worse than Joey.

"Fuck. None of that thinking, Jacky. Think of the alternatives." Even saying the word alternatives made me remember exactly why I had chosen the life of bar owner outside a small town in Texas. The other options I had made me want to gag.

I cleaned up my tiny bar quickly. It wasn't much work on the quiet nights. I didn't balance the books until Sunday, so once I was done loading my dishwasher in the back and sweeping the floor, I had nothing to do except go home, if I even wanted to. I had a small apartment above the bar, along with my office, but I really only used it on the long nights when going home and coming back didn't seem worth it. Tonight wasn't one of those nights, something I was thankful for. My skin itched, which was a sign I needed to head home and stay there for the evening.

I walked out the back, locking the last door behind me. I didn't really need to, since I had no fear of anyone breaking in, but I didn't like taking chances.

Turning away from the building, I dismissed the idea of driving home. It wasn't very far to my house. Kick Shot was surrounded by the pine forest that marked the area. Pine trees for miles, endless amounts of them going over the horizon. I nestled my bar in them so that I could hide a house out in the middle of my property. Most thought I never left the bar at all, and the few who knew my house was in the middle of my property didn't know how to get to it.

There was a reason for that.

My skin kept itching and I rolled my shoulders, trying to loosen them up. It wasn't a full moon, but it didn't matter, because it was close enough to one, which made all of this a bit easier and explained the small itch I had. I stripped slowly, dropping my clothes into a gym bag. Some women kept purses. Me? I kept a gym bag on me at all times. Normally it was tucked behind the bar where the boys never saw it, but I always took it with me when I left. Once I was naked, I zipped the bag up, making sure the strap was in a good position for me to grab.

Joey and his friends, always asking me if I was a werewolf. Always wondering what the mysterious woman behind the bar could possibly be. They had no idea. If I lived my life right, they never would. Unlike the werewolves, my kind were very private.

The change flew over me the moment I asked it to, taking me down onto all fours. For less than thirty seconds, my bones broke and rearranged themselves, my muscles and tendons moving to fit over the new structure, the new body. It was over in less than a minute, amazingly fast by werewolf standards. They took nearly twenty minutes to shift, the poor mangy bastards.

See, Joey and his friends were half wrong and half right, but that wasn't something I could ever tell them. I wasn't a werewolf.

I was a werecat.

Now, werewolves? They looked like wolves. Big wolves, but still wolves. Werecats? I looked like something out of a prehistoric documentary with bad CGI and some scientist talking over it. I had five inch saber fangs and a strange tan and spotted pattern. Whatever cat werecats were supposed to be was long extinct. It made things very interesting when people caught us out and about, which was exactly why that could never happen. The werewolves were out to the world, but not the werecats. We couldn't be.

And if people thought werewolves were big, they had no idea. I was just about as large as a male lion, which was to say, incredibly big. Human, I was five foot eight, weighing all of one hundred and fifty pounds, with a little bit of curve to me. Just a little, but I was proud of it, since getting any sort of curve as a werecat was practically impossible. As a werecat, I was four feet at the shoulder and roughly four hundred and fifty pounds. Massive, and roughly two hundred pounds heavier than most werewolves.

I gingerly grabbed the strap of my bag with my clothing and started to trot away, sniffing the air as I went. There were no humans anywhere near me or where I could see. I dove into the pine trees, heading straight for home. It was fun, more freeing than anything I could have ever imagined. I could really run when I wanted to, and while I sometimes hated what I was, I never hated this. There would never be a time when I hated the run.

As I went, my magic connected with the land, telling me everything I could ever want to know, like where potential prey was. I generally hunted whitetail since their population was always at risk of running amok in the region. I did my part, and it helped that even when I was human, I had a serious love for venison.

Werecats have a special magic with the land. We're a part of it and it's a part of us. We claim territory, which could be huge or very small depending on our strength and needs. Our connection with our territory means everything, from the day we claim it to the day we lose it. Mine was thirty miles in every direction from my home, a large circle if I ever bothered to draw it on a map. It was a sizable plot, but not the biggest I could potentially hold. I knew deep down I should have claimed a larger territory, but I never wanted to. I wanted a safe plot of land that was mine and didn't feel too threatening to any other werecats in the state. I didn't want to give anyone a reason to look in my direction, so I kept my magic close, never letting it reach out to try to claim more than I wanted. Six years before, I had claimed even less than what I had now, but had very slowly spread it out until I was comfortable.

There were a few reasons for that. I needed the leg room, for one. Two, a werecat could only safely hunt on his or her territory.

I had been warned that trying to keep my territory while roaming away from it would bite me in the ass. Like the idea of leaving my bar unattended, it was something I had learned quickly to correct.

It only took two minutes for me to find myself on my back porch. It took less than that for me to turn back around and run off, wanting to keep stretching my legs.

It felt so good. I didn't shift often enough, not nearly often enough. I tried for once a week, and there was really no excuse for me not to, but I was bad like that. I had never been a good werecat; I would never be a good werecat. I could only try, and even that felt too hard most of the time.

In the attempt to be a good werecat tonight, I sniffed out a whitetail deer nearly ten miles from home and took it down without thinking. Hunting came naturally, as I was ridden by animal instincts I couldn't control sometimes. It saw prey, and the feline beast I shared my body with wanted that prey. I had to be careful, thanks to that beast. The werewolves didn't admit it to the humans, but our animals thought they were prey too. It made things dangerous and was why I didn't worry about being closed on full moons. Everyone was. No one wanted to be out when the monsters were. Joey didn't know it, but it kept him safe too. I could never risk them visiting while some employee I didn't want was at the bar. It made them easy prey.

I don't know how long I ran, really. I could see the dangerous tinge of dawn just beginning to creep over the horizon when I was back on my front porch and triggered the change back into my human form.

"Fuck," I groaned, leaning against my back door. It was always painful, and the faster I could do it every year, the more it felt like it hurt. Maybe the pain was just too concentrated; I had no idea, but it wasn't pleasant. There was no fairy dust and seamless shifting for the moon cursed, wolf or cat. Our bodies just broke and healed into new bodies. It fucking hurt. Every time, it fucking hurt. For me, it'd been hurting worse, and my shifts had only been getting faster.

With that on my mind, I knew I needed to make a call. A call I would continue to avoid, because it was the worst call.

It was a call to family.

"Tomorrow," I promised myself half-heartedly.

2
CHAPTER TWO

Waking up to my cellphone blaring like a fucking police alarm wasn't the way I wanted to start my Friday. I didn't open my eyes, but I knew there was no way I was getting back to sleep. It didn't matter what time it was. I knew the ring tone. Even if it wasn't loud and obnoxious, the ring tone meant I was getting the call I had avoided making.

That was never good. In my world, it was possibly the worst thing that could happen.

Without opening my eyes, I reached out, groping for the phone. If I didn't pick up, he would just call again. And again. Then he would text, which was the last chance I would have to talk to him before he just showed up and invaded my territory.

Luckily, I grabbed my cellphone and yanked it off its charger before it stopped ringing. I was able to hit the bouncing green symbol before it stopped.

"Hi," I said blandly, hoping the caller wouldn't realize I had just woken up.

"It's three in the afternoon, Jacqueline. Is there a reason you almost missed my phone call?" His deep voice made my bones vibrate.

I still didn't open my eyes, and holding back a yawn took effort. "I don't open the bar until five, Hasan. There's no reason for me to be awake before three," I answered, trying not to grow impatient with him. The call had just started. I would have plenty of chances to lose my patience. The beginning of the conversation was not one of them. "What do you need?"

"To talk to my daughter more often," he said casually, but I knew him better than that. There was a tightness to the words that I figured only a few people in the world could notice, and I was one of them. Unfortunately.

Daughter. I despised the word to the very core of my being, but I wasn't foolish enough to refute it. I would never call him Father or Dad, but I wasn't stupid enough to tell him I wasn't his daughter. In the eyes of the werecats, I was. A werecat who Changed a human was that new werecat's parent. Mother or father to daughter or son. It didn't matter if there was any relationship previously. It was just their way. I had spent the first year of my new life as a werecat arguing against it to no avail. It wasn't even a bad thing. Just a thing I hated, and for very personal reasons, not because the system was flawed.

So I knew better than to argue.

"That's not why you called, though," I retorted, my patience trying its best to walk away from my brain and leave me agitated. I held it in place, however, and waited for the real reason for my *father's* phone call.

"Jacky...did you hear about what's going on in the Dallas area?" He seemed cautious now, even worried.

I resisted a sigh. Of course he would be. While I fought hard against the familial tie his Changing me brought, he treasured it. Of course he would be worried about a little coup or hostile takeover just two hours from me.

"I saw it on the news. It's not my business and there's no reason it should spill over and cause me any trouble," I said quickly, trying to assuage his fears. If he grew too worried, I knew he would show up, and that did no one any good. We'd be at each other's throats within hours, and it wouldn't stop until he felt like I was safe. "I'm just out of their reach. I made sure of it. None of them have holdings within an hour of me."

"Yes, I remember," he said patiently, the tinge of worry gone. An act, certainly. Or maybe the worry was an act. I could never tell with Hasan. He was a strange man, somewhat removed from the world around him. I knew it was because of his age, but I wasn't stupid enough to say it out loud to him or to anyone else.

He was over two thousand years old. When werecats got that old, and not many did, they tended to get a bit withdrawn, like any aloof cat could—or at least that's what I had been told. They didn't feel the need to interact with the mortal world. They no longer adapted, they just existed.

"So..." I tried to think of anything to say, knowing the

conversation wouldn't be over until he wanted it to be over. The last time I hung up on him, he'd called back. When I didn't answer, he showed up. He lived somewhere around New York, but he owned a private plane. He could get to me faster than I could get out of the state I bet.

"Other than that, I had a feeling you would need to talk to me. You're approaching the end of your first decade as a werecat. That's a milestone."

"Yeah..." I chewed the inside of my cheek, trying to remember what that was supposed to mean. Nothing came to mind, which wasn't good. I had probably forgotten a lesson, which reminded me of the reason I had wanted to make this very dreaded phone call. "I do have a question for you, actually."

"Anything, my dear," he said quickly. I could feel the anticipation. It was very rare for me to have a question for Hasan. I knew one other werecat that I preferred to call, but some things could only be answered by the one who Changed me.

"How fast do you Change?" I hoped the question wasn't insulting. There were some strange rules about werecats he'd once tried to teach me. I had told him to fuck off. One of those things was to never ask how old another werecat was. Not because it was a bad thing, but it was just rude. Like humans. As a human, I had never broached that topic since I had been good at eyeballing someone's age, but as a werecat, that changed. There was no way to tell someone two thousand years old from twenty-five. It made things sticky and a bit more complicated. Now I just had to hope that asking a shifting question wasn't rude.

"Hm. That's interesting. Why?"

I took a deep breath, closing my eyes again. I had been really hoping he wouldn't ask why. "I've been getting faster and it's been getting more painful. I want a baseline to compare to. You're it, as the werecat that Changed me."

"Ah, yes. I Change in less than two minutes. Fast by anyone's standards. Most werecats take about five minutes. You've been getting faster? You were at ten minutes when you left here. Good for a youngling, but not quick."

"I did it in your time last night," I whispered. It was actually a lie. I had done it faster, but he didn't need to know that. "The pain thing..."

"Worried you, I'm hearing. Yes. It's like growing pains. The body isn't accustomed yet to the speed at which it's doing it. It'll take some time to adjust to the new speed. Once you hit a consistent speed at which you Change, you'll rebuild your tolerance for it." He sounded like he was beaming with pride. "Two minutes at only a decade old. That's exceptional, my darling daughter. I hope you know that. It's unheard-of. If you were at five minutes, I would have been proud, but that's just..."

"Okay, it's good. Thanks. Now, I need to get up and get moving for the day, Hasan, so I'm going to let you go."

"Stay away from the dog trouble until their keepers get them well in hand, please."

"Will do. Goodbye." I wanted off the phone call and I

wanted off it now. I didn't like anything that I'd just heard. Not that his praise wasn't kind or anything, but I hated being different. He made it sound like I was very different. Different didn't fit with a quiet, ignored life. Different stood out. Different was challenge and change.

Different was bad and I wanted no part in it.

"Goodbye, Jacqueline," he said slowly, obviously annoyed my goodbye wasn't endearing enough. He knew I wanted off the phone. It was an interesting conundrum. I was the modern one. All of thirty-six years old in human years, including the ten I'd spent as a werecat, and yet I wanted to get off the phone call more than the ancient who didn't want an email until I forced him to get one.

I waited for him to hang up, and once he did, I dropped the phone and groaned. "Fuck me."

I hated surprise phone calls. I should have known it was coming the night before. Of course he was watching everything that happened within two hundred miles of me. Why hadn't I realized he was going to call? It was probably because I personally gave no shits about what the werewolves were doing. They were an annoyance and a headache, because I couldn't wrap my mind around their stupidity, not because they were actually a problem.

As long as it didn't spill into my territory, it *really* wasn't my problem. I might have my issues with it, but I was a werecat. I respected and followed the bounds of my territory. I made no actions outside of it, ever. I even went a step further. I didn't even shop in the city. I never left. I ordered everything online or made do with what I had in Jacksonville and the portion of Tyler that was my space.

I knew the dangers of playing outside my own land. It left me open to roamers, werecats who put no roots down. If they never entered my home, I could ignore them. If they did, I had to force them out, and fast, or they could challenge. If I left my territory and ran into one? It was a fight no matter what.

Werecats were nothing if not vicious. Territories were safer than roaming, even if they needed some defending. Another werecat would instinctively avoid my home unless they were looking for trouble. It led to fewer fights, or so Hasan told me. If eight fights in six years was less than average, I really didn't want to know what average was.

I tried to stop thinking about it as I got out of bed. That was it. A werewolf war nearby would also draw the eye of anyone I might have pissed off. There were a few—which was funny, since I had never done anything to any of them. Well, I had never done much to them.

"Stop thinking about it, Jacky," I mumbled to myself, shaking my head. There were things I wish I had never done. Things I wish I could get rid of, wipe clean from my history. This wasn't one of them, no matter how hard I tried over the last six years. "This better all blow over."

I showered and left for Kick Shot before my mind could get too stuck on the current situation. If I kept my head down, no one would remember I was here except Hasan and my only friend in the werecat world, Lani. I walked to Kick Shot today, smart enough to know that shifting in broad daylight was moronic. I normally had a dirt bike I took between, but it was in the shop getting repairs. I knew I would need to replace it soon, but I was attached to it. It was one of the few things I had bought with my own money once I moved here.

It also helped me escape the midday heat faster. It was ninety-eight and humid. Every supernatural creature had a problem with places this hot. It led to most of our kinds becoming more nocturnal than we already were. Monsters go bump in the night and all that. Humans were the only diurnal intelligent species. Everyone else? Werecats, werewolves, fae, vampires, witches, and who knew what else? We played in the dark. We played out of sight, out of mind, though some species started thinking that wasn't good enough. Hence, werewolves being on the news and everyone locking their doors around the full moon, no matter how safe their neighborhoods were.

Unlocking and walking into the bar, I sighed happily, thankful I left the AC on overnight. It didn't always help, but there was a difference between eighty and ninety-eight. I would take what I could get, really.

I got to work, trying to drown myself in it. I pulled stock around, opening my books to do inventory before opening the bar. I had several different crates and boxes of booze that I needed to get on the shelves, and what better time than the present?

I worked quietly and quickly, keeping my inventory in check. It was fifteen 'til five when I was done, right on time. Turning on the TV in the corner as I went, then the radio, because I knew better than to leave it off, I went to the door, watching the clock. The minutes ticked by slowly and the moment five hit, I unlocked the bolt on my front door. I was back behind my bar by five-o-two, like I was five days a week, Tuesday through Saturday.

My routine. I lived by it. When control over being what I was frayed and began to threaten to break, I could always rely on my routine. It was one of the most important things I could have, and my touchstone to reality to stop the Last Change.

There always came a time, werecat or werewolf, where our bodies couldn't keep the separation any longer and clashed into a war that would never end. It was the source of every horror story version of werewolves in Hollywood, though the humans were ignorant to it.

The last time a werecat hit the Last Change? My kind still whispered about it in dark corners, their eyes full of fear.

I tapped the bar, waiting patiently for anyone to show up. Joey and his friends arrived first. Then it became a constant stream of people, a few walking in every thirty or so minutes. I stayed behind my bar, serving out drinks to anyone who wanted one. Being the smart bartender I was, I kept tabs on everyone, my memory too good to fail me as long as I didn't drink.

"So, is tonight the night?" Joey asked casually, sitting at the bar in front of me.

"For what?" Rolling my eyes, I took his empty beer bottle and handed him another Blue Moon.

"For you to tell us you're a werewolf. Come on, Jacky. Jacky fuckin' Leon!" He gave me a desperate look, leaning over so that I couldn't avoid his face when I looked down to work on something.

"You know werewolves aren't the only things that go bump in the night, right?" My patience was wearing thin already. He was a smart human. He knew there was something off about me, but I wasn't foolish enough to ever tell him what separated us. The world was already dealing with the fact that werewolves were real. They even knew of the fae now, though the fae were still living in human disguises. A few witches were even going public, though it wasn't going as well for them. Salem wasn't that long ago.

"Are you a witch?" He blanched, and I couldn't stop a laugh. Of course he would pick the one everyone seemed most scared of. I didn't really understand it, but it was probably because witches were the easiest target. They didn't have the illusions of fae or the strength of werewolves. They were humans with some magic. They were the same, yet different from their own kind.

Different is bad.

"No, you fucking idiot. I'm just saying, you always ask werewolf and maybe you can shake it up sometimes. I mean, it doesn't change the answer!" I was still chuckling as he glowered at me. I pushed his new beer to him slowly. "I just wanted to own a bar, Joey. This happened to be a good place to do it."

"Fine." He swiped his drink off my bar top and walked away.

I felt stung for a moment until I reminded myself that Joey wasn't a friend. He was different than my other patrons, more willing to reach out and talk to me, but friend wasn't it. Really, if I thought he was a friend, I might have brought him into my life, exposed him and given him something better than what he had.

I also heard his friends, and several other humans in the area, talk about supernaturals. It made my stomach twist into knots. They always wanted to know if I was a werewolf. Why would I ever admit that to men who thought a werewolf skin might look good as a rug? Sure, they were joking. Texas was a hunting state, and I was one of those hunters, but they didn't make the small connection that a werewolf pelt to a supernatural was the equivalent to having human skin as wallpaper. It was disgusting and distasteful. It was inhumane. There was no way in Hell that I would ever tell them that I was a werecat. I would be a new and shiny thing, a unique pelt to adorn their walls and floor.

I ignored most of the humans for several hours, working and being pleasant, but not open to small talk. I couldn't find the mood. The werewolf drama already had me edgy, and from the TV and the news, it didn't seem like it was going to quiet down any time soon.

"The Werewolf Council of North America has stated that they are going to send in their own team to help stabilize the precarious situation. After the initial violence, there have been no injuries or fatalities reported, but we still recommend all humans lock their doors after getting home and not stay out past midnight. The deposed Alpha is still currently missing, believed dead. His family, two werewolf sons and a human daughter, are also missing as well."

I sighed, ignoring the woman at the bar waiting on a

beer while I listened. God damn. There was a human girl involved. By the Law, she was exempt from all supernatural politics. No werewolf was allowed to hurt her, no matter who her father was. I hoped that her brothers had taken her to safety and someone who could care for her, since their father was most likely dead.

"Jacky, I want my beer. Worry about your packmates later," the woman said, snappy.

I worked hard to keep my mouth closed and not bare my teeth at her. "Sorry, I'm not a werewolf—therefore they aren't my packmates. It's just interesting. I hope everyone is going to be okay up there." I grabbed a beer from the ice behind the bar. I wanted to be mad, as I finally got the human woman her drink. Mad that a child was out there, in the middle of the mess, but I couldn't. I knew the score. She was probably safe, no matter what side had her. Even the reckless wolves took that sort of thing seriously. Children were precious, and humans were supposed to be safe. End of story.

My grip on my rag tightened. It wasn't like this wasn't normal. It was just too close.

"How does a werewolf even have a human daughter? Did he adopt her?" The woman didn't leave, and I finally looked over to see who it was.

"Kelly, it's public knowledge that werewolves and humans can breed. Their children can be either. Some are born werewolves, some are born human. They've done DNA tests before to prove it." The same could be said of werecats.

"Who would ever want to breed with a dog?" She was laughing as she walked away.

I wanted to whack her on the side of her pretty blonde head. Werewolves weren't dogs and it wasn't illegal, though some states and countries were trying to make it. In my mind, as long as whatever was going down happened in human bodies, I didn't care. Werewolves were out and they had always been more lax about their secrets than werecats. They never had the rule to not fornicate with humans, and it was something that'd been going on for hundreds of years, if I remembered my history lessons from Hasan right.

It was near midnight and Kick Shot was as packed as it would ever be. I had nearly forty people in the bar, and the music was turned up louder than the TV now, much to my chagrin. It was still giving updates on the situation in Dallas-Fort Worth, updates I desperately needed.

There was a faint knocking for a moment and I frowned. I had better hearing than any other supernatural race, and that included the weird cousins I had in werewolves. Their sense of smell was a touch better than mine, but my hearing outclassed theirs by miles.

So the faint knocking I heard coming from the back of my building stood out to me like a siren. I tensed up, wondering what could possibly be making the noise. It wasn't something I had ever heard in my little bar. Ignoring my patrons, I started walking.

"Hey, I need a drink!" someone called out.

"Hold on!" I snapped. "If you reach for a freebie, I'll

take the hand. Clear?" I turned and pointed at the guy who yelled for me. "Two minutes. You can wait two minutes."

"Yes ma'am," the man said, settling into his seat. Normally I would never leave the bar during the busiest time of night, definitely not on a Friday, but the knocking was still going, and it wasn't just getting louder because I was getting closer. Whatever it was, it was hitting harder.

I swung the door open to my staircase and found nothing, so I looked at my back door. Someone was knocking on it. That someone now seemed desperate. I closed the door to the stairwell and opened the back door. I didn't see anything for a moment until my eyes trailed down to the eye level of my visitor.

"Oh for fuck's sake," I muttered.

I knew the face the moment I saw it. I felt the nearly undeniable urge to close the door immediately and without regret, but resisted it. I waited in silence, hoping I didn't hear the words I knew I was going to hear.

She searched through a backpack, the little human missing thanks to the turmoil in the big city. She couldn't be more than ten. I watched her pull out a wallet, obviously not hers—or maybe it was. I had no idea. Maybe it was a go-bag. I couldn't tell, but it was her size and that was troublesome for some reason. She pulled a business card out of the wallet and looked back up to me, big grey-blue eyes looking terrified.

"I am...I'm Carey Everson." Her voice trembled and shook, but she had to say it all. She had to. It was the only way she was going to be able to drag me into a small war I wanted no part in. There were questions I needed answered once those words were said, but she had to first get through the ritual. If I acted without the ritual, a war would start, one much bigger than the one her father was probably dead to. "I'm a human. Uh…I am eleven years old…"

"Just get to the important parts," I whispered softly. There was no reason to give me her life story yet. "I know you're human." I could smell it. There was a faint scent of werewolves on her, but she was human. There was no doubt in my mind about that.

"I need protection from the super…supernatural community. I am at risk of losing…" Tears began to spill from her eyes. "My life through…no fault of my own. I am requesting protection from fang and claw from another with fang and claw. I am requesting that the werecats uphold their duties to the supernatural… community and protect me from all threats inhuman." Her jaw was shaking, but her words were stronger at the end. Her large, lost grey-blue eyes were hidden by her limp, ash-brown hair. I figured that hair was normally a rich oak color, but running for your life had the tendency to wash the color out of someone. She looked up at me again, slowly and shaking. "Please. They probably killed Daddy. They want to kill me too."

I took a deep breath and reached out, pulling her to me slowly. I had to give her an answer. If I rejected, it would start a war, but I would never reject her. No, children were precious, no matter the species. There was only one correct way this could go down, even if I didn't want it. I had a duty, no matter how much I wanted to ignore it. This human girl had no reason to be in such fear.

"I, Jacqueline Leon of the werecats, hereby do swear to protect you from all threats supernatural until which time I feel you are in safe hands of family or friends that mean you no harm. I hereby do swear that your life is now in my hands and can be trusted there. I shall treasure your humanity and treat you as one of my own. You, from this moment until which time I know you are safe and no longer need me, are my child of this earth. You will be given all things in accordance to this. Carey Everson, you are hereby under the protection of the werecats."

The words were soft and broken by tears. "Thank you."

I was officially called to Duty. I moved to East Texas to get away from all the trouble of the supernatural community and it found its way to my bar.

Of course.

3

CHAPTER THREE

My world changed in that instant and I knew it. I held her to my chest, comforting even while I began to do my Duty. My magic roared in answer to my call, telling me every living thing that dared walk on this night. For the moment, there were no other supernatural predators to worry about. The moment any dared to come into my territory, I would know, and I only had one way to properly respond while protecting humanity from the threat of my cousins.

I would have to kill them. Brutally and without mercy.

"Come inside," I whispered. "Come in. I have an apartment on the second floor. I want you to go up the stairs and into my apartment. Get comfortable. I'll be there as soon as possible."

She only nodded, still curled into my chest, holding me like her life depended on it. It did, really. I removed myself, though. If her life was really in danger, and she was behaving like it was, then we couldn't stand outside the bar all night.

Once I was able to untangle from her, she ran up the stairs. I took a deep breath, locking my back door the moment I knew she was up and waiting on me. I turned back for the bar and walked in, knowing I probably didn't look like happy-go-lucky Jacky Leon anymore. I went straight for the radio, ignoring everyone talking to me, trying to stop me and find out what was wrong. It took ten long strides and I hit the power button with force, breaking the machine.

"We're closing early!" I roared. "I need everyone to leave now!"

Silence greeted me.

"NOW!" I didn't have time for this, and thankfully, my patrons realized. They started pulling out their wallets and I shook my head. "If you have an open tab, it's on the house tonight. I have a family emergency and I need all of you to leave so that I can go deal with it."

"Jacky..." Joey was the only one who dared come within five feet of me now. "Um..."

When he came closer, I could see it. I cursed, covering my face, rubbing my eyes. I could see the gold glow that had been reflected back at me. I should have realized that was going to happen.

"I'm not a werewolf," I whispered to him, looking back up at his face, hoping he knew to drop the topic and drop it now. "Please, Joey. Get everyone out of here."

This was a mess and there was no way I was going to be able to clean it up. I had better control than this, but the stress was already weighing on me and my feline was clawing and spitting to get out and defend its new charge, the crying human girl that I could hear in the apartment. Hopefully they only saw the gold and not the cat pupils that normally came with it.

"Let's go everyone! Jacky's got family problems and we need to let her handle them."

I watched them leave. I watched the glances over their shoulders, curiosity in their eyes. Most were harmless. Some were suspicious, wondering what monster was hiding in their community. It was a mess I couldn't clean up yet. Protecting humanity was higher on my to-do list than keeping the Secret. It had to be, especially if a little girl's life was possibly on the line. I locked the door behind the humans and watched their cars leave. All the while, I kept in touch with my land and my magic, hoping nothing crossed my borders.

"God damn it," I whispered, closing the blinds next. I turned off the TV and the lights as I walked out, heading for the back staircase that led to my apartment and office. I hauled myself up in record time, taking several steps at a time. The girl was still crying, and that drove me faster.

Werecats were protective to the point of insanity. Being solitary creatures, when we made a claim, no matter how temporary, we defended that claim to the death. It was part of what led us to the role we now played in the supernatural community.

I didn't burst into my apartment. I had more sense than that, even if the tears had me wanting to go in and destroy my own furniture for offending my charge. I walked in quietly, searching my dark apartment for her. My night vision was perfect. It wasn't in color, but it was perfect. I knew from the glow around my eyes that I hadn't been able to go back to my human eyes. There was probably going to be very little that made me feel safe enough now to calm down.

"Carey?" I called gently. "We need to talk." I knew she was on my couch, but I wanted her to know I was coming. I wanted her to feel safe enough to tell me where she was. I had never been called to Duty before, but I knew instinctively how to handle it. *Kind of*.

"I'm here," she answered, her voice gentle and broken. Scared. She was so scared. Her fear filled the air in my apartment, soaking everything with it. It would be weeks before I lost all traces of the fear she felt.

"Hi," I whispered, rounding the couch and sitting on the other end. She was a scared little doe and I couldn't invade her space without risk of her losing her ability to trust me. "We're safe right now, but we need to talk about a few things."

"Will we stay safe?" she asked, sitting with her legs pulled up to her chest. She seemed so small. There was probably a time in my life that I seemed that small, but those memories were gone now. Becoming a werewolf or werecat came with risks. One of those was that sometimes holes appeared in the human memories. No one knew why, and many were lucky it didn't happen to them. I wasn't one of the lucky ones. I didn't remember any time of my life from six to twelve. Her age.

"You'll always be safe with me," I promised. "I swore to protect you. If anyone wants you, I can and will stop the threat to you. You have to understand that a werecat takes the Duty more seriously than our own lives. We honor the Duty and *nothing* will ever stop me from fulfilling it. I will see you to permanent safety, Carey. Do you understand what that means?" It was hard asking a small child that. I was asking her if she knew I was going to kill anyone who came for her if they meant her harm. Not just defeat them. Not just scare them away. I would kill them, and I wouldn't feel guilty for it because she placed herself in my care.

From the blazing look that came into her eyes, she understood. "Yes."

I resisted a smirk because it was inappropriate, but I wanted to. She was the daughter of a werewolf Alpha. No amount of sheltering would ever protect her from the harsh realities of our world. It was a sad thing, but it also made her strong. She had come this far, which reminded me that she already had steel there in her spine, even if she was afraid.

"Okay, now I need you to answer a few more questions for me. How did you even know I was here?" That was important. No one outside of the werecats knew where I was, and most of them just stumbled on me, shocked at who they found in the borders of the territory. The werewolves should have never known. I was so careful.

"Daddy told me you were here. He gave me this." She thrust out her arm, holding that business card I had seen her read off. I took it slowly and read it, flipped it over and read the back.

What I read made me growl softly. Not because it was bad, only annoying. Her damn father had given her a business card with the words of Duty, which I had already guessed, but he'd also put on the Rules of Duty. She knew exactly what she was going to get out of this new...relationship we were about to have. I eyed the girl and her big eyes seemed fearful again.

I shook my head, handing the card back. "Smart father of yours," I said politely. "Did he think there would be trouble?"

"A smart and wise Alpha always thinks there will be trouble, but never gets paranoid. He trusts his pack fully, but always keeps his most trusted at his back, because if he didn't, he would be seen as arrogant. He must be strong enough to stand on his own, but know to use the strengths of the wolves around him so that he doesn't insult them." She recited it as if it came from a book. For all I knew, it did.

"Who am I protecting you from?" I had a very good guess, but if she knew any names, that would be swell. Once I was done talking to her, I had to consider a game plan. I was officially her werecat and she was my human and a child. Legally, there was no one who could stop me from whisking her out of the country until I felt it was safe. I wouldn't do that, but I had to recognize that I could. I had to keep on my toes and remember that this could go terribly wrong for someone, most likely her.

"There were wolves. I didn't see any of them in their

human forms and I don't know their wolf forms well enough because I'm too young to be around too many werewolves. We were having game night and they came in. My daddy wasn't home, working late on pack business. It was just me and my brothers. Landon told me to run. I heard fighting. I don't really know, but it sounded bad. I started running, grabbing my bag for this like my daddy taught me, and I knew I had to get here somehow. I saw on my phone that my dad was missing and my brothers, like me. That means you're all I have."

"Because you don't know which of your old guards are trustworthy," I stated plainly. She was a damn smart kid, that was for sure.

She only nodded and the tears came back. "Why would they do this? We were all a family! Daddy said a wolf pack is a family and family never hurts each other."

"Oh sweetie, it's okay. You can cry. Come here." I reached out for her and she half-crawled and half was hauled into my lap. I rocked her gently, my protective instincts flaring up. It wasn't helped by the fact that I was female and she was a child. All I could feel in that moment was the need to kill whoever made the tears come. I needed to protect this child. It was my sworn Duty and I wouldn't stop until every single one of those wolves was dead and ash.

While I rocked her, I began to consider my options. The best bet was to hide her in my territory and contact the werewolf government when things settled down. They would understand that I was keeping her hidden for her own protection until they cleaned up their mess. I couldn't go to the city and fight the war to protect her. No. Caring for her was my utmost priority, and the wolves would know it.

I grabbed my cellphone and texted Lani, telling her I was called to Duty, and knew she would text me back soon, probably offering any aid she could. I sent a second, requesting any phone number to the North American Werewolf Council that could be safely reached by supernaturals. If she didn't have one of those, any number would do. There were codes that any supernatural could use to get onto a secure line if needed. It was already past midnight, so all of those things would need to be dealt with in the morning. Right now, I just needed to lay the groundwork. She would be safe for the night, because if any wolf dared to enter my territory before I called anyone, I could and would just kill them, no matter what faction they might be in.

She cried herself to sleep, which was both good and bad. I laid her out on the couch and tucked her in with a blanket, hoping she didn't get too hot. The AC in the bar wasn't as good as the AC at the house, but it was the safer location in the end. It had the road access my home didn't and that would come in handy if a hunting pack came for her.

I waited for Lani, hoping she would answer soon while I watched the sleeping little girl on my couch. Of course, the damn werewolf Alpha had known I was here. How could I be so stupid to think that just because I never caught surveillance that there was none? In the end, it didn't really change my life too much.

Except for the fact that it meant I was now the only thing between his daughter and a possibly horrifying death.

Lani didn't text. My phone, at full volume, started blaring the annoying country song I had put for her ringtone. I fumbled with it like a fool as I tried to hit the answer button before Carey woke up.

"God damn it, Lani. I said text me!" I snapped, trying to keep my voice down. Carey was thankfully still asleep. If I guessed right, she had probably been running from the moment her brothers told her to, and that meant she was run ragged. The news of the takeover came out on Thursday. It was now Saturday morning. The poor girl had taken nearly three days to get to me.

"You were called to Duty, Jacky? Explain." The other werecat didn't waste any time, that was certain.

I quickly ran down exactly what I knew. Alpha's human daughter showed up at my bar. I closed down. I didn't tell her anything about accidentally exposing I wasn't human. Not yet. Carey was the number one priority. The rest of the mess would have to wait. It had to.

When I was done, I just listened to silence. Lani wasn't even breathing.

"Lani?" I sounded like a child myself in that moment. When I had run from my 'father' and claimed this private life in East Texas, Lani, a smaller-than-average female, had shown up at my doorstep. She had been confused at the presence of a new werecat in Texas. She didn't know who I was or who my 'father' was. She just knew I was new and wanted to get to know me. Since then, she's been my tentative ally, my only werecat to phone when I had questions or needed advice. Since I wasn't keen on ever talking to Hasan, I called her more than him.

"It's been nearly a century since something this big has been invoked for Duty," Lani answered carefully. "Do you understand that the Duty is going to put you in the middle of a werewolf turf war and you will potentially declare the winner?"

I swallowed. "Yes."

"Good. You cannot give her to anyone until they settle this among themselves."

"I know. I was planning on keeping her until the dust settled. What happens if the winner means her harm?" It was an important question.

"You keep her. Your Duty becomes a lifelong commitment. It hasn't happened in centuries, but it's happened. You need to tread carefully. Do you have a lawyer?"

"Yes." Well, not really. I had Hasan's lawyer, who I begrudgingly used when things were desperate. Luckily, I almost never needed a lawyer. Sadly, this was desperate. "I'll get him started on the paperwork needed for the human world once I'm off the phone with you."

"It doesn't have to be real. Just something to keep human cops off your back. What else are you planning?"

"To deal with the 'she's missing' problem, I'm going to contact the werewolves' council and have them make an announcement that she's been found, to call off the search and continue managing things in the city. They won't be stupid enough to think I can't protect her."

"Don't get overconfident. There's a lot of wolves in DFW. A lot. Last count I heard was seventy-five. Now, this turmoil might break them up, but a werecat your age might be able to handle five, ten if you're lucky. You can't take twenty or thirty. Hell, I've been around for a few centuries and I couldn't take the Dallas-Fort Worth pack."

"My Duty is to protect Carey Everson, daughter of the deposed Alpha of the Dallas-Fort Worth pack. I will do my Duty, Lani. It's not overconfidence. It's fact." I tried my damnedest to put as much truth in those words as I could. I couldn't fail. It wouldn't just look poorly on me. It would look poorly on all werecats—and Hasan. I might dislike the man for several personal reasons, but I wasn't going to fail in this. Not even for him or the werecats.

There was a strong, scared little girl on my couch who outweighed all of them.

There was silence. I could hear Lani breathing now, obviously trying to stay calm. "Be safe. Call if you need any more information. I'll text a number I know for the wolves."

"Will do. Thank you." I hung up first, not worried about Lani like I was with Hasan. My phone dinged only a minute later. I texted the family lawyer first, explaining I was called to Duty by a minor. I needed anything I could get my hands on to make it legal to the humans. He responded instantly, which wasn't strange. He might have been human, but he worked for monsters. He had to be nocturnal because we were. Thanks to client privilege, he wouldn't tell Hasan what was going on either. The last damn thing I needed was him showing up. He would start a damn war no one needed.

Finally, I punched in the number Lani gave me. It rang twice before a quiet and tired woman answered.

"Hello. This is the North American Werewolf Council's office. May I get your name?"

"Hello, I'm Jacky Leon and I need to speak with a wolf," I said quickly. "Fang and claw to fang and claw. Secure line, someone important."

There was an immediate beep. I had no hope I would get someone important, but it was worth a shot.

"George of the Atlanta Pack speaking."

"Are you important?" I asked immediately. "I need to speak with someone who has anything to do with the turmoil in Texas."

The wolf laughed at me. I gritted my teeth. "Like I'm going to give a stranger one of those lines. State your business and I'll think about it."

"How about this? I'm a fucking werecat called to Duty and you'll give me to someone in charge." I knew it would be easier to just explain what that Duty was, where I lived and the like, but I didn't give my information to random phone boys and that's all George was. He was some guy sitting in an office doing his pack's duty to support the council, and that was answering phones.

"Look here, kitten. I don't care if you're the president

of the fucking United States. You're a werecat and you're—"

"I have the Duty of protecting the deposed Alpha's eleven-year-old human daughter," I whispered harshly. "You'll give me to who I fucking want to talk to."

"Oh shit."

"Oh shit is right, you mangy mutt."

"One moment, Miss Leon." I was put on hold after that harried correction.

I nearly laughed. He wasn't the first werewolf I'd ever spoken to, and it was always a bit hostile, even though we've been at peace for over eight hundred years. A fragile peace, though. One that relied on two things. First, the werewolves had to stop hunting the werecats. Second, the werecats upheld and did their Duty. That was all that kept the peace between us. Not even the fae or vampires wanted the war to restart. It would spill into their communities, the human world, and probably beyond. It wouldn't end until one side was extinct.

That was why this was an entirely bad situation. If I screwed up, there could be an angry werewolf out there waiting to put a bullet in me, and then the war would kick off. There would be no peace if I got killed because of the Duty. Even failing the Duty wouldn't be grounds to kill me, though I had no intention of failing.

"Jacky Leon?" The voice was rich and calm, but tired. I could read the exhaustion in it, just by those two words.

"That's right. I take it you've gotten my message."

"It was explained to me. Where are you? I can send—"

I pulled the phone away for a second, giving it a confused look. "Excuse me? No? Why don't you tell me your name? Let's start easy here."

"I'm Harrison, Alpha of the Atlanta Pack. Forgive me, but you bring good news and we just wish to secure her—"

"She's secure now, and if you try to find and take her from me, I will consider it an act against her safety," I said softly, dangerously, letting violence roll through those words, knowing they would be clear. "Don't try to take her from me before I'm ready, wolf."

A moment of silence, at least over the call between us. Not complete silence, though. I could hear people talking in the background. I knew the call would have people listening.

"Then let me assist you. We will announce that she has been found and put into protective custody. What would be the terms by which you will accept that your Duty is over?" He was diplomatic and calm, but I didn't trust it. Really, in that moment, there were very few people I would trust. A life was my responsibility. I had no idea what threat level I was facing, therefore everything was a threat.

"There are a few factors," I began, taking a deep breath. "First, peace needs to be established in Dallas-Fort Worth. I don't care who's in charge, honestly, but peace. That way no one is feeling unstable and thinks to strike out against her in the future. Second, I would like someone of her family available—or all of them proven dead. I don't care how long that takes, but I need confirmation, because I won't hand her off to a family friend when I could give her to her father or brother." I considered if there was anything else. "Just so we're clear, I do have immunity from any repercussions that would come from me protecting my charge. That comes from the Laws."

"I understand the Laws," the wolf replied politely. "I will not have you get into any trouble for doing your sworn Duty, cat, unless you overstep them, like getting involved with the war itself. Don't forget your immunity only goes so far." He sounded severe, but sighed. "I agree with your terms, but they could take some time. Are you sure this is the course you wish to set yourself upon?"

I glanced at the little girl on my couch. "I'm positive."

"Okay. Please stay in touch with me. I will let you know if we catch any hunting packs leaving Dallas-Fort Worth that may be of concern to any felines in the state. Your phone number isn't even a Texas number. Did you know that?"

I grinned. "Of course I did. Do you think I'm an idiot?" I got the cellphone in Georgia, actually. He could trace me, certainly, but he also knew that coming after me would lead to dead wolves and a war. Or at least I hoped he knew that. "Don't track me." I figured the warning was necessary.

"We haven't been. I don't know if you keep up with the current Laws as they are applied to modern times, but once a feline on Duty declares they want privacy for their charge, using modern technology is considered just as criminal as using our noses." He was tired now and obviously a little shocked I didn't know that.

"Consider me paranoid." I had known, but it was always worth putting out the warning in my mind. No one could play the fool if the line was drawn early. "Goodbye."

I hung up before he said anything else. I didn't owe them anything more than that courtesy call, and that was all they were going to get. I looked around my apartment and decided it would be a fine time to get some work done. Carey was still asleep, and I left her on the couch so I could see her. I ducked into my office to grab my books and laptop, using the rest of the night to make sure my personal life wouldn't go to hell while I did this.

4
CHAPTER FOUR

I don't know exactly when I fell asleep, but I know when I woke up. Something touched my shoulder and made me jump clean out of my chair. I grabbed the broom near my dining room table, whirling around to find the threat, and stopped.

Carey giggled wildly, covering her face. She still looked worn and tired, with dark rings under her eyes, and in desperate need of a shower or bath or whatever eleven-year-olds did.

"Sorry. I've been awake for like an hour and I was getting hungry. And your phone was going off." She pointed to it on the table near my books. I sighed, rubbing my face as she continued to watch me like I was the most fascinating thing she'd ever seen. "My dad says that werewolves are a lot like real wolves. Are werecats like that?"

"I guess," I said, shrugging, trying to play it off. She had made me jump like people often did to their house cats and posted on the internet. I leaned the broom back against the wall and grabbed my phone, trying to act naturally. I called to the magic and it answered, telling me there were no threats on my territory. Good. That meant she wasn't followed, at least not yet. I had no doubt that a wolf or two would eventually show up, but as long as it wasn't a hunting pack, I could handle it. "What do you know about me?"

"He said you moved down here like five years ago. You own the bar below and you don't go anywhere or talk to anyone. He thought you had secrets, but as a werecat, those aren't my business or his." She shrugged. "I was busy learning about my family. He said I would learn more about things like you and the vampires when I was older."

"He's right. They aren't. I'll fill in some general things for you since we're going to be spending some time together." I considered what I should start with and went with the basics. "Werecats are very solitary by nature. We don't play nicely with others. We don't fit in with wolves because we don't play dominance games. We think we're the top predator and that makes us a challenge for werewolf Alphas. We can defeat them, but we don't want to rule because we don't want the community. It leads to chaos, and no one wants chaos." I yawned now, checking my screen.

There were a few texts and the most important were from my lawyer and Harrison, or so the text said. Each contained similar documents, and I sent the documents to my printer so that I could carry them. They were legal proof that Carey was in my care. I opened a browser and checked the news, letting out a long sigh of relief that the news was now reporting that Carey was in safe custody and removed from the danger in the cities.

"What else can you tell me? I've never met anything other than werewolves... and one witch. Well, kind of." She sat down and I eyed her for a moment. There was still a fear in her scent that wouldn't go away, which meant she was very good at hiding it. I wondered if it was because she grew up around monsters, predators. While they might have seen her as a member of their pack, she was still human. Her father, this oh-so-intelligent Alpha, must have taught her to never show that fear and she'd learned well.

"Um." I didn't really know what she wanted to hear. There was a lot I wasn't allowed to say, and she could definitely take back werecat secrets to the werewolves. I wasn't foolish. I didn't think she was spying, but I wasn't going to give her secrets to hold that weren't hers. "Nothing really. There's a lot of similarities between us and the wolves. Full moon makes shifting easier, and many can't resist the Change that night. New moons make it harder and some can't Change at all. You know, why don't you go take a long shower and I'll make us some lunch?" I checked the time. It was eleven in the morning. "Then we can figure out how this is going to work while you're here."

"Here?" She frowned at me and I frowned back.

"Yes. Here."

"You aren't going to go and save my daddy?" The

tears were back. "I thought you were supposed to..."

"Protect you. Which means we stay right here. I take care of you. I stop others from taking you. Your father is on a difficult road. He's an Alpha of a werewolf pack. I can't go save him. It's against the Law for my kind to interfere in that way." I knew the reality for her was harsh, but she needed to have it. There was nothing I could do against a wolf that wasn't a direct threat to her. If her father was fighting for his life, it was his fight. Not mine or his daughter's.

"That's not fair..."

"It's been the Law for a long time and it keeps a lot of people safe," I said gently, reaching for her.

She jerked away and stomped towards my bathroom. When the door slammed and I heard the water running, I had a feeling this was going to be a lot more aggravating than it really had the right to be. If this was the attitude I had just signed my life to, I was in for a long ride.

I sat back down and went back to my books, realizing that I had actually finished the night before. That was at least something. I checked my bank accounts from my phone and waited, yawning again as I stretched my legs under the table. I needed to shower and change after her.

When she came out, she was in the same dirty clothes. They weren't terrible, but they weren't good either.

"No changes?" I asked as kindly as I could. "We can run out and grab you something fresher."

"I have money," she said quickly, running for her bag near the couch. She pulled out the wallet and held it out to me. I took it and flipped it open, my eyebrows trying to crawl off the top of my forehead and leave. She had some serious cash and lines of business cards, all with important phone numbers all over the country.

"Whose wallet is this?" I asked softly, holding it up. I really hope she didn't steal it from another werewolf. There could be tracking in it.

"Mine. Dad and my brothers kept a bag made for me in case anything ever happened...like this. They put that in it with the money and the other stuff so that I had some ways to get ahold of people and find help." She took her phone out of the bag next and I snatched it, making sure it was off. I exhaled again when I realized it was. She grabbed it back, glaring at me. "What was that for?"

"I wanted to make sure no one was going to be able to GPS it," I answered, rubbing my face.

"I'm eleven. I'm not an idiot," she said with a prideful indignation that made me smile for the first time all morning.

"Fine. Good job. I'm going to shower. If you try to leave, I will come out, naked, and drag you in there to watch me. Clear?"

"Crystal," she muttered, rolling her eyes. "Like I would leave. You're all I've got."

"Yeah." I sighed again, walking away from her and heading to my bedroom in the apartment first. I grabbed a clean set of clothes and two extra towels, knowing she must have used the ones I kept in the bathroom. As I walked into the bathroom, I caught a glimpse of her making herself some cereal and let that ease me. She wouldn't run—hopefully. I didn't know why I was suspicious of it. It would be the stupidest thing she could do, but she was eleven, so stupid to me probably didn't seem so stupid to her. She was obviously angry that I wasn't going to go out and save her father and brothers, and that was a concern. Her father should have also explained that point when it came to werecats and their Duty to the other supernatural species and the humans of the world. The Law tied my hands, and it was for good reason.

I showered quickly, not giving myself the time to just enjoy the hot water pouring over me. I kept an ear open for her moving around in the apartment but no one was below and she never tried to leave, which was good.

When I stepped out, I was greeted by my reflection and it reminded me why I was doing this. My gold feline eyes were still there, the only marker that I was anything but human. Here I was, thirty-six, looking twenty-six, a werecat and beholden to rules and a lifestyle I didn't have any say in.

When I was human, I hated my brown curls because they were so normal. Now I loved them for that. I had a soft face which many took as me being a soft girl, but they couldn't be further from the truth. My body told a similar story. It wasn't cut or lean, but it didn't carry much excess fat either. It refused to put on any more weight, and I ate a lot to keep my calories up. As I kept staring at myself, my pupils constricted into the feline slits seemingly on their own, but it was probably my own anxiety over what I'd just gotten pulled into. I would need to wear sunglasses to make sure no one saw that outside, since I hadn't been able to convince them to go back to my hazel.

"Fuck me," I groaned softly, finishing up by brushing my teeth and pulling my hair back into a ponytail. I dried off and dressed, walking out into my living room, finding Carey immediately and watching her play on my computer. There wasn't anything there for her to find, so I wasn't sure how to react to the violation of privacy. I could stomp over and slam it closed. I could ignore it and let her know it was okay, even if I didn't feel that way. I wasn't good with children and it was becoming more obvious every second I stood there. She finally looked up and closed the laptop on her own.

"I was just wanted to…I don't know. I wasn't doing anything." With a shrug, she stood up and left my chair, going to another and crossed her arms, seeming smaller every second.

"You're fine. I have a few games on there if you want to kill the time, but maybe we should get you some clean clothes first. The best thing here is a Walmart, but it'll have what you need." I didn't know what sort of lifestyle this girl was used to and I didn't want to make any assumptions.

"Yeah, thanks." She stood up and grabbed her bag as we walked out. I led her out the back of my bar to my hatchback and held the door open for her. The strong shell of curiosity had obviously faded and now I was stuck with a somewhat sad little girl. Not that I could blame her. She was in a rough spot and one that I had the utmost sympathy for.

"So…" I had no idea what I was doing with an eleven-year-old. If her father was alive, I hoped he realized he sent her to possibly the worst werecat he could find for this sort of thing. I might have been the closest one to his pack, but I wasn't good with kids.

"Why do the Laws say you can't help?" she asked, and I could hear the sadness. Hopelessness and sorrow. She had really thought that I would help her dad. "I'm human, so I'm not taught a lot. Dad says if I decide to try and be Changed, I'll learn a lot more, but I'm too young to consider that, and now this…"

"The Laws," I said softly, staring out into the bright sun. I grabbed my glasses from the center console and slid them on. I didn't want to consider her being Changed one day. It wasn't my business, and I knew she was now seeing realities of her world that she thought would never touch her. Children thought their parents were indestructible. The shattering of that belief was something that shook everyone eventually. "Over eight hundred years ago, there was a very big and very deadly war between werewolves and werecats. I don't really know the why, but because of it, humans were starting to notice we existed and were not just scary stories. They started hunting all of us. Vampires, fae, witches. They were all caught in the crossfire too. They forced werecats and werewolves to sit at the same table and talk. The werewolves aren't as strong as werecats, but my kind were being driven to extinction. We wouldn't give up until one of our most ancient werecats forced us into the peace talks to save us.

"Well, the sides all sat down and we made the Law. The witches and fae used their magic to make the Law binding. Now, I'm really young. I've been a werecat for less time than you've been alive, so this is all secondhand." I stopped for a second, glancing at her. She just nodded, accepting that I might have some of this wrong. I didn't think I did. Hasan was ancient, and the likelihood he got anything wrong was low. It helped he was there when it happened. "The end agreement was simple. If we wanted the wolves to stop hunting us because we started the war, then we needed to give them something back. We're viciously protective over something we consider ours, and they used that. Now, we're not allowed to meddle in werewolf politics. We must also uphold the Duty to protect any human at threat through no fault of their own from supernatural species. It doesn't matter the threat; it doesn't matter the human. If a human approaches a werecat and gives me the ritual request for me to defend them, I do." I sighed.

"Do you know how the war started? I mean, you just said werecats did it..."

"No. No one has ever told me exactly how the war began, only the Laws we were left with. And the Laws aren't just for werewolves and werecats. The other big species all sat down as well, or sent representatives for the collective. Like the fae. There are hundreds of types of fae, but we look at them like a collective. There's Laws covering everyone." I shrugged. "There you have it. The Laws. Do you see why I can't help your father? I'm sure he's a nice man." Not really, but I knew I needed to make her feel good. "I just can't break an eight hundred year peace for one werewolf. I can't do it."

"I understand," she whispered, pulling her legs up to her chest.

The drive to Walmart was a short one and I got out before her, scanning the parking lot. There were no other supernaturals in my territory, no other predators that needed to be handled, but my own instincts drove me to even look at humans as possible threats. That wasn't a bad thing either. Every supernatural species employed humans. Normally it was for simple tasks like accountants and lawyers if the supernatural didn't have those skills or the time, but sometimes it was for dirty business.

Dirty business like capturing a little girl to use as a hostage, or worse.

"Come on, Carey," I said, thumping the hood of my hatchback as I walked around to her side. I got the door for her and closed it behind her, playing the perfect bodyguard. "What kind of style do you have? Anything in particular? We can also pick up some groceries—"

"You don't need to try and be my friend," she mumbled.

"You think I'm trying to be your friend?" I began to chuckle and it broke into a full out laugh as we walked across the parking lot. "Eleven-year-olds are not my friends. I'm trying to make this easier on you. There's no reason for you to starve while under my protection. There's no reason for you to do anything except hope your father is going to show up, okay?" I looked down at her, suddenly sad for her again. "Let me try to do this for you. You aren't the only person out of your comfort zone here."

"My dad might be dead," she muttered, crossing her arms as we walked. "He might be dead. My brothers might be dead, and..."

I saw the tears come and reached out for her, wrapping an arm over her shoulder. Gently, I pulled her to me and let her hide her face in my side as we walked. It was all I could do.

Grabbing a cart, I took us to her section for clothing first and waved over it. "Pick enough out for a week," I ordered gently. "This shouldn't last too much longer than that." I hoped, anyway.

She did as I asked, going to the racks and just taking things off, her eyes lacking any sort of spark of light. There wasn't anything I could do about that, no matter how much I wanted to. Seeing her, all I wanted was to go to the city and find her father and deposit him at her feet. I wanted to find the wolves that ripped this family apart and left this girl in my care, alone, possibly forever.

I couldn't even ask for updates, though. It would appear to be meddling. I couldn't find out anything for her, and I didn't feel comfortable with giving her a cellphone and having her talk to anyone. She needed to stay clear of everything too if this was going to be safe.

I should have paid more attention to my surroundings, but I jumped when someone came up behind me and began talking.

"Family emergency?" he said softly.

My heart wanted to climb out of my chest and go on vacation. I turned quickly to find Joey, his eyebrows raised. He looked slowly around me at Carey, his eyebrows going further up.

"Yes." I didn't have really much else to say. Well, except one thing. "I'm not a werewolf."

"That's getting hard to believe," he replied quietly.

"She's not a werewolf," Carey said, dumping more shirts into the cart. "I would know."

He eyed the little girl, looking back at me when she walked back to the racks, hopefully picking out jeans now.

"Don't ask questions with answers I can't give you," I warned. Maybe coming out into public wasn't the best idea, but she needed the clothing and there was no evidence that anyone would come out to Jacksonville to take her, not yet. Hopefully the wolves would be too busy fighting amongst themselves to cause any trouble for them. It was really all I had so far as a plan. "But I can tell you this is legal and calling the human police will just cause more problems for everyone involved."

"Ok." He shrugged and started to walk away. I sniffed the air, tasting its particular flavor as he walked farther away. He didn't trust what I had to say, but I didn't smell anything to worry about.

"Fuck," I muttered, then closed my eyes for just a second. I was cursing a lot in front of a kid. I needed to quit, but it had been a long time since I had to worry about who heard my mouth. I owned a bar, damn it.

I opened my eyes again to find Carey right in front of

me. She was watching me carefully, frowning. She was an odd child, or maybe I was an odd adult and knew nothing about eleven-year-olds. I had no idea which was right, but something about whatever we were was odd. Maybe it was the whole 'sworn to protect and maybe die for her' thing.

"You okay?" she asked, that frown never leaving.

"It's not a problem you need to worry about," I answered, giving her a tight smile. She didn't need to worry or care about how I would probably need to pick up and move after this. I was always careful about who and what I was. This was exposing me as anything but human. Sure, the annoying question about being a werewolf would probably happen anywhere, but my lack of oddness had kept suspicion at bay.

After this, nothing would be the same. They're all going to know I'm a freak, if not a monster.

"So, you want to pick up some food, too?" she asked, kicking one of her feet, looking as uncomfortable as I felt.

"Yeah— hey, do you play video games?" I wanted to find something to help pass the time and I personally loved them, but I didn't think Carey would be interested in anything I played.

"Yeah! I don't get to play them that often since my dad limits my screen time. Can we get some games?" Her face lit up into a real smile for the first time since I had met her. All I could do was nod, enjoying how lovely her eyes were when she was happy. They didn't seem so grey-blue anymore, instead looking more like the summer sky.

I ruffled her hair, smiling back. "Come on. I own a

Switch and you can get some games for it."

"You own a Switch?" Her jaw dropped and I couldn't hold back a laugh anymore.

"Yeah, though I never use it. I use my PC for everything." I started pushing the cart, keeping her next to me.

We hit up the electronics section and then I let her pick out a lot of junk food and snacks. I knew I needed to feed her real food, but I was already stocked up on everything I needed for a couple weeks. If I could treat her with a mini vacation during the mess her family and life had become, I would.

She was happier when we were back at the bar. Together, we managed to get everything upstairs and she changed into cleaner clothing. I kept her old, dirty, and torn things, putting them in a plastic bag. I didn't know why I wanted to keep them safe, but the urge was there so I followed it.

As I cooked dinner later that night, I figured things would be great for the week. Her father, no matter what happened to him, raised a good kid and she would be fine in the end. I just had to keep her distracted and happy.

That was, until my magic screamed at me. I gasped, dropping the wooden spoon I had been using to stir the chili I was whipping up. My chest tightened as I closed my eyes and focused, trying to decipher what my magic was telling me.

"Wolves," I whispered, knowing she couldn't hear me. Then I snarled loud enough that she jumped. "Wolves are coming."

CHAPTER FIVE

It took less than a minute for me to get all the information I needed. I started rambling, hoping Carey picked any of it up, since it was unnatural for me to tell others these sorts of things. Normally, I went on instinct. My magic would tell me of an intruder and that drove me to chase down the new predator in my territory. I couldn't do that this time, not if I wanted Carey to stay safe.

"They just entered my territory. They're moving too fast to be in their wolf forms, so they must be on US-175. That means they're coming right this way, or close by. They might be following a trail—or maybe they had a lead on where we are. It gives us roughly thirty minutes until they get here if they stay on the road." I locked eyes with her across the room as I turned the stove off. The chili was practically done anyway. "Carey, when I say hide, you will, is that clear?"

"Yes." She dropped the Switch and jumped off the

couch, twiddling her thumbs. "Um. What if they're my family? What if they're here to get me and take me somewhere safe?"

"That's not how this works," I answered. "Your father, if he knew how this works well enough to send you here, would know that I can't give up claim on my charge until I know without a doubt that he or she is safe. I told the big honchos that run things on this continent that I had two conditions for that. One was peace in the Dallas-Fort Worth area. The second is that I know your family is alive or dead and that no more trouble is coming their way." I ran a hand through my hair, looking up to my ceiling, trying to think of the best way to say what I needed to. "Carey, if these wolves are here, they *can't* be friends. Any allies we might have wouldn't come to try and take you from me or give away your position. Did anyone in the pack know I was here except your father?"

She only shrugged, which didn't bode well for me. I figured when she arrived that her father wouldn't tell anyone who he was planning to have protect his daughter, but secrets always got out. That meant I had to adjust. After this, I had to get her packed and into my car.

"Anything? Do you have anything that could tell me who these wolves might be? Who was in your father's inner circle? Who were his top five?"

"I don't know! They kept me pretty far away from pack things!" Carey threw her hands up.

I sighed, nodding. "Okay. I want you to grab your bag and the new clothes and take it all to my bedroom. I'm going to go down and secure the bar. You have to stay up here, okay? No matter what you hear or what anyone says to you, you have to stay here."

"Until?" Her big grey-blue eyes were wide in fear now. At least the severity of what was happening was sinking in.

"Until I come get you and we leave. They've come on my territory and they know better. There's only one way for this to end." I started walking, not bothering to grab shoes or anything. It would all be in my way anyway. When I reached the door, I turned back to her, watching her grab everything she could hold and begin to haul it out of the room. "Carey. These wolves might have been a part of your father's pack, but I need you to remember one thing for me."

"What's that?"

"That the loyalties don't matter anymore. Right now, every wolf from your father's pack is on their own until stability is brought back to the area. You can't trust them."

"But I have to trust you."

I winced at the bitterness in those words. I was telling her to not trust men who probably guarded her, helped raised her. They were probably honorary uncles and friends she watched grill with her father. She was probably friends with their children.

"He sent you to me," I said gently. "He didn't send you to them." Why? I had no idea, but I was absolutely planning on finding out when I got my hands on him. If he was dead already, I figured a witch might help me contact his spirit. That wolf needed a piece of my mind, and I fully intended to give it to him. "He sent you here, sweetheart."

"I know..." She continued walking after that, disappearing into my bedroom.

"Lock all the doors, then hide in the closet!" I called, turning to leave.

I jumped down the entire staircase, checking my back door first. I bolted it closed, then the secondary lock. I didn't need it for the area I was in. No, the extra locks were only because of what I was and the potential trouble being a werecat could bring me. Now they came in handy.

With that door secure, I pushed open the door that led to the bar. I propped it open. I needed to be able to see the staircase in case any of the wolves tried for it. I kept the blinds closed and went to the front door. It was locked, but that's not what I wanted. I flipped the latch, hoping the wolves would try it first. It was past dark now. Perfect.

Then I went to the bar, my cat clawing to come out. I couldn't let the monster play, not yet. Closing my eyes, I focused on my territory and my land. The wolves were still moving, closing in on my location on the highway. Damn, I had really been hoping they would abandon the car and run the woods instead. I had twenty minutes now. I turned off all the lights from my spot, letting my eyes adjust.

I poured a drink once I was done. I could hear Carey above me, moving things around and probably getting ready to run once this was over. I hoped so, at least.

Fifteen minutes and my hands began to twitch. The full moon was tomorrow night, which meant every single one of the wolves would get faster shifts, but then again, so would I.

At ten minutes, I began to pull off my clothes. Thankfully, my normal patrons didn't even bother showing up today, or they must have checked the door, saw the closed sign, and turned around. None of them were around, and I hoped it would stay that way.

Five minutes to go, I Changed. The pain tore through me as the bones broke and reformed, taking me down onto all fours. I snarled as the pain flared and took the air from my lungs. Hands became giant paws. My canines became five inch saber teeth. My eyes focused and adjusted to the dark, even better than in my human form.

Roughly a minute. That was my Change time now. A shift between forms faster than even one of the oldest werecats could do. It was much faster than any werewolf would ever be able to perform.

I jumped onto my bar and lay down. It was high enough to make me feel level with anything that walked through the door. I focused on my territory. The wolves had stopped five minutes out and were going through the Change, most likely. It made my hackles rise.

In human shape, they could speak to me. I would get information, then probably kill them. In wolf form, they were a hunting party. There would be no talking. There would only be a fight.

I could have left and hunted them down, but my instincts were against the idea. Staying close to Carey was my number one priority. If I left to hunt them down, I could miss one, and it could come here and take her or kill her. That wasn't an option. This was my first Duty and hopefully my last. I wouldn't fail it. I *couldn't* fail it.

The wolves were running now. I flexed my paws, extending my razor-sharp claws. I heard their paws hit the gravel of my parking lot, though one wasn't in wolf form. I could hear the hum of a small engine and the tires hitting the gravel, kicking it up. It was a sound I was familiar with, like a small dirt bike. I bared my teeth, licking between my fangs. One stayed in human form. Interesting.

I stood up slowly, all four hundred pounds of me, tense and ready to pounce as I heard the footsteps toward my door.

"We come in peace. We're only here for the girl. If you give her up, you'll live," the werewolf in human form called out.

I snarled, making my answer known. They had already broken one rule by coming onto my territory without my permission. They were here for my girl, my charge, my Duty. They were idiots if they thought I was going to let them leave with her and just go back to my life. I was in this now. There was no turning back.

The door opened and a wolf ran in. I took my shot, leaping off the bar and barreling into the smaller predator. The yelping noise it made as bones crushed from the impact would stick with me. I would win. Only fools came after a werecat.

Something bit into my back leg, trying to yank me

from my prey. Snarling, I pushed the wolf I was on down more as I turned to swipe at the other wolf. I could smell them now. Even if one or two lived through this fight, I would always remember them. I would always know which idiot wolves thought they could come into my territory and take something precious.

I missed the wolf, who jumped back, releasing my leg at the last second. I spun around completely, snarling, sizing them up. The average werewolf was normally between two hundred and three hundred pounds. Only smaller werecats were close to three hundred. I probably had each of them by nearly two hundred pounds, and one of them already knew exactly what that meant for them. The wolf I pounced on wasn't getting up for a long time, if it even could.

I roared, letting the sound shake everything in the room. The werewolf in his human form walked carefully behind his wolves, glaring down at me. I gave him a very feline grin.

"It didn't have to be this way, cat," he said almost casually, but I could smell the rage and hate in the air. It was a cat versus dogs problem. Unlike house pets, though, I would win.

The wolves jumped. One landed on my back, trying to push me down. Another ran for my back leg, grabbing hold of it. The third was coming straight for me, probably trying for a neck bite.

I swung a paw, slamming it on the side of its head. I heard the bones break and crunch, heard the yelp of pain as the wolf flew to the side and hit a table.

It was on now. I bent, trying to bite the one on my back. When I couldn't reach it, I shook and directed my teeth and claws towards the one hanging on my back leg.

A gun went off and I growled from the burning pain that hit one of my shoulders. Silver. Of all the dirty tricks, that one had a gun full of silver bullets.

It was a weakness werewolves and werecats shared, but no one knew where the weakness came from. It wasn't an instant kill, damn near nothing was, but it stung and would kill us eventually. The metal would hit the bloodstream and slowly poison us if we didn't rest and recover and remove whatever the source was. It also made healing slow, another serious problem if I was going to be tangling with wolves.

I was able to shake off the wolf on my back, but I didn't get my fangs into the other wolf. Something hit my side and caught me off guard. I roared as I tumbled to the floor, clawing at whatever hit me. Teeth sank into my belly, and the next roar I made was one of pain. I kicked with my back legs, feeling flesh rend and a howl greeted me. It was painful music to my ears.

Fur flew as the battle waged on. I lost track of the ability to really judge and plan my movements, instinct kicking in and taking over. I snapped and clawed at whatever flesh was around me. Anything that smelled like a wolf was a problem.

The wolves were fast and agile, something I wasn't expecting. They dove in, got a hit on me, opening up my flesh and tearing through my muscles. One of the knocked down wolves was up again and rejoining the fight.

Finally, I was able to gain purchase on one and sank my fangs deep into its neck, holding it down as the other two tried to pull me off. I made sure it was dead with a hard shake, breaking the neck of the wolf. I felt good now, blood in my mouth, my vision sharp.

I spun and grabbed another, who was too slow to get away now. It must have been one of the wolves I had already injured. I tore open its gut, roaring in satisfaction.

A scream was the only thing that pulled me out of the blood haze I was in. Carey. I had to get to Carey. Where was that wolf in human form?

Releasing the wolf without killing him, I just ran, heading for the staircase. I barreled up it, ignoring the hounds on my tail. I slammed into my apartment to see Carey trying to pull away from the werewolf holding her. With a snarl, I leapt, tackling the fool still not in his fur. They should have killed me before trying to take the girl.

Not her! She's mine!

He was dead on impact with the floor, but that didn't stop me from tearing him open, blood going everywhere. I even swallowed a piece of meat, just to prove my point to the wolves that followed me into the room. This was my girl and they were lunch if they didn't start running.

Idiots never run, though, and I was fine with that. They both jumped for me, snarling as they realized their mission was a loss unless they ended this now. Carey was still screaming, therefore I still had a cub to protect. Nothing was going to take that cub from me.

It lasted only seconds. I met one of the wolves in the air, and it didn't stand a chance. I was able to get my fangs into its gut and take it to the ground, ripping it open with a satisfied snarl. The second wolf jumped on my back, a safe place normally, but now there was nothing to stop me from rolling, forcing it off before my weight crushed it.

When it was off, I jumped back to my feet and went for it, so fast that it didn't seem to have the time to react. Furniture was knocked around as I tore it open and half played with the body, making sure it was dead.

Panting, I realized I had won. I never thought I would lose, but there was always a pause at the end of a fight to breathe and take stock. I could feel the blood dripping from my jaws, hear it hitting the floor. I could hear the sobs of a little girl and turned, seeing her huddled in the corner of my living room. Her grey-blue eyes were wide with a petrified fear I understood but could do nothing about yet. I couldn't shift with a silver bullet lodged in me, which meant there was no comforting the girl.

I sniffed around and found the gun, nudging it to her. She was shaking like a leaf but I needed her. I needed her to help me so I could help her. She was watching my every movement, which meant I at least had her attention, which was good. Then I went into the bathroom and gingerly pulled open one of the ground level cabinets and pulled out my first aid kit. It would have what she needed to get the bullet out. I just hope she understood the message I was trying to send her. I dropped it at her feet and took a moment to sniff her.

There was so much blood in the room and on me that it was a bit amazing I could smell anything, but I needed to know if any of it was hers. Once I was satisfied she wasn't truly harmed, I sat back and angled so she could see the bullet wound. I made a pitiful noise, hoping to garner any amount of sympathy from her to get moving and help me out.

It worked. She blinked twice and opened her mouth before closing it again. She grabbed the first aid kit and looked down at it, as if she was realizing what it was.

"The gunshot," she said softly. "Oh! They shot you!"

I bobbed my big head and tried to nod towards the hole. It was on my left shoulder and I was hoping she could see it. I was probably covered in claw marks and bite wounds, but a bullet hole looks different from those.

"You…Oh. Okay. I've never done this. I don't know if I can. Is there anyone we can call?"

I shook my head. *Come on, kid. I need you. Please.*

"Oh fuck," she said, anxiety and fear all I could hear. I bared my teeth. I cursed a lot, but she was eleven. She had at least a few years before she was allowed to be a mouthy teenager. "Okay." She unzipped the bag and found what I was hoping she would. Every werecat carried everything needed to get a silver bullet out. It was paranoid and ridiculous, but we had mini surgery kits, honestly. When you didn't have backup, you had to have everything you needed. Lessons young werecats normally thought were jokes, overly paranoid, but I was never stupid enough to be completely unprepared, so I had taken those lessons to heart.

I hissed but kept to myself as those tongs were shoved into my shoulder. I could feel her shaking through them and down to my bones now. She was terrified and it was my fault. I should have taken the werewolf with the gun out first, and it was a mistake I promised myself I wouldn't make again.

I even heard the ting of the tongs finding the bullet. All the while, Carey was quiet—shaking, but quiet. The poor thing would need therapy after this, that much was clear, but the loss of her innocence was something that would need to be addressed later.

I wanted to drop my head on the floor in relief when I felt the bullet leave me. That much silver was stopping me from shifting, but now I could, so I started the process. It was slower than normal. Carey's free hand never left me as my bones broke and changed.

Finally, I was a naked human woman lying on her stomach on the floor, covered in blood. I was still panting, though, my tongue out and everything.

"Are you going to be okay?" she asked me. "Please be okay. I never wanted this. This wasn't supposed to happen. Why are they doing this? I would have never told them if…"

I let her trail off, letting that sink in. Of course. "Did you call them?" I asked softly.

"I…He was one of my guards," she answered softly, pointing at the dead one in his human body. "He had texted me and I said I was being protected by a werecat and that he didn't need to worry. You were going to take care of me. He just needed to find my dad. Then he came up here and he had a gun." Her voice broke and I could hear the tears begin. Regretfully, I was bleeding and in too much pain to push myself off the floor for a moment. Shifting with silver in the system was *hard*.

"It's okay," I said gently. "You told him not to come. You tried. You didn't know that they were the bad ones."

"I thought...I thought he could never betray Daddy! He was texting me, begging to know if I was okay and I thought that was a good thing! I told him Daddy wanted me here and he needed to stay away, that I was safe! He... he came up here with his gun and said he needed me! He needed me to get Daddy to come out of hiding and d-d-die like a good Alpha."

"Oh honey," I breathed out, trying to move closer to her. I reached out and grabbed one of her hands. "It's going to be okay. Me and you, we can do this. Give me a few minutes to get over that last Change I made and we're going to get out of here. I'm going to protect you."

"I know!" She was sobbing now and fell over, her face on my back. I could feel the heat of her tears as she clung to my prone form. "Get better! Please! This is my fault! Please get better!"

"Give me a moment." I tried to push up, my arms shaking. The pain was fading, though, which meant I really needed to get moving. I could see where the wolves hit me now. It would take time for everything to heal. Normally, after injuries like these, I would take four to five days letting them recover, but the silver was going to make that into a few weeks unless it bled out of my system sooner.

I didn't have a few weeks, though. Carey needed me right now. I was able to sit up completely thanks to that thought, that need. I stared at her, probably as wide-eyed as she was staring at me.

"This wasn't how I thought our night would go," I said, trying to smirk. "Run off and pack a bag. I have a few suitcases in my closet. Use one of those and put the Switch in your go-bag. You can play on it while I drive."

"How are you so calm?" she demanded, seeming even more shocked by my quick bounce into what we needed to do next.

"Because freaking out and crying isn't something I can do right now. I know what world I belong to, and that means I don't get to pause and think about things like this until I know we're safe. I have to be strong for you and direct you or this is never going to work." Oh, I wanted to. There was violence in the supernatural world, and there was no escaping it, but there were types of violence. A werecat territorial fight wasn't fatal. There were too few of us for it to be that way. It was brutal, but never to the death. This...I didn't have it in my heart to tell Carey this was the first time I had ever killed anyone with the *intent* to kill them and that I wanted to fall apart just as much as she did. I was a monster, but this was the first time I had truly lived up to the reputation.

She nodded, trying to stand. I attempted to help her as she slipped in the blood covering my hardwood floors. I didn't move as she walked back into my bedroom. I had my own things to deal with for a moment while she packed.

Grabbing my first aid kit, I looked over my injuries. I dried them with a towel nearby and somehow not soaked in blood. Werecats bleed slowly, something I was eternally grateful for in that moment, so it wasn't hard to stop the bleeding. I grabbed a suture kit and looked at my thigh, seeing to the worst of my injuries, hopefully. There were scratches all over my back that I couldn't do anything about, but I could deal with my legs.

My shoulder burned with every movement too, but I sutured three deep injuries on my left thigh, then two on my right. I had training in it, and more than enough practice at doing it to myself. I was done before Carey and pushed myself to stand as she brought out her go-bag and put it on the couch, which was five feet off its previous spot.

I let the destruction sink in, sighing as I realized this was going to have my bar shut down for weeks, if not months. If I could even come back at all.

Pushing that aside, I went into the bathroom, wiped off as much blood as I could, then followed Carey into the bedroom. I threw on something to wear, then began emptying my drawers, grabbing whatever I could to pack. I took my big suitcase and began to fill it, probably taking too much, but if I was going to end up covered in blood at every turn, I needed spares.

"Carey, can you find my cellphone?" I asked. I needed to text a few people and let them know that we were attacked. It was time to go deeper into hiding, and people needed to know that so that they didn't worry when they came here and found this. Which reminded me that I needed to tell the wolves to come clean up their own. The council would do it because it was their fault.

Once the cellphone was in my hand, I shoved it into my pocket. I would call everyone from the road.

The last things I needed to grab were weapons. I took the gun off the floor, thankful for the unintentional gift the werewolf had given me. I also had a silver dagger, a gift from Hasan, who had decided when I left that I needed some way to defend myself. Finally, in my closet there was an aluminum baseball bat. I threw all three weapons into my gym bag, then proceeded to help Carey finish.

We had to leave this carnage behind and disappear. I wasn't even sure where to begin.

6
CHAPTER SIX

Carey and I were on the road within twenty minutes of me getting off my floor. It wasn't particularly fast, but it was the best we could do. I was limping and she was scared. There was only so much two girls could do under those circumstances.

I had no idea where I was going, but it was far away if I had anything to say about it. Thirty minutes and past Jacksonville, I guessed my direction was the Texas-Louisiana state border. I knew I couldn't drive all night, but I was going to at least make some distance from my own territory. Hopefully that would shake the wolves off our trail for the time being.

Carey fell asleep only a few minutes into the drive, and I let her rest. Something like that had the tendency to either keep people awake for days out of fear or drain them of all their energy. I took her sleeping as a good sign that she was tired, scared, but felt safe with me. Safe enough to close her eyes anyway.

I looked down at my phone for a split second and saw the number I needed. Hitting it, I put it on speaker and on my lap, then turned the radio down. He answered before I finished doing that.

"Harrison. What do you need, cat?"

"We were attacked. Five werewolves, four in wolf form, and one with a gun loaded with silver," I started, not stopping for pleasantries. "They wanted Carey to flush out her father."

"Damn it. We've been looking for Heath since this all started, but no one has gotten a bead on him."

Heath. A good name, a strong name. Also, one that made me think of a particularly sexy actor. So that was the Dallas-Fort Worth Alpha. I finally had a name. Not that I needed one, but it was nice to know. I couldn't have asked for it since it wasn't pertinent to my Duty, but now I didn't need to wonder.

I stayed silent, because I couldn't think of anything to say that wouldn't be potentially meddling in affairs that weren't my business. He must have noticed, so he continued instead.

"I don't know if this is going to help you or not, but maybe it can help you keep her alive and safe. Here's what we know." His volume dropped and I raised an eyebrow. He was going to tell me more. Interesting. He didn't want others to know, either, since while it didn't break any Laws, he was giving a lot of trust to a werecat. "Right now, the coup's leader doesn't want anyone to know who he or she is. Whenever two werewolves meet on the street, even in broad daylight, they ask if the other is for or against Heath. If they answer different, it's a fight, normally until the death. We've got ten dead wolves from just that. The initial coup has five more bodies, a few in Heath's inner circle. His sons are still missing as well, and some are even saying the family might already be dead except for Carey."

That gave me chills, and I couldn't resist commenting now. "That's not how wolves do things. There's no such thing as assassinating an Alpha and his family. Any resulting pack made from that would be unstable. It would result in anarchy in the region."

"Hm, so you do know a bit about our kind. You're right. This doesn't happen. Alphas are normally challenged publicly, and getting permission from the Council is preferred. We don't assassinate people. It's a sign of weakness."

"So I'm dealing with wolves who break your rules," I said quietly. "That is helpful, thank you. I had my suspicions when five of them came into my bar and demanded I give up on my Duty and hand Carey over."

"And?"

"I killed them all. What do you think?" I snapped, suddenly tense again. Five wolves, all dead by my fangs and claws. I could still taste the blood when it rushed over my tongue, hot and heady. I tightened my grip on the steering wheel.

"Of course. Of course. I take it you're about to demand something of me because of this, aren't you?"

"Get people to my bar. It's on US-175, just outside of Jacksonville, Texas. It's called Kick Shot. I know they left some sort of vehicle somewhere on the road and there's a dirt bike in my parking lot. There's going to be bodies everywhere. Two downstairs and three in my apartment above it. Clean it up and tell me who to scream at for repairs." I damn sure wasn't going to pay for it. I could afford it, but I wasn't going to let the wolves destroy my life and not pay for their part in it.

"I'll send a team," he agreed. "How is she? Was she injured?"

"Fine and no. Do you know her? Would she feel comfortable talking to you? I want her to have some comfort, but I can't trust any of the wolves in Dallas. The ringleader of the ones in my bar…he was one of her guards. She had told him she was safe with me and he came after her."

"No. I only know Carey through her father and what he tells us. He would show us pictures every time the council had a meeting."

"Damn it. He was a council member?" Not every Alpha was. Generally, there could be a few packs in a region, and the strongest pack was the region's council representative, the Alpha who answered for all of them. Kind of. I pulled over and cut the engine, getting out of the hatchback and taking the call off speakerphone. "It fucking changes things if he's a council Alpha, damn it."

"He is…was. All of the packs in Texas, New Mexico, Oklahoma, Arkansas, and Louisiana use him as their representative on the council. Be careful not to meddle, cat."

I did the mental math. "That's...that's ten wolf packs," I said quietly. "That's probably a thousand wolves." Maybe more.

"Yes. Why does this—"

"I'm protecting Carey from potentially a thousand wolves." The realization sank in slowly. This could reach well out of his home city. I couldn't take her to another werecat in the region because the wolves were now probably watching every werecat they could find, hoping I showed up with her.

I was well and truly on my own with an eleven-year-old girl, and I had to treat every wolf like the enemy. I was strong. I was a werecat, for fuck's sake, but I couldn't kill a thousand werewolves, especially if they were carrying around silver bullets.

"I wish you the best on your Duty. Thank you for the update. Good luck, Jacky Leon."

My name rattled me out of my fear of impending doom and death. There was nothing more to say, then. "Thank you for the information and clean-up." I hung up on him, leaning against my hatchback in the dark. I was out of my territory now, so I kept my nose up, hoping to pick up anything important on the wind. It wasn't the safest thing to do, but I needed a moment to think instead of just driving.

There was nowhere safe for Carey, not if this was bigger than Heath's home pack. If this reached further, it meant I would need to run her out of the entire southern half of the country, and even that might not be far enough.

I called Lani next, trying to collect my thoughts.

"Hey. I was hoping you would call. I have werewolves all around the borders of my territory," she said immediately when she answered.

"Figured as much," I replied. "I was attacked." I ran through what happened to her, since repeating it seemed to make me feel better. Not really, but I liked to believe it might one day.

"Well, this is a right mess, isn't it?" Lani snorted on the other end. "Yeah. They must be watching all of us in the region now. A council Alpha…That's the sort of information that gets dangerously close to meddling in their politics, Jacky. You know that, right? That's against the Law."

"Yeah, but it's information I needed to know to help keep Carey safe. I'm off my territory and every wolf could be a threat. It's important." I closed my eyes, suddenly exhausted. "I haven't even had her in my care for twenty-four hours and they tried to take her. It took everything in me not to eat them after I killed them. I wanted to. If I have to break the Law to keep her safe, I'm going to. She's so strong. Hell broke loose in her father's pack and she still made it to me, dirty, tired, and alone. She's so…she's a good kid and she's scared and now her life is a mess. I can't let them have her."

"Okay. If this goes sour and you end up breaking the Law about meddling to keep her safe, you'll have my support. I'll make some calls to my other allies, other werecats in the region. I know a couple in different areas of the country. I'll see what kind of backup I can get to protect one of our own against the Law when Duty is involved. It's not like you started the coup or anything, and your involvement only started when Carey showed up."

"Thank you." I let go of a breath I didn't know I was holding. This couldn't get worse, could it?

"Too bad Hasan has been missing for the last century. He knows the Law better than anyone and would be able to defend you the best if it needs to happen." Lani sighed. "You might not have heard about him, but he was there when the Laws were written. He would know best what to do. Regretfully, he went missing when his youngest daughter died."

I kept my mouth shut. I wasn't the dead daughter. I was the next one he made. Hasan, by his own words, made many children over the centuries. Four sons and three daughters. Only one was dead, his previously youngest daughter. He was still in hiding, still refusing to interact with the rest of the supernatural world thanks to whatever happened. I didn't want to consider what would happen if people started finding out exactly who made me because it made me a sort of feline royalty. Not announcing who Changed me gave me a reputation, but it was one I was willing to live with. The royalty aspect of being Hasan's child wasn't one I was ready to deal with.

"You weren't there?" I asked, changing the topic. I knew Lani was pretty old, but not exactly how old.

"I was in Africa at the time," she answered,

something wistful to the words. "Still human. I was Changed just after the Laws were written."

"Ah." That made her just over eight hundred years old. Now I had that answer. Werecats tended to get old, very few died under a hundred years of age, but most alive were also Changed after the Laws. That was because most before the Laws were killed in the war between the werewolves and werecats. "Stay safe, Lani."

"You too, cub. I'll get to work." She hung up on me.

I shoved the phone back into my pocket, considering my options. I needed to find a motel or something, but nothing in a city center. Something off the beaten path where a fight wouldn't risk innocent humans.

I got back into my hatchback and saw Carey still sleeping there, easing me just a little. My charge was safe for now and that helped crush the restlessness in me. I got us back on the road and stopped at the first gas station I could, jumping out without waking Carey.

I grabbed some snacks and drinks before going to the counter.

"Where's the nearest motel?" I asked quickly, dumping everything on the counter. The human gave me a look that made me concerned. Did I miss some blood on my face? Was it in my teeth?

"Next door," he answered.

"Oh!" I wasn't expecting that answer. Sure enough, when I paid for the goodies and walked back out, I cursed my own tunnel vision and smirked. Perfect. It was a run-down little thing, not even one of the chains. No one would expect us to stay there. I got back into my hatchback and rolled into the adjoining parking lot, stopping in front of the main office. This time when I got out, I paid more attention to the world around me. I looked over the pine trees that seemed to run for miles and sighed. This was actually perfect. It was right off the highway, but there was nothing else around. It was a pit stop, a gas station and a motel. All one needed for a long drive and more secure than sleeping at a rest stop.

I left Carey in the passenger's seat and walked into the office, stopping at the desk. There was no one there, so I dinged the bell. I chuckled as I heard someone jump in the office behind the desk. An older gentleman walked out and looked me over as I raised an eyebrow.

"I need a room, preferably on the first floor and not close to the office."

"Not a hooker, are you?" He huffed, giving me a confused look.

"No. I just want to be able to listen to loud music without pissing people off." I didn't want anyone to hear me talking about a sensitive topic, and the place seemed deserted enough that the only person around was this guy. "Do you own the place?"

"Yup, and the gas station next door." He was still eyeballing me pretty hard and I took a sniff of the air and bared my teeth.

"Damn it," I muttered, shaking my head. "What's a fae doing running a little motel and gas station combo in the middle of bum-fuck nowhere?"

"What's a werecat doing here?" he fired back.

"On Duty," I answered. "Do you have a room for me or not?"

"Oh shit. Yeah." He grabbed a key from the back wall and I resisted shaking my head again. The motel was so old it was using keys instead of cards. One would think a fae trying to live in the modern world actually would update, but apparently not. "It'll be sixty a night. Cash or card?"

I considered my answer before pulling my wallet out. I could have run to the gas station and used the ATM for cash but I had multiple names for this very reason. Everyone in Texas knew me as Jacky Leon, so I could use my fake ID cards. I handed him the credit card with Jane Brown on it and let him do his thing.

"I'll close out the account when you check out. Be safe and good luck on your Duty." He was respectful now, and I knew it was because one day, he might need it. No one fucked with a werecat on Duty, except, apparently, for the werewolves dead in my bar. I grabbed my credit card back from him, tucking it away safely in my wallet again.

"Keep an eye out for something, would ya? Werewolves. I don't care what they say. If you see any, please let me know."

"Can do."

I nodded once to him and left with the key, not bothering to say thank you. I wasn't an idiot. No one thanked the fae.

When I parked my hatchback in front of my room, I sighed, looking over to Carey. It was time to wake her up and bring her back to the nightmare that was her life now. I knew the idea of it was depressing, but it was the truth.

I didn't wake her up immediately, though. I grabbed our things and bags, taking them into the room, leaving her for last. It was night out and no one was around. The fae was trustworthy in a sense. He wouldn't get involved in werewolf politics, no matter what they offered him. If he was caught messing around outside his own kind like that, his kind would kill him, probably in a painfully slow way. He could help a feline in her Duty, though, and that was what I needed.

Finally, I was bent over Carey, undoing her seat belt. The pop of the seatbelt was what finally did it. She jumped awake, gasping for air.

"Woah. Woah, Carey. We're safe. I found a motel we can hide in." I grabbed her shoulders, holding gently. I really didn't need her screaming bloody murder. "Please calm down."

She stopped moving, closed her mouth, and gave me a baleful stare. My heart broke a little more each time I saw those grey-blue eyes. Once, just once, I had gotten them to lighten up to a pretty summer sky, but now they were just a dreary sky.

"Come on," I whispered, holding a hand out for her to take. "Everything else is inside."

She just nodded, grabbing my hand and letting me help her. She was so tiny, only about four and a half feet tall. I remembered being taller at her age. I think. Eleven was a dead spot in my memory.

I locked my hatchback as she went inside. Not

following her, I rubbed my face. How did I end up here again? Oh yeah, that's right. Not even twenty-four hours before, she showed up at my back door and called me to Duty to protect her until she was safe again and would be safe if I let her go.

Sighing, I turned and walked into the room. It had a single queen and a decently large flat-screen television. For being a poor, seemingly run-down motel, the fae who ran it kept it updated in some ways, which made it odd. Carey was already sitting on the bed, kicking her shoes off.

"Want to watch a movie?" I asked as I closed the door and locked it. Then I looked at it and realized there was more than one lock and did the second.

"Sure."

I grabbed the remote from the dresser the TV was sitting on and sat on the other side of the bed. The comforter was scratchy and a floral print, like most motels or hotels. The carpet was beige and the furniture was all a light wood I didn't like. It was a long way off my dark hardwood floors and deep red furniture, that was certain. The bed wasn't particularly comfortable either, but I knew better than to vocally complain. I needed Carey to think I was fine, even if my shoulder hurt and my legs burned. My back wasn't much better, but those injuries were shallower and already healing.

I turned on the TV, ordered a pay-per-view movie for her, something Disney, and dropped the remote, yawning. I hadn't watched a Disney movie in years, since I was human. Carey seemed interested and enjoying it, but there were shadows in her eyes. She was probably thinking about her family and what had just happened to us.

"We should talk," I said about thirty minutes into the film.

"About?" She glanced at me, wary. I couldn't blame her. Watching a werecat kill three werewolves and take a bite of one of those probably didn't endear her to me.

"How you're feeling. You can talk to me. I would understand—"

"Don't. How could you possibly understand? My dad is missing and so are my brothers! Werewolves I was raised with are trying to take me prisoner!" She went from subdued to shouting in less than a sentence. "You probably have done this tons of times! How many werewolves have you killed before?"

"None. This was the first time I've ever fought another supernatural with the intention to kill them." I didn't let her anger penetrate my exterior calm. "This is the first time I've ever purposefully killed anyone, actually."

"Really?" The disbelief on her face hurt.

"What do you think I am, a killer?" Suddenly insulted, I paused the movie. "Do you think your father would send you to a murderer for protection?"

She sniffed, holding back tears again. I closed my eyes, rubbing my face as I tried to find what to say. There was really nothing except telling her about myself, and I had to be careful about that. I didn't want to expose this girl to my life and give her secrets and stories to carry that weren't hers. I just couldn't.

"Carey..."

"My dad said that werecats are solitary, but social. That when a werecat moves around, everyone hears about it, knows who they were Changed by. That you have all sorts of...politics, I guess. But no one knew where you came from. He said I needed to be careful, because you were the closest werecat but maybe not the safest, because no one knows anything about you. He said you would follow the rules of Duty, but..."

I started to chuckle darkly, my shoulders shaking. Tears threatened my own eyes now. Even the werewolves wondered where I came from. Wasn't that something?

"I'm not going to hurt you. I could never..." I swallowed my own emotion for a moment. "No one knows where I come from because I don't tell them, but it's nowhere bad," I promised softly. "I just don't agree with some of the decisions my...father made. You know that part of our culture, right? A werecat that Changes a human becomes that person's...parent. They teach us about our new life and world and introduce us to people and help us learn all the rules. I don't tell anyone who that is because I don't want much to do with him."

"Oh. So you've, like...run away from home?"

I huffed, nodding. "That's a good way of putting it. He didn't want me to leave, but I did. Normally, a new werecat stays with their older 'parent' until they're about a decade into their new life, then they slowly begin to separate. I left four years after I was Changed, and while

I still talk to him, I don't let him into my life anymore. He doesn't even know this has happened." *Not yet.* "I was an EMT when I was human. When I say this is the first time I've killed anyone intentionally, I mean it. I lost people when I was an EMT. I saw their life fade, and no matter how many times I defib'ed them..." I pantomimed a defibrillator, seeing recognition dawn in her eyes. "They were never coming back. So it's not that I'm dangerous, though I understand why some think that. I'm private, Carey. Very private. I don't like getting into things and generally want to stay out of them. I put my territory pretty far from your pack's for a reason, and your father's pack are the closest supernaturals to me that I know of." Though maybe the fae and his little family were now. I would have to check a map.

She nodded and opened her mouth, pondered saying something, then closed it again. I resisted rolling my eyes.

"What?" I wanted her to feel like she could talk to me, and if this was going to be story time, I wanted her to get it all out.

"Are you lonely like that? I mean, there's so many werewolves, and they say that pack is super-important. Isn't living by yourself with no friends or family lonely?"

"Very, but it's the life I chose, just like a lot of people choose to be Changed into werewolves or werecats. I chose this life of mine."

"Did you choose to be a werecat?" She was tentative and curious now. "Dad says one day I'll get to decide if I want to try and be Changed...it's scary. It's scarier now."

"One out of ten people survive the Change, but you'll

have it a bit easier if you go that way. Human children of werewolves and werecats almost never fail. You should be fine if you decide to." I reached out and grabbed her hand, pulling her towards me. It was hard, ignoring the throb in my shoulder, but I figured the girl needed some physical comfort. I positioned her next to me, under my right arm. Thankfully, she scooted in and got comfortable, leaning in like I was her best friend.

"You didn't answer my question," she pointed out once I went to turn on the movie again.

I couldn't hold back my groan and dropped the remote again, realizing I couldn't distract her. "I didn't. I was in a car accident and had no idea that werecats or werewolves or any of this was real. I thought witches were in movies and Harry Potter. I thought fae were the monsters in old fairy tales. A werecat found the accident. I had met him before and had struck up a casual friendship while I was on vacation, with no idea what or who he really was. He decided to Change me."

"Do you ever regret it? My dad says I should think really hard because I might."

"I didn't have a choice like you will, sweetheart. At first, no, I didn't. Things changed. They might change again. But for now, yeah, I regret it a little. Or at least I did, until you showed up at my door. I haven't had the chance to consider it since." I couldn't leave it there, so I continued. "But if I was never Changed, who would be here protecting you?"

"Dad says fate is real," she whispered.

When she yawned, I yawned with her. It was a sign

that the movie needed to come back on. She was asleep in a few minutes, the fear and recent events finally putting her under again. I rubbed her hair and dared to even kiss the top of her head. I tucked her in, checked the locks on the door, then proceeded to pass out myself.

CHAPTER SEVEN

I woke up to the sun coming through the window. Carey was still asleep next to me, and I was thankful for it. It was safer that way, really. It would give me a chance to check my injuries, find some real breakfast, and get us ready for the day.

Not that there was anything to get ready for.

My plan was to stay low here at the motel until everything blew over. Over an hour away from home and out of my territory, there was no reason to think the wolves would have a way to track me or Carey here. It was concerning to know that they had abused Carey's trust, something that really stuck a bone in my teeth. She had trusted that werewolf to respect her father's plan to keep her out of harm's way. He'd betrayed not only her father, but her, and I was the only line of defense she could probably trust now. Even that was tentative, unsure. I could smell it on her and see it the night before.

I stumbled into the bathroom with my first aid kit, did

my business, then got busy looking over my shoulder. When I pulled off my shirt, it tore something, making me wince as I felt a small line of blood flow down my chest. Once I could see it, I sighed. It was angry red and scabbed over, but not healing, just like I knew it wouldn't. I grabbed the kit and tore it open, frustrated. I couldn't be injured while I was protecting her. It wasn't fair. No one should have challenged my Duty the way those fucking wolves did last night.

After cleaning up my shoulder, I checked my thighs and calves. They weren't healing well either, but the stitches were holding and that was something. I cleaned them up with peroxide, hissing at the sting, but didn't let it deter me from the job. I had to keep them clean if I didn't want to get an infection before the silver left my system.

Once I was done, I jumped into the shower for a quick clean, making sure I didn't get shampoo or conditioner on them. It was tricky business.

When I was done, Carey was blessedly still asleep, so I left the room and went to the main office. Maybe I could catch the fae and finally grab his name and learn where breakfast might be. I was nearly there when he walked out of the main office, juggling a tray.

"Hi..." I slowed down, confused until I realized he was having a hard time. My manners kicked in and I grabbed the door so he had an easier time leaving the main office with whatever he was carrying. I was able to catch the scent of it on the air and frowned. "Food? Where did you get it?"

"My wife made it for you, and before you ask, she's human and this isn't fae food. You can eat it safely." He looked up at me, lifting the tray to me. I didn't take it, puzzled. I hadn't realized I was taller than him the night before. Distraction at its best, which had to stop. There was another problem.

"Does your wife talk to werewolves?" I asked softly, dangerously.

"No, no!" That made him go stiff, the accusation sitting between us still. "She knows a lot about the supernatural world, but she doesn't talk to anyone, not even her own human family. We have a nice quiet life here and don't want any trouble."

"Did you tell her who or what I was?"

"I told her some, but only because she already knows about the Law of the supernatural species and the Duty of the werecats. It's why she made you both breakfast."

I raised an eyebrow. I hadn't told him who I was with.

"She's the one who put it together. You asked for me to keep an eye out for werewolves. Dallas-Fort Worth area is having issues with their werewolves. Human daughter of a council Alpha goes missing, then is said to be safe, but her location isn't publicly announced..." He frowned now, sniffing around. "Are you bleeding?"

"Fuck," I muttered, touching my shoulder. "I didn't know your nose was that sharp. What are you? Fair trade, considering you know so much about me it seems."

"I'm aes sidhe," he said casually.

"Yes, which is just another general term for fae," I retorted, narrowing my eyes.

His brown hair fluidly shifted before my eyes to a bright red. Freckles began to appear on his face. I knew it had bad been an illusion, a glamour to appear human. Then his ears became pointed. "No, lass. It's Irish fae. Get it right." He chuckled, finally pushing the tray at me. I grabbed it before he let go, but neither of us moved. He looked me over, calculating. "You could also say I'm one of the Daoine maithe. We're known for being...human-like with supernatural abilities."

"Yes, and you're divided into Clans that give people an idea of what you are and what you can do." He was beating around the bush, and I knew it was because he probably wanted his privacy. Or he was fucking with me. I didn't know much about fae—never really cared for them or about them— but I knew some basics. I didn't, however, know any of the Clans or what they meant, just that there were Clans and a Clan passed on their abilities like humans passed on hair colors.

"Well, I've given you an answer, werecat who hasn't announced her lineage," he said softly, his smile turning sharp.

I shrugged as best I could while holding the food. Answers for a different day, then. I walked away from him but stopped after only five feet.

"Then give me your name at least," I ordered, turning back to him.

"You can call me Brin," he answered. "I would give you my wife's name, but I don't plan on letting you meet her. My sons are Eamon, Fergus, and Rian. They work the gas station."

"I'm Jacky." I inclined my head after I offered him my name. I left him there, thinking about what I knew about the fae, but I had no conclusions about him by the time I made it back to the room. I knocked, hoping Carey was awake by now, and thankfully, she unlocked the door and opened it for me.

"I bring food," I declared, holding up the tray. "Sit down and we'll eat." I gestured to the small table next to the window AC unit and she did as directed. I put the food down and revealed it. Pancakes, eggs, bacon, sausage, and even a couple of muffins. There were two clean plates and silverware too. It was a good setup. I made her a plate before making my own, sitting down to quietly eat.

This time, it was her turn to interrupt the silence. "When do you think this is going to end?"

"I don't know, but I'm with you for the entire ride."

"Don't you have a life, though? You own that bar. Don't you need to get back to it?"

"The bar will be fine," I told her, taking a bite of the eggs first. Protein was perfect. "It would have been closed tonight anyway."

"Why?"

"Full moon, and it's Sunday. I'm always closed on full moons and Sundays." I chuckled, shaking my head. "You know that. I'm going to have to shift tonight, from sunset to sunrise. It's going to make protection a bit sticky, but we'll make it work."

I could smell her worry now. "Will it be safe?"

"I'll probably shift and run out in the woods, but I

won't go far. I expect you to be in bed when I leave for the night. It'll be easier for both of us if I'm not cooped up in here." I didn't want her to fear me or the feline that lived under my skin, but she had reason to be worried. If I shifted while locked in the motel room, there was a chance I could get hungry and lose control. Hunting was important on the full moon, to give the predator an outlet that was safe. "Don't worry about it, please. I've got it covered. The good thing is, the werewolves won't come tonight, even if they find us. If they want you alive, it'll be too dangerous, so there won't be anymore running for you, at least not for the next twenty-four hours." I had to be practical. There was a chance running still needed to be done, but not on the full moon.

"And what about tomorrow night? Will you have to go back to your bar—"

"My bar is not the concern here," I said forcefully. "I could close its doors indefinitely and not be worried about it. I could pick up somewhere else and it's not a problem. Don't worry about me, Carey, please."

"I think my dad would describe you as practical." A shy smirk formed on her face, daring and precious, even if it was a little sad. The sadness wasn't in the smirk; it was in her eyes.

I hope so, but it's only because I won't get snarky with a child who's scared. "What would your mom say?" All I had heard so far was about her dad and brothers. There was a key person in the family missing that I knew nothing about.

"I...I don't know. Dad said she was a human, and she

must have been since I'm one. She gave me to him after I was born and left." There wasn't anything sad about those words, just an acceptance that made my heart clench. "It's fine, really. Lots of people feel bad for me, but I have Dad and he's great. My brothers are super-cool and teach me all sorts of things, and I have great friends in school."

"I mean…" I missed my human parents more than life itself sometimes. I couldn't imagine just never knowing one of them. It was beyond me to consider. "Don't you ever want her? To teach you…mom things like how to bake, or…" I was at a loss. My mom had never really taught me a lot of those things either, but there were moments when she was the person I needed most, the rock by which I could anchor my life.

"Can't miss something I've never had. The female werewolves do all those things with me. I have a big family." Her weak smile assuaged my worries for her just a tiny bit. I figured if it weren't for the war going on that her father and 'family' was in the middle of, it would be huge. "Like Emma? She's great. She's half-witch too. She teaches me a lot. She has a werewolf son my age who's really cute too. He's a quarter-witch. We're all wondering if his powers are going to come in or not."

"Your pack has werewolf witches?" I chuckled, considering that. Werecats didn't change anyone with witch blood in them, considering it too high a risk, too much power. There was no reason to give mortal witches the near-immortality of the werecats.

"Well, her dad was a werewolf and her mom was a

witch. She came out both. Then she fell in love with Dean, who's one of my dad's inner circle. Dean is cool." Now she was rocking in her seat, grinning. It faded quickly. "I hope they're okay."

"I'm sure a half-witch is just fine during all of this," I promised softly. It wasn't a promise I had any right to give, but I didn't want Carey's mind wandering off to think about what could possibly happen to the people she loved.

The reality was different than what I was promising, which hurt the worst as the words came out of my mouth and brought some light to Carey's eyes. If this Emma was loyal to Heath, then she was a target. She would be harassed at every turn as people would see her as a threat that needed to be eliminated. If she wasn't already dead, there was a chance she would be soon. If she was with the coup or neutral, that was a betrayal Heath wouldn't be able to stand for, if he was like any Alpha I had ever heard of.

"Jacky..." Carey pushed her plate away now, all of the food half eaten. I was pleased by that, though I wished she would eat more at the same time. At least there was something in her stomach that wasn't junk food, and that was what kept me from pushing the plate back in front of her. "Tell me about your family."

Looking for a distraction, little human? "My dad, my human one, is a real Texas gentleman with all the flaws that come with it. He's a good man, though. I'll love him dearly for the rest of my life. My mom is...Well, she's unique. She can be selfish and ridiculous, or she can be the most loving woman in the world. She's great at her job, but terrible with money. What do you want to know?"

"Do you ever see them? Do they know you're in danger?"

"No. No, Carey, I don't see my family. Werecats... we're not like werewolves. We keep things separate for our own secrecy, our privacy. My human family knows I'm alive, but I left them no way of finding me or getting ahold of me. They know there was a terrible car accident and that I'm an adult that doesn't want anything to do with them."

"So you're alone. You left your werecat dad and your human family. I'm alone too now." She blinked those blasted big grey-blue eyes at me. "We can be family. While we have none, we can be family together, right?"

I was flabbergasted for a moment before smiling brightly. "Yeah, we can be family. So what does your family do together?"

"We play video games..." She smirked.

"I do think I told you to bring the Switch along, right? Go get it while I clean up. Can you set it up on the TV?"

"Yeah!" She jumped up and ran for her bags. I resisted chuckling as I cleaned up our breakfast and left the room with it, taking it back to the main office for Brin. He was behind his counter and nodded to the place I should put it down. I left without saying anything to him, not wanting to disrupt his reading or cause more of a problem for him than I already was.

Once back in the room, I chuckled louder as I

watched Carey plug in cords and turn on the Switch on the big screen. She pulled up some weird board game-looking thing with that red plumber. I really hated that guy, but I wasn't going to dampen her good mood, so I took the second controller and sat down next to her on the bed.

"You ready?" she asked, flying through menus to get the game started.

"Let's do this!" I grinned down at her, glad to finally be able to distract her for longer than a few moments. That was the thing about kids, human ones especially. If you were willing to lie, to give them hope, they bounced back; they acclimated and adapted. Did I despise lying to her about her friends Emma and Dean? Yeah, but it was better than having a broken-hearted little girl, so much better.

We played four rounds and to my disappointment, I lost every single one of them. I had been playing video games since I was young, born in the Eighties. I remembered the NES and SEGA better than most, small fragments of the dead zone in my memory. Yet Carey stomped me, and hard. My pride took a beating, and each time I lost and she won, she would cheer, jump up and down on the bed, and rub it in.

"I win again! I thought werecats were supposed to be the best supernatural creature! Ha! Humans forever! Got you! Trained by werewolves, you'll never beat me!" She tossed her head around, brimming with confidence.

"I'll never beat you? Are you sure?" I smiled slyly. It was time to cheat then. "Start a new game," I ordered, pointing at the screen. "I think I can take you down next time."

"Really? Are we doing best out of nine now? You would have to win five in a row to beat me!" She hit start anyway, and when the first mini game came up, I took my chance. Instead of playing the mini game, I dropped my controller and pounced on her, going for her ribs. "NO!"

I was laughing as my fingers danced, tickling her until she screamed, trying to hit me away. She laughed until there were tears in her eyes.

"Stop cheating! HA AH!"

I didn't relent until the full two minute countdown of the mini game was over and she was breathing hard.

"Well, I didn't win the game, but neither did you," I said lightly, going back to my spot on the bed.

"That's not fair!" she cried out, kicking a foot at me. I caught it, laughing. "My brothers do that!"

"Good for your brothers. You should learn to win better." I held her leg by the ankle and tickled the bottom of her foot until she screamed again, the laughter bouncing off the walls. When I was done, it was my turn in the game and I wasn't even paying attention. I was just watching the bright-eyed little girl glare at me.

"My dad says the same thing, but he doesn't get it either. It's hard being the winner when all the other players are werewolves. I take my wins where I can get them." She stuck her tongue out and I kept laughing. Kid had a point, but it was a good time to teach her an important lesson.

"My sister was better than me at everything, too," I

said gently, forgetting the game. "Our parents wanted us both to be doctors. She made it, I didn't. They wanted us to get scholarships to college with sports. She got them, I didn't. I understand trying to be good at one thing no one else is. But...you should be nicer when you win. My sister never rubbed it in my face. She encouraged me to get better." I ruffled her hair. "Understand?"

"Yeah..." She might have understood, but she obviously didn't want a lesson in the morality of being a gracious winner and good sport. "What sports did you play?"

"Changing the topic on me again. Sneaky." I pulled her under my arm again and she curled in, giving me that childish, curious look. "I played soccer and softball. I was good, too, but not the best. My parents were proud of me, but I wasn't her."

"Do you like your sister? Sometimes, I don't like my brothers very much..." She frowned. "They're older than me. A lot older than me. Sometimes I wish I had a brother or sister my age or younger. Someone who would look up to me and let me be the big one."

"She's my twin, so it was closer than most, and I did love her, but I didn't always like her. We weren't very good twins. It was like she got everything. All the talent, all the ease, while I floundered and screwed up a lot. It was my life, though. I loved it all the same."

"And now you're a werecat protecting me. I'm sorry."

"That's not your fault, Carey. Don't ever think that. Werecats, we made this decision, and it's an honor to keep you out of harm's way and protect you." Though I wished it had never came to this. I wished this had never stumbled on my doorstep or ripped her from her life.

"But you're so sad and it's my fault! It is!" She crossed her arms, pulling away from me. "This would have never happened to you if my dad didn't have me."

"This would have never happened if your father wasn't betrayed. He sounds like a strong Alpha, and I have full faith that he's going to fix this and take you home. You just need to relax and wait for that to happen."

"But you're sad..."

I closed my eyes for a second, letting that statement sink in as she repeated it. "I am sad. My life is a lonely one, but it's mine, and that's something. Even better, Carey, I wasn't sad playing that game with you. You don't make me sad. I was already sad when you came to my bar and needed help. If anything, right now, I'm pretty happy, even though this has been so bad. Even though those wolves hurt me." I wasn't lying. My sadness had nothing to do with her, nothing at all. She was a bright spot that came out of a dark mini-chapter of my life and hers. "I haven't talked about my human family in...years. Not since before I came to Texas. Thank you for talking to me about them."

When she launched herself at me, I opened my arms and accepted the hug, holding her tight. I buried my nose in her hair and inhaled. There was something to be said about Duty and the werecat drive to protect. It forced me to build a deeper bond with Carey than I ever would have. I was willing to take risks and talk to her, make her feel better, and that I never would have done under other circumstances. She belonged to werewolves, but for a moment, my body was her shield and my heart belonged to her.

Tears pricked my eyes. It was sad that death and destruction were needed to give me something in the world to hold on to. And I had to hold on to her.

CHAPTER EIGHT

"Lock the door behind me, kiddo," I ordered, feeling the overbearing call of the full moon. The sun was setting and that meant I had to get going, but I was reluctant to leave Carey by herself all night. We spent all day playing a variety of games on my little Switch, jumping between laughter and tears. It was a roller coaster of emotion, two girls in hiding, each wondering what their life would be like when it was all over. Needless to say, emotions were always high, even when they were good.

"I will, I will!" she whined, stomping over to me and beginning to push. "Now get out of here. I won't do anything or contact anyone. I think it's perfectly clear that that's a stupid idea. I don't want to spend another night looking for a new place to hide, so just go!"

I groaned, turning to walk out of the room. She was right. The lesson about talking to anyone was perfectly clear now. This time yesterday, we were getting ready for dinner in my apartment. Now we were in a run down motel owned by a fae-human family.

"Be safe and careful. I won't be more than a five minute run away, I promise." I didn't stop walking because she didn't stop pushing. When I turned around again to look at her, she was in the doorway and I was firmly outside of it.

"Just come back," she whispered. "I need you."

"I will." With a smile, I closed the door for her and stayed there until I heard both locks click into place. The sun was dropping fast, but I had to know she was secure, even though my body was beginning to burn with the need to become a monster.

I stepped back as my brain became more feline and hissed at me, mad that I locked easy prey away. After that, I knew I needed to start running.

Full moons were rough. The call and pressure to change was irresistible, and no matter how hard I tried, I could never overcome it. And I tried. Every full moon, I tried. This time was more important than the others, and I gasped as the Change began to force itself.

I barely made it into the woods behind the motel, yanking my clothes off desperately. As pieces of my clothing fell, my hands became more useless, forced into paws. The sick sound of bones breaking marked every Change, and this one was no exception. It was a slow Change for me, too. I was fighting it as I tried to get everything off.

Once my underwear was on the ground, I dropped to

all fours, resisting a scream or snarl as I let the full moon take me away.

I was panting at the end of it, angry, hungry, and out of place. I was a werecat off my home territory, which made my feline edgier than normal, something I could ignore in human form thanks to the distraction that was Carey, but not now. I hissed as I began to sniff the new woods around me, unsure. Needing to find prey, I picked up the faint scent of a doe and took off, silent and powerful.

This was why I wasn't worried about the werewolves attacking. During a full moon, the animal was mostly in charge and I was pretty much along for the ride, the human part of my soul taking refuge as its partner decided to kill, eat, and run.

It was a strange detachment. I knew there was a doe in front of me. I knew I was hunting it, but it felt like I had no control over the steering wheel. The control would slowly come back as the cat satisfied itself, but not in the beginning. Not right then.

I felt my claws sink into the earth. I felt the powerful muscles twitching under my skin tense. I felt my body crouch. Stalking in the underbrush, I approached, already considering what sort of meal I was about to have. I had skipped having a human dinner because I knew this was coming and the feline was going to gorge herself on the wild raw meat.

I was not even five yards away when its head came up, looking out into the darkness directly at me, but not seeing me. I was downwind, so my scent couldn't have carried to the doe. It was dark except the light of the moon, barely able to get through the thick canopy over my head. I must have made a heavy step then that drew its attention.

It didn't matter. It was too late for the doe.

I pounced, silent and fast, taking it down in that single move, I clamped my mouth over its throat, sinking my long saber fangs through the windpipe and jugular, maybe even the carotid artery. It was the perfect kill, something the cat was pleased with as blood filled its mouth and the struggle of the doe ended before it ever really began.

Eating wasn't pleasant, not for my human side, but necessary. I never begrudged the big cat for taking what it needed and leaving the carcass for the rest of the wild.

Once full, my girl was content to let us wander the woods, soaking up the new atmosphere. It looked, to my human perception, just like any other piece of East Texas forest, pine trees. Well, those were the standout, anyway.

She took me further from the motel than I wanted to go and even picked up speed when a new scent hit our nose. I was just along for the ride until she wanted to give it back, so I didn't bother to fight with it. It would have done me no good.

We stopped on the edge of a pond and she took a long drink before lying out under the moonlight, finally letting us relax and digest the meal.

"Ah, good evening, cat," a male voice said politely. Both sides of my soul jumped at that, hissing as we spun to see the intrusion. Brin walked slowly towards us, smiling gently as he drew near. "It's a wonderful evening, isn't it? Not too hot, not too cold. Perfect August night."

I bared my teeth, but the cat also bobbed our head. Fantastic. She liked that a fae walked in on our full moon nap. Full moons. It was the worst time for me to be a werecat. Normally when I Changed, I retained a majority of the control and blended nicely with my feline half, but not tonight. Tonight we were on opposite pages. Not a good place to be and not safe for Brin, who could make easy prey or a serious threat.

"You know the fae love cats, right? I'm not going to harm you. This is my pond, I'll remind you, and this is pretty far from your territory. Show respect where respect is due." He folded his arms behind his back, patient with me.

I lowered my head in what was supposed to be a bow.

"Very good. I actually wanted to talk to you both. You're protecting Carey Everson, human daughter of that werewolf Alpha. Sad business, that. It got me thinking."

Oh hell. Fae thinking was never good. My cat didn't seem disturbed though, completely at ease with him and his presence. For once, I wanted the more defensive and aggressive cat and I didn't get it. Perfect.

"You are going against wolves. Have they attacked you? You got those injuries from somewhere. Normally werecats on Duty find strength and protect their territory at the same time. You must have been driven away."

I just nodded my large head. He had the right of it.

"That's not good. While it's happened before, generally once a human is under the protection of a werecat, it's a safer bet to just leave it alone. The werecat is as much of a deterrent as it is a warrior." He hummed thoughtfully before continuing. "I have a human wife. I don't like that. I don't like that some wolves have decided to pick a fight to take the charge of a werecat. That's not good."

I could relate to that. It didn't make much sense on the wolves' part. There was no way five werewolves could have taken Carey from me, but the fact that they *tried*? That was bad business for everyone, which was why I took her and put both of us into hiding.

"They would have attacked you in wolf form as well. I could smell the blood from you, along with a touch of silver. That's foul play in my books. I'll have to contact my own. If they're willing to use silver on a werecat, who knows if they might use iron on a fae..." He growled and it sounded feral. Not like my deep, wild growl, but a rabid animal that was barely held back by its leash. "I'm probably paranoid, but it says something that I'm as old as I am and just a little paranoid. Well, fae problems aside, I wanted to offer you a gift."

That had my hackles rising. I should have noticed he was fae and moved on. Fairy gifts weren't trustworthy. My cat lay down, fighting my urge to leave. Damn girl thought this was perfectly normal.

"The human and the feline, warring for control. Jacky Leon, how much do you know about fae? You know enough to not get caught up saying thank you and you know how to barter. I caught that earlier, don't think I didn't. Well, your cat knows more instinctively than you do, so trust her for a moment." He smirked, kneeling in front of me. "See, cats and the fae get along. We always have. Dogs became man's best friend, but the cats and their fickle natures appealed to us. Cait sidhe are more common than Cu sidhe, even. Ah...cat fae and dog fae, respectively." He reached out slowly. I tried my best to jerk my head away, but my cat thought a scratch was a great idea, lowering my head further and letting him get his fingers behind my ears. For a moment, I was positive he must have spelled us, removing my ability to leave, but the feline half disagreed.

"I'll keep explaining. I can feel you fight, but there's no reason to. This gift isn't for you, Jacky, it's for your charming feline half. I would never give a gift to a cat and expect repayment for it in the future. I just hope that maybe one day you will consider my family and I, and this gift. Maybe one day, I'll need you to protect my wonderful wife and this will help you." His smirk turned into a large grin. "There's a lot you don't know, but one day you might need to know. For now, I just want you to accept this gift and stick it to the werewolves who have decided to try and harm a human girl. Unacceptable on their part, and against the Law."

Something burned in my mind, even making my cat uncomfortable. Finally, the smart thing happened, and I snarled, swiping a paw at the fae for whatever he was doing.

But as quickly as it started, it was over. He wasn't in front of me either. I jumped to look behind me and found him, his arms once again folded behind his back.

"Werecats. Strong, smart, territorial, and beautiful. You take the form of a beast that no longer walks this earth and you hold on to life with all your fangs and claws, fighting against the tide that would see you wiped out. A shame, since wolves are smaller and weaker than you. They have one advantage, though. Pack magic."

I bared my teeth. I knew what pack magic was. The ability for wolves to talk telepathically with each other, among other things. It made their hunting strategies the best in the world, and even though I could defeat a small group, the pack magic helped them to the bitter end. They were able to change plans and react while I fought alone and against the very tide he spoke of. It was the direct counterpart of a werecat's territory magic, our ability to connect with our land and know damn near everything we needed to know about it, like if there were other predators entering it.

"You do know," he said softly. "I should have expected that, really. Well, I gave you a boon that will even the playing fields, kitten. Now you can talk to anyone while in your werecat form. That means you can still communicate. Isn't that nice?"

The puzzlement must have been clear even on my feline face because he laughed.

"Focus on me and think. *Speak* to me."

I did as he asked, narrowing my eyes on him. *"Like this?"*

"Very good!" He clapped excitedly. "Perfect. Now if you'll excuse me, I'm done for the evening and—"

"Why? Why did you do this for me?" I needed

answers. He'd just forced a fairy gift on me, god damn it. I had to know why.

"Because they broke the rules, the wolves. Their own and the Law. Don't think I don't follow the news and can't put it all together. Keep Miss Carey safe, please. Just remember that I have human family. This sort of thing could encourage others to play badly. They *must* understand that there are consequences to it. If you fall to the wolves, there won't be any repercussions for them. No one would dare try, including your own kind. But it would make your kind vulnerable to it happening again. This was a selfless, and yet selfish, gift. I ask nothing in return for it and cede the right to it. I would ask you to just remember. That's all."

Meddling. He was meddling in the affairs of werecats and werewolves for his own personal reasons. I had given him the opportunity and his reasons were, in a sense, sound. He had a point, a strong one. Werecats were only allowed to exist at this point because of the Duty. It was something I had been repeating to myself since Carey showed up. Failure wasn't an option. Apparently, I wasn't the only person who thought so, and his gift was a good one. A very good one.

"*Thank you,*" I said softly. His gift, freely given, deserved a thanks. He wiped the debt, but I gave it back to him. I would remember tonight. Forgetting it could prove deadly.

He waved once, then disappeared.

I felt edgy long after his disappearance. I jumped at

small noises. Even my feline, finally letting go of control, didn't know what to think about what had just happened.

Carey's father, Heath, believed in fate. I was beginning to as well.

The night wore on and I trotted slowly back towards the motel, keeping my nose in the air, just in case the wind wanted to tell me anything about what might be nearby. I found nothing and went to the door of the motel room, thinking about Carey.

I lay down, waiting for dawn, protecting her door. I wasn't worried about humans anymore. The cat and I were sated, and there was no one else at the motel. It was too dark and wooded to see the road. I was safe, and so was my human.

And I had a fairy gift, a permanent one. The world was a weird place.

9
CHAPTER NINE

I was still awake when the sun came up. Instead of waiting outside the door, I headed back into the woods, finding my clothing before the sun asked me to Change back into my human form. I collected everything and let my human form rush out, trying to mentally block out the pain.

What a strange night. I couldn't really believe it, even though it had happened. Fae were meddlers, and if they could make something about themselves, they would. Brin was a fae. I really should have seen it coming. Hasan had spent years warning me to stay clear of them, but idiot me thought I would just be a customer and get ignored by the one here.

I was wrong. Now I was going to live with the fairy gift and hopefully it wasn't going to bite me in the ass. It wasn't the priority—Carey was. The politics weren't the priority—Carey was. Was I trying to be mindful of the politics? Yes. Hasan would have my head if I wasn't.

It was the same mental debate I had all night. Kicking myself but also being grateful. Hating my place in the world, but accepting it.

"This was supposed to be simple," I muttered, pulling on my clothes. "Keep the human girl safe while werewolves were fighting it out. Simple. Keep her in the apartment for a week, maybe two. Fucking simple. So why do I feel like I'm knee-deep in some shit I don't want to be?"

I growled as I finished getting dressed and stomped back to the room, knocking to hopefully grab Carey's attention.

"Carey!" I knocked harder and heard the moan of a sleeping child not wanting to get up yet. I knew the noise because I had made it my fair share of times in life.

"Let me get the door," Brin said behind me. I sighed, turning on him to see him holding another tray. "I won't ever bring you lunch or dinner, but my wife believes everyone should have a healthy breakfast." He shoved the tray at me, his smile not fading. "And about last night... It's not a secret. I don't care who you tell or show off your new ability to, but please, don't tell them who gave it to you. Just say that the fae respect our felines much like humans respect their dogs or something. I don't want to be harassed by people for it."

"So you know that if the wolves find out I can now communicate in my werecat form, they might try to kill both me and you?" It was another thought that had already gone through my mind. It evened the playing field, something no werewolf was going to be fond of. I would have to be very careful with it.

"Yes, but also, I don't want any fae coming to bother me about it. The Law doesn't say we can't get involved with the going-ons of other species, but it's preferred that we keep our dealings confined to humans. They're more gullible and less dangerous."

"Less dangerous." I couldn't hold back a disbelieving snort. "With their iron, guns, and weapons of mass destruction."

"They don't believe in us anymore, and that makes them harmless for the most part. They no longer believe in the old, old stories." He pulled out his keyring, jangling with a dozen different keys, and found one, finally unlocking the door for me. He opened it, even, being quite the gentleman. "There ya go. Enjoy your breakfast."

"Tell your *wife* thank you," I replied, stepping in. I kicked the door shut next, leaving him out there. After I dropped the tray, I walked over to the bed and looked down at Carey, pushing her hair off her face. "Hey, kiddo. Time to rise and shine. Another day is here."

She made that noise again and pulled the blanket over her head. I gave up immediately, in no rush to force her up. She was lucky that Brin showed up with a key. I should have been worried about that, but there was no point. Somewhere in the back of my mind, I always knew he had to have a master key to the motel he owned. There was no reason to get freaked out over it now.

I decided to shower, not caring if breakfast got cold. I

was dirty and tired, something I was going to have to accept. Maybe Carey would let me take a nap later. She was sufficient at keeping herself busy and out of trouble.

As I rinsed off the grime of the forest, I considered my game plan again. It hadn't changed at all, but I was paranoid just like the fae. When I was done in the shower, there was really nothing new for me to think about except the fae gift, which could prove useful, but hopefully wouldn't.

I didn't try to wake her up again when I was dry, either. I just threw on a pair of sweatpants and tank top, passing out right next to her.

I WOKE up to her shaking me this time. I opened one eye at the young girl over me, knowing it was glowing and gold.

"That's cool. Werewolves just have different color eyes, but you get the cat pupil thing, too." She didn't seem as impressed as I had hoped. "You've been asleep for awhile. How was your night?"

"Fine," I mumbled. This was why I liked having a bar. It meant my nocturnal schedule didn't seem weird to my patrons and I wasn't trying to live a life I couldn't. Carey, however, was human. Her body naturally wanted to be up with the sun. Not early enough for her to get the door, but up sometime in the morning. "What time is it?" I asked, not moving.

"Nearly noon. That guy, Brin? He picked up the tray

and said you were on your own for food. Don't worry. I ate breakfast."

"You seem like you're in a better mood today," I remarked, pushing the conversation off the fae. I hadn't told her what he was and I didn't plan to. The less she knew, the less trouble she could get into.

"Well, I said I wouldn't contact anyone, but this morning, I checked my phone, just for a second."

I growled, low and deep. Damn it. "What happened?"

"Nothing. I only had it on long enough to read some texts. That's all. Well, one of my brothers contacted me! He said that he and Landon were okay!"

"That's good." I finally pushed myself to sit up. The new day was bringing good news. I didn't like her turning on the possibly-trackable phone, but it was good news. She would have someone at the end of this. "I'm happy for you." I was able to manage a smile, but part of me was sad.

It meant eventually I was going to have to give her back to her family. It was the natural way of things once my Duty was complete, but it made me ache. She wasn't my human in the end. It was temporary, and everything we talked about would just be memories for both of us. The transient life of a werecat called to Duty and asked to care, only to have the object of that near-obsession taken away once it was all over. There was nothing that could be done. But until that moment, she was still mine. Still my child of this earth and due all the respect and treasured as such, just as I promised.

"Are you okay?" she asked softly. "I turned the phone off right after I was done. I don't think anyone would have found out anything. I promise! I know the phones can be tracked, but…"

"It's fine. You deserve to hear from your family," I said, pulling her into a hug. I might have been Duty-bound to consider her family, and she might want to pretend while she was in my care since it made it easier for her, but I had no real aspirations that she seriously believed it. She was trying to be nice, comfort herself. I would be second fiddle to her real family, no matter what.

And that was how it was supposed to be. Werecats lost a lot thanks to the peace recreated by the Laws. Making real families with humans was one of those things. We were only allowed the temporary attachment of Duty. Not that it was against the Law, but it was werecat law.

"Let's play some games," I said softly, grabbing a controller.

The day passed slowly, and so did the night. Nothing to do except play video games and wait until things were cleared up in Dallas. Nothing to do until her father was found, dead or alive. Nothing to do until she was gone.

I barely slept that night. Maybe it was because I was restless, my mind attached to everything over the last few days. Maybe it was because Carey was unusually restless next to me. I didn't know.

But I was awake when she started to whimper in her sleep. I sat up quickly, looking down at her. Oh no. I had no idea how to handle nightmares. She kicked and began to thrash. I raised my hands but couldn't bring myself to touch her. Everything had been going so well. Why now? Why did the nightmares have to start in on her now? I knew they could come after all of this, but I was so woefully unprepared.

Then she screamed and I grabbed her, hauling her over to me.

"Carey, wake up. Please. Come on, sweetheart. It's just a nightmare."

"Help," she cried out, weak and tired. "I don't want to die..."

"Open your eyes, Carey," I snapped, shaking her just a small amount. I got what I wanted. Her big eyes popped open, looking up at me. I exhaled a terrified breath, hugging her close as the tears started immediately. She sobbed into my shirt, clinging to me like her life depended on it. "It's okay, baby girl," I whispered, rubbing the top of her head. "It's okay."

"There were monsters. They tried to take me away again. They killed Daddy and Richard and Landon. I didn't know what to do. I was so scared. You weren't there!" She was shaking like a leaf. "There was so much blood an-and I didn't know how to stop it!"

"Shh." I could only hold her as she told me what her nightmares had brought.

"There was roaring and howls. It was so scary, Jacky."

"I bet it was, but it's not real. The nightmares aren't real, Carey. I promise."

"You'll never let them take me, right? You'll keep me safe?"

"I'm doing everything in my power to keep you safe. I promise. I would die before I let them have you." I meant every word with a conviction that should have scared me. I should have been terrified of what I had just said, but I wasn't. Nothing could have Carey and I wouldn't let anything else give her new nightmares. She obviously had enough. One was one too many.

I consoled her, the tears pricking my own eyes again. After this was long over, she wasn't going to be the only girl in the room with nightmares, that was certain. There was blood on my hands now that had never been there before, and the only reason I was holding it together was because she needed me to be strong. It was her vulnerability, her need, that made my spine steel to all the things this was throwing at both of us. As she cried herself back to sleep, wrapped in my arms, I knew there would come a moment when I didn't need to be the strongest person in the room anymore. I was *not* looking forward to that moment.

As dawn approached, I knew why werecats actively avoided getting roped into Duty and our place in the world. Why we really didn't advertise where we were or educate people. If some vampire didn't know the Law and what it meant for werecats, it wasn't our business to fix. Out of sight, out of mind.

Every moment I grew more attached thanks to my instincts and every moment I knew the end was drawing nearer. She was long asleep again when I stepped out of the room, pulling my own cell phone from my pocket.

I dialed a number, my heart pounding.

"Daughter. To what do I owe the pleasure?" Hasan's voice was like honey, always pulling me in and trying to make me feel cherished and loved. I didn't trust it, but I let it make me feel a little better just for a second before telling him why I was calling.

"I was called to Duty," I whispered, leaning on the door. Behind me, inside the room, she was asleep, dreaming hopefully of her family and how much fun they would have together again.

"Explain," he demanded, the honey gone, only steel left in its place.

I did as he wanted, telling him about the last three days. I started with the facts. The who, the what, the where. Ish. I didn't tell him where I was at the motel, nor about the fairy gift. Only that Carey and I had been driven further into hiding thanks to an attack by a small hunting pack.

He snarled as I explained I took a hit from a silver bullet and that I was recovering slowly. He sighed when I reached the end. "There's nothing I can do without breaking the Law," he informed me gently. "As much as I hate it…"

"I know. You taught me the Law pretty damn well, Hasan. No, I wanted to talk to you about something more personal. How do you deal with it? How does anyone expect a werecat to let go when it's over?"

"You have it harder than most. A minor brings out all of your protective instincts, but also your parental ones. Most of the time, it's not children. Adults who accidentally worked for the wrong supernatural, who crossed someone else. Normally, they aren't even targets, it's just an added measure of safety. Things this big were common back when the Laws were new, but in the last two to three hundred years? Practically unheard of." I heard him playing with something in the background. He was probably in bed with a drink on his nightstand or a book he'd been reading. "You'll have to give her up, though. You can't keep her."

"I know." That was the hard part. "In the end, it's for the best right? I'm not doing anything wrong, am I?"

"Ah, my confident daughter. The world has finally found a chink in that armor you wear, has it?" He chuckled, but it lacked any humor. "No, you aren't doing anything wrong. Just keep her safe and then give her to her rightful parent. You'll know when the time is right. It will come as naturally as the rest of this has. Being so young and facing this must not be easy, but I believe in you."

"Thanks. Well…I need to get back inside and check on her." I didn't, but Hasan wasn't there. He wouldn't be able to smell the lie. Then I remembered something else that had happened in the last few days. "Do you know a werecat named Lani?"

"Hm. Yes, and I know you talk to her, though she doesn't know I've been snooping around. She's not a bad werecat to call an ally. Next time when something is wrong, though, call me first. I am your father." He was chiding me now, and I wanted to roll my eyes. Hasan and I were complicated. We would always be complicated. There were times when I despised him and wished him dead, and others, like this exact moment, where all I wanted was to curl up and cry on his shoulder. He was beginning to tip the balance out of his favor by that statement, however.

"Don't get on to me for that. She's a local, and knew more about the werewolves in the region." I tried not to get snappy with him and failed, hearing the unintended bite to my words. "Look. I just wanted to talk to someone who's…She said you were there when the Laws were written. I don't know if I knew that, but…"

"You hate calling me for help. Admit it. You would never talk to me if I didn't call you. Now you're choking on the bone of calling me and being vulnerable." He had a bitter note to his voice now, which I knew was my fault. "Stay safe, protect your charge, and get done with this. And Jacqueline? Don't die on me."

"Okay." I hung up. I shouldn't have, but I did. I turned my phone off before he could call me back to chastise me for not letting him say goodbye. When I walked back into the room, Carey was sitting up in the bed, staring at me.

"Who was that?" she asked.

"Another werecat," I answered.

"Why do you get to call people, but not me?" That was a demand.

"Because they won't know my number and be able to track my phone," I retorted. "Finding my bar is one thing, since it's in the middle of my territory, but my cell phone number is guarded and private. Only two werecats even have it and I've never given it out." Crossing my arms, I waited for the eleven-year-old security expert to tell me I was wrong in making the call. When she had nothing to say, I continued. "It's the third phone call I've made since we left...Damn it."

"What?" She crawled across the bed towards me, but I refused to answer.

I *had* called wolves with it. There was nothing I could do about it now if the number had leaked to the wrong wolves. I had to hope that the Alpha Council kept my number under lock and key. Even then, like Carey, I probably didn't have it on long enough to have anyone tracking it.

"Get back to sleep," I asked gently. "I know there's nightmares, but please. You'll feel better if you sleep through the night."

"I'll try," she promised softly. "Only if you promise that tomorrow you'll go to the gas station and get some more snacks for us before I wake up."

Bargaining. Good sign? I hope so. "Yeah, Carey, I can promise that." I smiled gently, leaning down to kiss her forehead.

She crawled back to her half of the bed and was thankfully old enough to tuck herself back in. I turned on the TV, keeping the volume low, and let that background noise help lull her back to sleep. Considering it was four in the morning, the show that came on must have been too boring for her and she was out within a few minutes.

With that, I decided to finally nap myself, and only a nap. I set an alarm for when breakfast would show up, which was normally around eight, then curled into a ball on the other side of the bed, closing my eyes.

I didn't have any nightmares. Maybe it was because I was one of the monsters she heard roaring in her own nightmare.

10

CHAPTER TEN

I was up before Carey, a blessing since I had promised to hit up the gas station for snacks and the very idea of disappointing her gave me anxiety now. I could hear footsteps, which told me the alarm wasn't only useful, but my timing for breakfast was also perfect. I opened the door to the motel room without bothering to get decent and found Brin, took the tray in silence, and left it on the table. He didn't say anything to me either—another blessing. I wasn't in the mood for conversation.

Taking a quick shower gave me the chance to look over my injuries again. I had to swallow my shock when I saw there were none. I was healed. That wasn't right. There was no way I should have been healed already. I thought back, frowning. Did I still have them yesterday morning after the full moon? I had no real idea. I couldn't remember if I had checked them or not.

But it didn't really matter, since today the only thing I

had was a small scar where the bullet had hit me. Silver burned like that, leaving scars. I didn't mind the scar or being ugly, but part of me really wished that I wouldn't have a permanent reminder of everything that had happened.

The gunshot was thankfully the only scar, as the scratches and bites I had gotten were long gone now. I ground my teeth as I figured it was probably Brin that had done this, and I fully intended to ask him why.

With that in mind, I got dressed, opting for one of my favorite pairs of jeans to make me feel normal. I needed normal. I needed anything that reminded me what normal is. I needed anything that reminded me that I did have a life and one day I would go back to it, for good or bad.

I left Carey sleeping, only pausing to write a note in case she woke up before I returned. Once I was in the main office, I slammed my hand on the bell, waiting impatiently. Brin was yawning as he walked out of the back office.

"Do you ever go home to this wife you have?" I asked, snappy and vulnerable.

"Yes," he answered nonchalantly, as if he didn't realize I was angry.

"Did you heal me?" I demanded softly. "Without my permission?"

"No. Kind of." His smirk gave me a firm idea of what the truth was. "I pushed the silver to leave your system a little faster while giving you the gift. Silver likes fae where it hates your kind. It answered my call. It was such a tiny amount to be causing you as many problems as it was, and since I'm meddling already, I didn't think that was too much."

"Why me?"

"You could be any werecat. I don't really care about *you*. I care about what you're doing. Get over it. Accept what I offered graciously and move on."

That had me baring my teeth, a growl vibrating my chest. His eyebrows went up slowly. "I have enough on my plate. I don't need to be looking over my shoulder, wondering if the fae are trustworthy."

"Oh, I can answer that. We're not, not if we want a trade or bargain, but I didn't ask for those. Look, I explained already, but it didn't seem to sink in. It's in my personal interests that you do your Duty. Not this specifically, but in the general sense. You have a reputation to uphold that is much older than you, and that reputation keeps everyone feeling comfortable. We're allowed to breathe a little easier if we know the werecats can and will do what's needed to protect our humans from each other." He sighed, crossing his arms as he looked me over. "Anyone with a human in their lives would relate to what's going on here and offer assistance. Anyone. Don't kid yourself by thinking we all just turn a blind eye to werecats and their Duty. That kind of thinking can and will destroy your ability to make valuable allies."

I bit back my anger. "I wish you had told me before actually doing it."

"Sure. You would have told me no and I would have

done it anyway. I decided to skip the act of betrayal and just get to the gift-giving. Plus, you're in my motel, my territory. By the grounds of hospitality, seeing that you come to no harm and helping you is part of the deal."

I curled a lip, turning away from him. "I should have kept driving when I realized you were here."

"Maybe, but it's too late now. I actually gave you the time to run, too. I was thinking you would notice me and get moving after you and your charge got some sleep, yet here you are, still in my motel, still eating my wife's home cooked breakfasts." He started to laugh. "Not everyone is out to get you, Jacky. Some part of you must realize that, because you're *still here*."

I waved a hand dismissively at him and walked out, shaking my head. I should have told Hasan about Brin. I should have kept driving. He was right, though. Some part of me did just want to stay in the motel. I had an ally, no matter how out of the blue it was, and it was someone who could really help and not some human bystander. I had someone to talk to, who understood what was going on.

I headed to the gas station, seeing it was Rian behind the counter this time. Unlike their father, who kept a glamour up over his red hair, the three half-fae sons didn't. Rian was a punk, his flaming copper red hair in a mohawk with blue streaks. He had more metal in his face than I had seen before on a person, and I wondered if he set off metal detectors with that sort of assortment.

He seemed stiff when I walked in, which he hadn't been the last time I had seen him behind the counter.

Over the last few days, I had visited the gas station on a number of occasions, and Rian was my favorite.

"What's up?" I asked him, not going to the food, but directly for him.

He nodded his head to the back of the room. "Just came in." His voice was a hushed whisper.

I turned slowly, breathing in the air and paused, fear flying through me.

Werewolf.

"Haven't had the chance to call my father. I don't know if there's more."

"There's always more," I said softly, my heart racing. I couldn't will it to calm down as I stepped around a display to get a better view of the werewolf. He was grabbing some cold coffee from a cooler in the back. He was dressed to kill with beaten-up jeans and a thick leather jacket. I could see the gun in its holster at his waist.

I started walking to him, determined. I had no idea what I was going to do when I finished closing the distance, but I wasn't letting him go unnoticed.

When he was in arm's reach, I saw the moment he noticed I was there. He hadn't been paying attention, the fool. I reached out, grabbing his shirt with one hand and his gun with another, snarling. He raised his hands as I threw the gun away.

"What are you doing here?" I demanded, my voice rough and animalistic. "Who do you work for?" *That's what they ask in the movies, right?* I was throwing it out there. Maybe I would even get an answer.

He growled back as I knew my scent was finally registering in his brain. Wolves have a much better sense of smell than I did, which meant he was truly not paying attention when I walked in if he let me get the drop on him.

"You must be the werecat he sent her to. We're not here to kill you or Carey. We need her." I smelled the lie. Fucking idiot must not have realized I could do that just like him.

I slammed him back, hearing the glass door crack, then break, drinks falling out and going all over the floor. "Don't fuck with me! How many more wolves are here?"

"Like I'm going to tell you that," he snapped back, now starting to struggle. I was six inches shorter than him, probably a hundred pounds smaller, but that didn't matter. I was a god-damned werecat. He wasn't breaking my hold. "Did you really think you could hide her? That we don't have the resources to find you wherever you go?" Now he smiled. "Like we haven't been watching you since the full moon?" He chuckled. "One wolf in the gas station and no backup...really? You must be new at this."

Ice ran through my veins and the shock of what he said must have loosened my grip. He took the chance to bring a knee up into my gut, forcing me to let go of him. I had no time to recover before a fist connected with my jaw. I shook it out before he got in another hit and pushed away his leg. I ducked down, small enough to get under another swing, and pushed forward, slamming my shoulder into his gut.

We both went down, into displays and shelves, things

flying everywhere. In the midst of the struggle, he rolled us, forcing me onto my back. I went for his eyes as he got two hands around my throat. I started to Change, knowing deadly claws were replacing my finger nails, my hand was becoming a paw, and longer than it was in my human form. A quick swipe and the spray of blood that followed told me that I hit my mark. His scream made my ears ring as I took a deep breath when his hands were done. I pulled back on the Change and stalked after him as he tried to stagger away, holding his bloody face.

I jumped on his back, forcing him into another set of shelves. Rian was screaming something but I ignored it, too focused on killing the other predator who had come into my domain to take what didn't belong to him. The wolf tried to pull me off his back as I tried to adjust my angle on him, going for his throat this time. I felt flesh rend under my nails and another scream dominated everything. He staggered underneath me, going to his knees.

I was relentless, pushing him all the way down and rolling him over. When I was on his chest, I snarled victoriously. I sank my fingers into his neck and pulled, taking out everything except his spine.

I was dazed the moment it was over, looking down to see what I had done. The last wolves I had fought, I had done so as a werecat in my animal form. This time I had killed a man with bare hands.

"Jacky, you have to go!" Rian yelled. "There's a fucking hunting group in the parking lot. There's too many for us!"

I jumped up, letting his works sink in. I picked up the gun off the tile floor, my mind reeling, trying to put together any sort of plan.

No.

All I could do was run. I flew out of the gas station towards the motel, covering four to five feet with every stride. I could see them clearly. Brin was trying to talk them down with his other two sons backing him up. The problem was, there were a dozen wolves this time, maybe more.

This was a true hunting party. Werewolves only ran in that number for one reason, and that was when they were killing a werecat.

I saw Carey there as well, held roughly by her upper arm by one of the brutes. Luckily, everyone was still in human form. Regretfully, they all had guns too.

I never slowed down, even when they realized I was coming. One lifted a rifle, but was stopped. He said something I didn't hear, but I didn't honestly care what that was.

"Stop! We don't have to kill you!" he yelled.

I jumped.

The thing about cats was that we could and would jump long distances when it was required. I cleared fifteen feet, landing on a wolf next to Carey, who screamed at the top of her lungs. It might not have been my smartest move, but the only thing I really cared about was that she was next to me and maybe I could get her out of the middle of the hunting party and running with the fae before I died. I lifted my gun and fired before the one holding Carey had time to react. His eyes were wide with shock as he dropped, a bullet hole on the right side of his forehead. I grabbed her, pulling her into my body and kicking another wolf. I fired at the same wolf, putting it down before it was a problem.

Three down. Ten to go.

I'll kill all of them before they take what's mine.

One tried to grab me away from Carey, so I kicked back, stomping on a foot, feeling the steel toe of the werewolf's boot bend and crush the toes underneath. I held her with one hand, and fired with the other, hitting another wolf in the shoulder. I spun around, bringing her with me, and fired at a wolf bringing his sidearm out as fast as he could. I was faster than them, stronger than them.

They can't have her. She's mine.

A gun went off and this time, it wasn't mine. I yelped as pain lanced my thigh.

"Incapacitate her!" someone yelled. I fired blindly at the next wolf I saw. I knew I hit him from the scream, but I don't know where. Next to me, Carey huddled close and finally, I saw a gap as I turned again. Brin was there, wide-eyed. I knew he couldn't —shouldn't—get involved. He couldn't leave his wife and sons at risk if the wolves decided to kill him. A human woman and three half-fae wouldn't have it easy in the world if he was gone, and if he pissed off the wolves, they might kill his family too.

But that didn't change that I did trust him just a little bit and to me, Carey was the most important thing in the world. I shoved Carey at him and into his arms. He lifted her, backing away. His sons pushed off a couple of wolves trying for her. I lost track after that as something hit my face and sent me to the pavement. I was dazed for a second, but I didn't let the wolf kick the gun from my hand. I shot his foot instead. I had no idea how many bullets I had, but if I had to use every one of them, I was going to.

Another gunshot hit my back and sent me to my chest, knocking the air out of me. I pushed up, standing slowly as another bullet tore into my shoulder. That one didn't knock me down, but a fourth gunshot to the stomach did, sending me back to my knees.

All I could hear was screaming at that point, the fighting fading into the background. I looked down, shocked at the blood pouring out of my abdomen. I was an EMT—at least I once was. I knew what it meant. Being a werecat, I knew the bullets were all silver.

There was a very strong chance I was going to die.

I didn't let it stop me from standing up again. I pushed into the wolf closest to me and took him to the ground. I was weak, much weaker than normal and I was barely able to hit him before I was yanked off and thrown a few feet away. When I landed, my head smacked the asphalt. My vision went blurry.

No.

I heard Carey screaming. I heard others yelling and another gunshot. For a second, I thought they had shot me, but they hadn't. I was just in that much pain already.

My vision went dark to the tell-tale sound of trucks driving off.

CHAPTER ELEVEN

"You have to get up, feline."

I didn't want to. Everything hurt. I felt weak and sluggish. I didn't want to get up. Where was I, anyway? Why wasn't I at home in my bar? Who was talking to me? It wasn't Hasan. It wasn't even Joey, the damn human.

"Jacky, please. I did all I could to get the silver out of your system, but I can't force you to rise."

Silver? Why had there been silver in my system? I didn't get into trouble that normally had silver involved. I didn't get into trouble. I actively avoided any sort of anything, really.

"They shot me and my son, Eamon. Nothing fatal. Just some warnings that they were willing to kill us if we didn't hand over Carey. I'm sorry, but I had my wife to think about and my boys. I'm sorry."

Carey...

I took a sharp breath, my eyes flying open. The

breath made my chest tighten and hurt beyond imagining. It took me a few moments to be able to breathe again, whimpering a little as I tried.

Carey.

"There you are. You had my wife and I worried. You were dead for a little while, cat." My eyes found the man talking. Brin, the fae owner of the motel. He had a human wife and two...no, three half-fae sons. "Rian showed up after making sure the one in the gas station was well and truly dead. He also called the fae Kings and told them what happened. This is considered private property and there's going to be repercussions for them if the wolves don't handle their own."

"Carey...they have Carey?" My heart sank as that revelation settled in.

"They have Carey," he confirmed softly. "I'm sorry. I couldn't risk my family."

"It's okay," I said hoarsely. "I knew that when I jumped in, but I had to try. I-I..."

"I know. We tried to say she was now fae property, but they weren't buying it. They weren't going to allow me to keep her and when they shot me, I was fine, but then they shot Eamon..." He reached out and patted my shoulder, ever so gently. "You're on the mend, but it won't be fast this time. There was too much...too much damage, too deep. Internal organs and such."

"Yeah...Thank you." I was able to get one arm to move and put my hand over his. "Really. I'm in your debt for trying. You must have slowed them down just enough for me to get there." My lungs hurt, but I didn't let that stop me from saying what needed to be said. I owed him for so much.

"We tried. I think some of them were hoping you wouldn't get there before they could sneak off with her. They showed up the moment you entered the gas station and had her before I was even able to cross the parking lot. It was like they were waiting for the right moment to get her in hand without needing to go through you." He seemed concerned, worried. "They must have been watching us. I only own and have my own claim on this side of the highway. They could have been hiding in the woods across the way and I would have never known. I'm sorry."

"Heh. I still killed a few of them," I managed to say, even as the pain and regret filled me. *I lost her. She's gone. I failed.*

"They also managed to kill you for nearly two minutes," he snapped, glaring now. "And I have six dead werewolves to deal with."

"Call...Call the Alpha Council. They'll clean up. I've already used them." I coughed now, my body rejecting how much I wanted to use it just to speak. The problem was, I couldn't stay down. They took Carey. With that thought, I sat up slowly, trying to work my stiff muscles and ignore the pain. "How long have I been down?"

"Ten hours," he answered, his voice going gentle again. "You can't be thinking..." Realization dawned in his eyes. "You're going to go after them? Are you mad?"

"I swore an oath to protect her."

"And you failed. I'm sorry, but you did. At least you're alive. Let the wolves deal with their own now."

"Is that really what's expected of me?" I couldn't believe it. "Is that really what you think I should do?" I tried to move so that my legs would fall off the edge of the bed. I had a few things I needed to do now that I was awake.

"It's what everyone would tell you to do. To get involved now puts you directly in the line of meddling in the politics and affairs of the werewolves, which is a very bad place to be for a werecat. They won't let it stand."

"I swore an oath to her!" I growled, louder than anything I had been able to say before. "She's *mine*!"

"You lost her. I'm sorry." Brin stood up and stepped away, heading for the exit. He looked back once and sighed. "Let it go, Jacky. No one would fault you for walking away right now, not after the beating you took."

No. I stayed silent until he left. No. I'd promised, and I wasn't going to back out of it now. My Duty was to keep her safe as if she were my own child until I could put her back into the hands of those who have the longer claim, her family or legal guardians. Neither of which were the ones who took her, which meant I wasn't done.

I was slow to get up—which was to be expected, since it was only ten hours after I had been shot four times and died for two minutes. I stumbled to the doors, checking each. One was a closet, one was to the hallway, and just my luck, the very last was the bathroom I needed. I caught a look at myself when I sat down to do my business, seeing the dark circles under my eyes and the pain in the gold. I wondered if I was ever going to feel in control enough to get my hazel back. Someone had washed the blood off me, cleaning me up quite nicely, which was one small blessing.

There were bruises, too. One on my jaw and another on the opposite cheek. My neck had hand prints. The smaller injuries would be gone before the end of the week, but the more pressing ones, the gun shots? I would be nursing those for a while, and they would become a myriad of new scars I would have to live with.

Just like the night I left the apartment with Carey, I knew I didn't have weeks to get back to my best. I had to act, and quickly, so I began to formulate my plan as I washed my hands, then my face. I gingerly tested my body, bending over and wincing in pain as scabs tore and my muscles screamed in revolt at my movement.

When I went back into the bedroom, I found clothing set out on top of the dresser and got dressed. That took longer than anything I did in the bathroom.

Plan. Take Carey back and protect her to the best of my ability, which admittedly hadn't been too great so far.

How? I really had no idea. Brin was right. If I showed up in Dallas-Fort Worth, I would have to get involved with the mess going on there. I figured the wolves attacking me were working against her father, which meant if I took them all out on their own turf, I was giving Heath the upper hand in his fight, if he was still fighting. It was everything a werecat shouldn't do. We were supposed to be impartial protectors, guardians for humanity when the supernatural ruined their lives.

I curled a fist as I sat back down on the bed. It was a defensive role. I was tired of defensive, and in the end, I had failed at it. The only course of action I had now was to be on the offensive.

I had sworn an oath. Carey was mine and they took her from me. My throat tightened as I thought about everything that had happened. Tears flooded my eyes, even as I battled with a deep, unsettling rage growing in my chest. I killed people. A lot of people. I tore a man's throat out with my bare hands after I blinded him.

Ten years ago, I was just an EMT. I had saved people. Now I was killing them.

I'm a monster.

And the other monsters had taken something that belonged to me.

Hasan once told me there would come a moment when I had to embrace what a werecat truly was. That I would have to accept the beast instead of just living with it. He'd said there was nothing wrong with violence in our lives, because we weren't human. We were built to be the top predators of whatever region we claimed, and it was in our nature to defend that claim to the last breath.

He probably never thought it would be over a human. He had probably just wanted me to stop feeling bad for knocking around other werecats when they accidentally or purposefully walked into my territory. It had always felt like needless violence to me.

Fighting for Carey didn't feel needless, though.

"She's mine," I growled, continuing to feel the instinctual pull to protect and care for her, accepting it and holding on to it with everything I could. *And I'm going to defend that claim to my last breath.*

I found the energy to stand up again and walked out of the bedroom, staggering only once and using the wall as my support. I found the fae-human family in their dining room.

"I need to go back to my room and get my things," I said softly, grabbing their attention. Brin was the one who sighed. I saw the young men around their human mother, who wore such an expression of worry that I nearly opened my mouth again to comfort her. I decided against it as Brin closed the distance and pointed to another door.

"Follow me," he ordered.

We walked out of the little house and down a trail that led to the gas station. We were silent until we reached the far side of the motel's parking lot and he stopped.

"This is where we scraped your body from the asphalt," he whispered, pointing down. I could still see the dark stain of my blood there, and it gave me chills. "This is what they're willing to do to capture a little human girl. Are you sure you want to do this?"

"I'm going to show them what I'm willing to do to save a little human girl," I answered.

"And you know what that means? You are going to break so many Laws—"

"They started it," I hissed. "They came into my home to take her and I killed them. They came here and I killed as many as I could. They took something that belongs to me, and yes, I know what it means. I have people I can call and warn. Maybe, just maybe, I'll get some backup. I don't need you questioning me, fae. This has nothing to do with you once I drive away."

"Of course." He inclined his head. "I'll charge you for everything."

"I have the money," I told him, walking past my bloodstain on the asphalt. The money wasn't a problem. The card was limitless. Hasan would never let me go out into the world poor, and I stopped arguing with him about money years ago.

I wasted no time in throwing all of my things back into their suitcases. Then I got Carey's, growling as I saw that the wolves took nothing of hers. She had nothing but the clothes on her back again.

It took me less than twenty minutes to load up my hatchback, my body aching in protest. Brin never stopped watching me, shaking his head in obvious equal parts disappointment and dismay. I was about to get into the hatchback when he grabbed me.

"You could start a war against your kind, Jacky. Please. Remember that there will be other humans who need you one day."

"I am," I whispered harshly. "I *am* thinking about them. They took Carey from me, and let this be a warning to whoever tries to take something from me again. Next time, they'll need to make sure I'm dead. Let the world get angry. I'm going to put fear in their fucking hearts before I rip them out of their fucking chests." I slid in, wincing because of the pain and slammed the door shut before he could say any more.

Duty was defensive. I wasn't going to let it stop there, though. I turned the engine on and screamed out of the parking lot, hitting the gas harder when I was on the highway. I pulled out my phone and punched in a random spot in Dallas as my destination. I didn't care if wolves were going to track me anymore.

I hope they know I'm coming for them. I wonder what they're going to think when they realize I'm not dead and I'm coming for their mangy asses. There better not be a hair out of place on Carey's head.

I turned on the Bluetooth between my hatchback's system and my phone.

"Call last number," I ordered.

It rang twice.

"Jacqueline—"

"They took her from me. I'll be in Dallas." I hung up right after that. I didn't need to have a long conversation with Hasan, but I felt he deserved to know that much. He tried calling back and I hit reject on the touch screen on my dashboard. Then I flicked through to another number and hit it.

"Jacky Leon. I heard some news, and I was worried something happened."

"Something did happen, Harrison. At least a dozen wolves showed up where I was hiding with Carey. Ten or so hours ago. I was shot four times with silver bullets and they took her. There's six dead wolves at the place. You'll get a call from the owner soon. He's called Brin. Get a clean-up crew out there for those guys."

"And what are you going to do? With Carey back in the hands of the wolves, I guess this is the last call—"

"I'm going to get her. You're going to stay out of my way. Before you ask, damn right I know what Laws I'm breaking. You should ask a more important question than that when you speak next."

"And what question would that be?" he asked softly. He was tense, and I couldn't blame him. I was about to say something stupid, and do something even stupider.

"Do I care?"

I hung up on him too.

I rejected another phone call from Hasan once the line was dead and called Lani.

"Jacky. I hope everything is okay." She sounded normal. I nearly felt bad for what I was about to drop on her head.

"What exactly does the Law cover when it comes to a werecat's Duty?" I knew the Laws as they were written but I had never sat down and really considered the nuances of them. I knew for a fact that I was about to break the Law, but the wolves had first and I was still, in my opinion, under the oath of Duty. If there was ever a dangerous grey area, I had found it.

"You are required to protect the human from all harm until the conditions are met. I take it, you promised Carey to take her back to her family or another keeper when things settled down, so that's two conditions."

"Exactly. That I knew, but...what does it mean for me?"

"In what case? Jacky, what happened?"

"Wolves took her from me and left me full of silver. I'll be fine, though. I'm still under oath, right? The problems in Dallas-Fort Worth haven't been resolved and I didn't give her into the care of someone I knew she was safe with. She was taken."

"Yes, but if you go to there...if you go after them, you're going to have to choose a side. That's...you can't do that!" Lani must have figured out what I planned. I knew it wouldn't take too long.

"What's more important to the werecats? Our Duty, the thing that keeps us useful and safe in the world since the war with the werewolves, or the Law that binds our hands and leaves us lonely?" I demanded. "What's more important? Do I abandon Carey and walk away? That would be breaking my oath, Lani. I can't do that. Or do I break the Law and go get her and do what I'm supposed to, do what's *right*? There's a loophole, a conflict here. I need to know that something, anything, is going to back me up in my case on this." Because if I lived through it, I would be going before the Tribunal for a crime the likes of which I had never heard of. They would probably decide to kill me then and there.

"You can argue that you were only fulfilling the terms of your Duty. It's stupid and risky."

"I promised to treat her as one of my own, as if she were my child. Now, I don't have kids. I...wanted to, though, a long time ago. I would never let someone carry any child of mine away and give up on them."

"So you're going to Dallas," Lani said softly. "I can't promise it will help, but when they ever get around to putting you in front of the Tribunal, I'll be there to defend your choice. And they will. Jacky, if you live through this, they will come after you. Probably immediately. You might not leave Dallas."

"I know," I whispered. "I'm driving. I'm going to let you go."

"I've got your back, cub. You young ones always know how to keep things interesting." She hung up first, and I focused on the road, staring down the long highway.

Eventually, I passed through Jacksonville again, and then my bar. As I passed, I was able to see that the dirt bike was no longer in my parking lot, a good sign that the cleanup was either under way or finished. Not like I had the chance to really worry about it, but it was interesting to note.

An hour out of Dallas, I considered my game plan. I had to find a werewolf and hopefully use him or her to help me find Carey. They could be anywhere, but I figured it wouldn't be hard to look up some basic information once I was in the city. It wouldn't be hard to look up Heath Everson, Alpha of the cities, and find out where he worked or maybe even lived. For once, I was kicking myself for not having any connections to begin with. I should have been more active in the supernatural world. I should have known Carey might run to me if there was trouble.

Even Lani, who was reclusive as well, at least met the werewolf Alphas near her, even if it was to shake hands and show respect both ways. Me? I just dropped into

East Texas and proceeded to ignore the world until Lani showed up and started to build up a tentative, if distant, friendship.

Which brought other questions to mind. How did the werewolves track me? Where did they get their information from? Was it my phone or Carey's? Was it my credit cards, even though I was using ones under a fake name? Did they know all the aliases I used? If so, how?

Nothing makes any sense and I'm way out of my depth here.

I winced as I adjusted in my seat. Out of my depth and wounded. Couldn't forget that second part if I wanted to live through whatever wasp nest I was about to kick.

CHAPTER TWELVE

Dallas was a beautiful city, one I wished I visited more but never did. Werecats didn't find comfort leaving their own territory and were definitely not comfortable in the territory of a large werewolf pack. Or really any werewolf pack. I had only been in the city once in the last six years, and the visit had been rough on my mental state. Just a two hour drive away from home and I'd hated every second. I hadn't been able to do anything since I had been terrified wolves would find me and put me down for encroaching on their space. I hadn't liked leaving my territory undefended either, constantly worried about it.

What could I really say? I was a homebody.

I drove through downtown looking for a place where I could essentially dump my car for the entire time and finally found a grocery store parking lot and parked in the very back. With my luck, someone would tow it anyway, but it was the only place I could think to drop it. I popped my trunk and took stock of everything I had. I tucked my knife into my boot and considered what to do with either of the stolen guns. Gun laws in Texas were more lax than other states, but I still didn't have any sort of carry permit.

Hell, up until recently, I barely used the damn things. Hasan always told me to practice, just in case I needed to defend myself...

I groaned, thinking about the ancient werecat and how he'd now called over a dozen times. They were more spaced out as time passed, but he still called, trying desperately to convince me not to do what I was doing. Probably. I was his 'daughter' and he was protective of his family.

I grabbed one, checking its ammo, and then the second. The first, also the first one I grabbed from the dead, had a lot more ammo, so I decided to take it, tucking it into my jacket pocket. I checked my reflection in my car's window, then shook my head. That was way too obvious. I couldn't put it in the waistband of my jeans either. I didn't own anything loose enough to handle that and didn't want to shoot myself.

"No gun, then..." I didn't like the decision, but I didn't want to get arrested either. I put it carefully back into the trunk of the hatchback and closed the trunk.

With a deep breath, I pulled my phone out of my pocket and began the haphazard research I was planning as I walked to the nearest place to find some food and coffee. Coffee sounded great. I was out for ten hours and it was already past dark. If anything was open on a Tuesday night, it would be quiet.

After dark, the werewolves would be out too.

I kept my nose trained on any scent that might come by, my eyes on my screen, and my ears listening for anything interesting.

"We should probably get home, love. With the werewolf thing happening, the governor thinks it's too dangerous to be out and about," a woman said to the man next to her.

"They should call in the fucking National Guard and put those animals down. It's all fine and dandy until someone gets turned, or even better, gets their arms torn off." The guy was cruel, but I could admit he had a small point. Werewolves were great for a community and its economy, being long-lived, nearly immortal, and sometimes incredibly rich. Wolf packs were generally self-sustaining. They employed most of the pack and a lot of humans on top of that to manage their day-to-day lives and the myriad business Alphas and many old wolves ended up with.

Until they went and pulled something like this and turned a city into a war zone.

There's always a trade-off when humans play with monsters. The wolves were about to learn what trade-off they were going to get by picking a fight with a bigger monster. I let that settle my nerves. I was a god damn werecat. I was built for fighting werewolves.

In full werecat form. Don't get overconfident, Jacqueline.

Oh god, even that thought was in Hasan's voice. What is wrong with me?

I stopped, smelling not werewolves, but coffee. I was near Union Station and followed the scent and frowned when I realized it was a hotel.

Fuck me, I guess. No coffee for me.

I continued walking, hoping to find anything. As I walked down the street, another scent hit my nose, one that had me grimacing and baring my teeth.

Werewolf. Got your number, asshole.

Coffee and food would have to wait. Now I was hunting.

I tracked the scent down an alley and onto another street. It was fresh, maybe only minutes old. *Lucky me.* I continued, casually looking at my phone still, trying to learn something about Dallas as I walked. I needed to appear like a casual tourist because I couldn't go running if I couldn't see who I was chasing. There was no fear in the wolf's scent, or really any obviously discernible emotion. He seemed like just a guy on a walk, that baseline everyone had when they were just having a normal day.

I followed it down the street, wishing I knew more about the city. I didn't know anything, honestly. The tall buildings could have been from any major city, and the little restaurants dappling the streets could have been New York or Seattle or Atlanta for all I knew about Dallas. I was never a city girl, but then again, I was never really a violent person either. Things were changing fast on me.

I followed the scent down another alley and up

another street. It went on for nearly an hour, but I was slowly gaining, walking a little faster than my target.

By the alley, I could see him. The back of him, anyway. He was broad. Really, he was fucking huge, and I was going to have to play this one carefully, injured as I was. My thigh was burning from the walking now, but I knew what I had to do.

As the shadows covered both of us, I started running. He looked over his shoulders, first confused, then his eyebrows went up as shock hit him next. Once that was done, I was only ten feet from him, but my thigh wasn't ready for me to make that sort of jump. He took off, and suddenly the hunt was really on.

He turned right at the end of the alley, and I followed. When he shoved through a pack of people, I followed through the hole he made. My thigh screamed in revolt, wanting me to slow down and stop the madness, but I wasn't having any of that, so I pushed through it until my legs began to feel more like gelatin. Maybe not much of an improvement, but it was better than pain.

He tried to duck into another alley, but I was too close to him for that to work. As he tried to scramble over a fence, I grabbed the back of his jacket and pants, yanking him back down as hard as I could, snarling viciously.

"Who are you loyal to?" I demanded. "WHO?"

"Fuck you, cunt," he growled at me from his back.

I put a knee on his chest, pulling my silver dagger and pressing it to his Adam's apple. That brought fear to his scent.

Good boy, pup. "Answer the fucking question," I whispered. "Or I'll end you right here. Not even our kind can come back from a fucking open throat. I would know. I've torn enough of them out over the last few days."

"Why the fuck are you even in this city, cat? Huh? You're breaking some serious Laws, taking me down like this."

"So were the wolves who stole Carey Everson out of my protection and threatened her life enough for her to come to me in the first place," I snapped, digging my knee into his chest until he screamed.

"Hey, what's going on back here?" someone demanded from the light of the street. I looked over to the human, knowing my gold eyes were glowing and my pupils were feline slits. I definitely wasn't human.

"Werewolf business. Get out of here. This doesn't concern you or the mortal police," I answered. The human, a smart man like I hoped he would be, took off running after a second. When I looked back down at my werewolf, I grinned. "They're so easy to appease, aren't they?"

"Like you're a fucking werewolf. If you kill me, every werewolf in the city, probably the state, is going to come after you."

I had to give it to him; he had some real balls for the wolf with a silver knife slowly poisoning and burning his flesh, one that could kill him the second I decided to.

"Did you not hear me? My name is Jacky Leon. I live outside of Jacksonville, Texas, and have for the past six years. A few days ago, Carey Everson—the *human* daughter of werewolf Alpha, Heath Everson— called me into Duty and I became her oath-sworn protector. Werewolves took her from me before I returned her to safety. I'm not here for werewolf business, just her. So if you're a good boy, you're going to tell me who has her and where. If not, you can tell me whatever you know."

"I can't help you. I've had no idea where she's been. Not everyone in the pack had even met her before shit went down. Heath is really protective over his little girl. If anyone knows where she is, it'll be someone higher up than me," he answered.

"So, back to my first question. Who are you loyal to?"

He didn't answer, baring his teeth.

"I'm going to take that as...not Heath Everson."

Again, he stayed silent.

I'd never thought that I was capable of torture, but I moved the knife a little, creating a small slice across the werewolf's skin, just under his Adam's apple. A scent hit my nose as I realized he'd lost control over his bladder.

"A little human girl, all of eleven years old, is in danger, wolf. It's against the Law to use humans against other supernaturals, or endanger them in any way with the purpose of causing distress to them personally. Accidents happen, but nothing that has happened to her has been accidental. They came with guns and silver bullets. They're going to use her to get to her father, who has the right as a supernatural being to know his daughter should be safe with a werecat, thanks to the Law." I was bordering on the edge of violence just by speaking. My rage grew. Part of me, a very big part of me, just wanted to end it and kill the wolf underneath me.

The wolf, bless his damnable heart, had the smarts to realize he was underneath a very dangerous, very mad, and maybe a little crazy, werecat who was tired of the fucking games.

"I support the bid against Heath, but you-you have to understand. I never knew they were going to take Carey. I thought we were going to do it right. That our leader was going to challenge the Alpha and it would be a clean fight."

"Who?" I demanded.

"I don't know! I take orders. It's kind of like the military in a wolf pack, lady. Sometimes you don't know who's above the guy, only that they're going to make things the way you want them."

God damn it. Fucking morons. I would never let orders come down from someone I didn't know. "Who do you answer to?" I asked.

"A guy named Timothy. We call him Little Tim. He's a wily shit, but he's a good man."

"Obviously not," I growled. I had three options now. Let the wolf go with a message, kill him, or follow him into some shit that I might not be able to handle. Since the last two options were both potential trouble I couldn't afford, I pulled the silver dagger and stood up. "Get out of here, and you tell Little Tim the werewolf that big, pissed-off Jacky the werecat is in town and I'm coming for whoever took my girl. I'll kill anyone who stands in my way and anyone who tries to stop me from keeping her safe or taking her back."

He nodded as he stood up, touching his neck. Then he started running, a single werewolf who was smart enough to know that he needed reinforcements if he wanted a piece of a werecat.

I was somewhat proud of him. Most meatheads saw women like me and thought they could handle me.

With him gone, I stood in the alley for a moment, catching my breath finally. I thought back on what he said. He had no idea who led the charge? I actually was wrong. When I was human, I didn't know the names of all of my coworkers, or all of my bosses. There were tons of middle men and things coming down the pipeline, and I didn't have any idea where they came from.

As for the rest...Little Tim. Hopefully the werewolf took my warning seriously. I had no belief they would just hand Carey over, but they had the small right to know that if they killed her, I was going to eviscerate them. Probably in terrible ways.

I started walking, tucking my knife away and shoving my hands in my pockets to keep them from shaking any worse. I went back to that hotel using my phone's map and went to the front desk.

"I need a room. I do have a credit card, and I don't know for how long I'll need it. Family emergency," I told the woman at the front counter. I pulled out my wallet and held out the credit card while she took in my words and probably my appearance. The bruises on my face. I'd forgotten about them. I was suddenly self-conscious. Now the words family emergency had a strange and more concerning meaning. The woman probably thought I was having trouble at home.

She took my card silently and glanced at her desk phone.

"Don't call the cops. I'm fine."

"You have strange eyes," she said softly, glancing over at me again. "Contacts?"

"Yup." The best lie was something easy to agree with and believable. The human woman had given me the best lie, even though it made me feel morally bankrupt. "My man didn't like me going out, with the werewolf drama, and decided to let me know. I'll get it sorted. The cops already know. I'm just looking for a place to stay until everything cools down."

"Of course. You're all set up. You'll be on the third floor." She handed the card back to me and I tucked it away. "Here's your room key for room 304, and if you need anything, please let me know."

"If I get any visitors that don't have official uniforms or badges on, don't let them know I'm here," I told her softly.

"Of course, ma'am."

I walked away, heading for the door again. I could bring my Nissan to the hotel parking lot now.

It took nearly an hour, but I managed the streets of Dallas and parked. I went straight to the twenty-four hour coffee place and grabbed one for myself, then headed up to my room with my single suitcase and gym bag, the guns were in the gym bag just in case I needed them. It was better than leaving them out in my hatchback.

When I got into my room, I knew I needed to look over my injuries and take a shower, which I got started on immediately, leaving my cell phone on the bathroom counter. Hasan had tried to call five more times since I had left my car, and I was still unsure about answering. He was wearing on my patience, though. Lani called once, and so did the number I used to call Harrison. None of them could have known I was already kicking the damn hornet's nest in the city, so they must have called either with information or to try and talk me out of it again.

I sat down on the queen bed in the middle of the bland hotel room and went back to my research. So far, I knew that Heath Everson was on a few boards of directors and that seemed to be all he had or did. He was always the guy on the side, never the one in the middle. The pack itself had a variety of businesses and holdings all over the Dallas-Fort Worth area and outside it.

It didn't make a lot of sense to me, but I was thankful for the laws governing werewolves in the United States. A lot of their information was public, even though it was unsafe for their kind. It made it easier for me to learn about them.

The impression I got? Heath didn't want the spotlight—strange for an Alpha. From my understanding, Alphas liked to be in the middle. They owned things, ran businesses, and were good in charge. Heath was never that guy in any of the businesses I saw his name attached to. He seemed...quiet.

Always the bridesmaid but never the bride, huh, Heath? I feel you. When I finally had the chance to be the bride, I got into a car accident and became the family pet.

I snorted, but I still dropped the phone as the memories assaulted me. All the things that had changed in my life since that accident. EMT to werecat. Engaged to single and alone.

My hands were shaking as I covered my face, the tears coming. What was I even doing? I was jumping into the middle of a werewolf civil war for a girl I barely knew. My shoulders and chest hurt as I fell to my side and cried.

Ten years ago, I was on a road during a storm, my fiancé in the driver's seat. We were singing, not caring about the weather. We went over the edge of a cliff.

Now I was in fucking Dallas, Texas, between two factions of werewolves and trying to save a little girl because I was honor bound and couldn't bring myself to let go of it.

My phone started ringing and this time, I saw Hasan's name and felt pure rage. The tears stopped flooding my eyes as I answered. "Stop fucking calling me, Hasan. I'm doing this!" I snapped immediately.

"Have you already caused trouble?" he asked quickly. "If you haven't, you still have time—"

"It was the first thing I did when I got here. Found a werewolf, roughed him up, and told him to send a message back to his fucking master. Obviously, I caused some trouble."

"Why are you doing this?" he asked quietly. "Why are you taking this so far?"

"Because they took her and she was mine."

"If you wanted a human pet, I would have—"

"No," I snarled. "No, Hasan, this isn't one of those cases where you throw some fucking money or your connections at it and make the problem go away. She..." I took a deep breath as I realized my own problem. "She filled the hole for a minute," I whispered. "She filled what he left. She filled what you lost for me." My throat tightened as I remembered Hasan's role in my life. Doting werecat 'father', who gave me a second chance in life and opportunities to make it a long, healthy, immortal one.

Who let my fiancé die by only saving me.

Complicated didn't begin to describe him and I. Fucked up was a better description.

"For the first time in ten years, I had something that was *mine*. That I could take care of. That I could treat as family—"

"I'm your family!" he growled. "Don't forget that I would do anything for you, Jacqueline. How dare you—"

"You let him die, remember? You took my broken body out of that car and Changed me, but you didn't even try for him." My love. We were going to be married only weeks after that vacation, deciding to have our honeymoon first. We were trying to have a baby, too.

We'd been trying really hard, actually. It was fun and wonderful, and then it was over.

"He was too far gone. How many times do I need to tell you that?"

"Until you stop lying and tell me the truth," I answered. "So yeah, I'm here in Dallas because for a fucking short moment in this fucked-up world, I had something again with a human being. She's someone's *daughter*, Hasan. She could have been mine. She's nearly the right age. I'm not letting this go, because it's the right thing to do. These werewolves are going to learn never to fuck with me. Respect that. If I'm a sinking ship, then fine, save yourself and tell the other werecats to do the same, but I'm doing this."

"I love you, Jacqueline. Just as much as any of my other children. You know that, right?" He was quiet, so quiet. "But I can't come and help you do this. I was there when the Laws were written. I know what the Duty is. I don't know how to justify you doing this."

"I do," I mumbled, the heat gone now. "I never fulfilled my Duty. That's what I'm going to say to the Tribunal. Carey left my protection due to the illegal actions of the werewolves, who are equally as guilty in this as I am."

"That means you failed—"

"No, it doesn't. It means I need to step up my game and fight harder." I hung up on him, turned my phone off, and pulled a pillow over my head.

I had failed. I let them take her.

Now I needed to get her back.

After I got a needed short nap, because there was nothing else to do for the night except roam the streets looking for more werewolves to rough up and I hurt, a lot. Healing was harder when I was awake.

A short nap.

13

CHAPTER THIRTEEN

I woke up before dawn and didn't waste any time in getting out on to the streets again. As I stepped outside, I checked the time, smirking to see it was five in the morning. While that might have sounded terrible to humans, it was a great time for werecats. I was full of energy, even though everything ached. I didn't carry much as I started back out onto the streets of Dallas. A simple outfit, which amounted to nothing when it came to protection, but it covered up the injuries I already had. Jeans, a t-shirt, and tennis shoes. I looked normal. I also had a pair of sunglasses hanging from the front of my shirt's collar in case my eyes went even more haywire than they already were. I couldn't risk more humans seeing cat-eyed women running around the city. There was an accidental slip and then there was being stupid. Though I woke up with gold eyes again, I didn't have the cat pupils...yet. Lastly, I had my silver knife, sheathed and stuffed into my hoodie pocket with my cellphone and wallet.

I didn't have much of an objective, just like the night before. Find a werewolf and get to someone important. The leader of the ones who took Carey was the best option, but finding her father was a good second option. If he didn't already know his daughter fell into the wrong hands, he needed to. Whether that would make him my ally or my enemy, I didn't know, but I had to make sure he knew in case I needed him to get her back and out of the danger zone again.

I was walking past a large skyscraper when I 'accidentally' bumped into a man in a suit, who cursed at me, glaring angrily.

"Sorry, sir," I mumbled, bowing my head a bit respectfully.

"Damn street whores taking over the fucking city," he muttered, shaking his head.

Wow, dickhead. Who pissed in your coffee? It's not like I'm going to give you some transmitted disease from a shoulder check.

I brushed off my shoulder where I'd touched him and smiled at his back as he continued to hurry where he was going. It wouldn't be too hard to do that several hundred more times throughout the day, but hopefully the rest would be a bit nicer about it. It would help spread my scent, taking it in buildings and cars across the city. It would let any werewolf with a brain catch my scent and let them know I was around.

I walked into a Starbucks, glad it was open, and

purposefully ran my hand over everything that seemed natural. The door, which my shoulder checked as well, as if I was too tired to push it all the way open. The counter, which I rested my hands on lazily, letting my scent cover it. When I got my drink, I took a seat near the front door, took a few drinks, then played up an act that the spot wasn't good enough for me and moved to the back of the room, trying to find dimmer light.

It was ridiculous, planning out how to do it, but I left with my coffee thirty minutes later knowing that for the next hour, any human who touched my scent would carry it. That was why I'd hit up the counter. The only problem with a Starbucks was that it had a variety of its own strong smells. Those would fade faster, but they had the potential of covering me up. I went for quantity over quality.

"What to do?" I asked myself softly as the dawn finally started coming. I couldn't force a werewolf to show up during the day time, not if they didn't want to. "I can check out the pack's shit..." I nodded, pleased with that idea. Hitting up their businesses would get some attention, and a bunch of humans would be around for me to bump into. Humans who were possibly employed by the wolves.

I pulled out my phone and searched for the closest one to me. I chuckled as the GPS sent me back to the skyscraper where I'd bumped into the human businessman. I stepped in, appreciating the strong AC they ran in the building. It kicked scents everywhere, telling me only humans were in the room.

I walked quietly to the security desk in the front and smiled. "Hi, sir. I'm looking for a friend. I'm with the Werewolf Council of North America." I knew my gold eyes were going to work in my favor, so I blinked them innocently. The more innocent a supernatural monster tried to be, the worse the reaction they got from humans. Humans had a natural prey instinct, really. They might have dominated the globe and became the smartest and most advanced creatures, but they were prey. Actually, the earliest believed ancestors of humanity had a problem with big cats eating them.

I knew the sort of response I could elicit from the round security officer, who was just trying to enjoy his bagel.

His face blanched. "The wolves work on floors sixteen and seventeen," he said quickly. "Welcome to Dallas..."

"Thank you." I patted the counter and started towards the elevator. It was funny that he didn't notice what I was wearing, or maybe he thought it didn't matter. I was obviously not human and I presented myself as someone he had no chance of identifying. Maybe my casualness seemed like a display of powerful disrespect to the petty human contrivances around me.

None of that was true, since for all I knew every human in the building was smarter than me, but appearances were important. I wasn't dressed importantly, so I had to act important. Above it all. Werecats didn't survive if they didn't know how to blend in a little bit. It was like Joey and his friends in

Jacksonville. They knew I wasn't human, but I presented myself as mostly harmless and as human as I could. I didn't try to be innocent and disarming, just normal, talking about things they found interesting, like the football team that I pretended not to care about. They found me less of a threat because of it.

But they still knew I wasn't human.

Part of me wished I wasn't using all my instincts to make this work, though. I was running on pure instinct, the hunt driving me and keeping my feet moving. The only time I stood still in the building was when I stepped into an elevator with several other people, all of whom gave me a wide berth. A lady looked over her shoulder at me and I could smell the shock in her scent.

Yeah, lady, realize you and your power suit aren't the most powerful thing in the elevator.

My mom was a power suit kind of woman. It kind of made me want to gag, honestly. Not just the women, either. The men too. What was the point of wearing suits to sit behind a desk all day? Professionalism? What even was that? Wasn't the definition of professional whatever someone decided it would be?

I mean, I understand not wanting people to show up in booty shorts...Actually, I own a bar. If I hire a couple of waitresses and let them wear little cut-offs, I would own the most popular bar in town. So I don't really understand that either.

That put an immature smile on my face, as I slid between a few of the humans to get out on the sixteenth floor. Stone and Mortar, a construction company of the highest caliber and with the most boring name. Realty and construction were popular for the wolves. It gave them positions of employment for their less intelligent, but still very strong, lower pack members. Imagine houses built by werewolves in the suburbs, and then consider that werewolves have been known to heal broken backs. Worker's compensation took on a different meaning when it was harder to injure and disable the workers.

I stepped through double glass doors and walked up to the front desk, taking a long sniff. There was a werewolf in the office, or there had been one recently. I grinned as I leveled a stare on the woman at the reception desk, who was watching me cautiously.

"I'm looking for a werewolf," I told her, stepping closer.

"Which one?" she asked, her hand moving. I wondered who she would call if she needed help. A werewolf, or the building's security? I didn't plan on letting it get that far. I had no intention of hurting any humans, no matter who they worked for. Scare them a little? Sure, but not this woman, who was already on the edge of screaming just by seeing me. An interesting reaction. It showed me just how bad things were getting for the pack if their human employees didn't feel very safe.

"Doesn't matter, actually. I'm not here to hurt anyone, just talk." It was a half-truth. I was in Dallas to hurt someone. A lot of someones, really. I wasn't in the building to hurt anyone, just trying to find anyone I could get information from.

"Why?" she demanded. She grabbed something, pulling it towards her slowly. I sighed, reaching over to stop her from doing whatever that was. I tried to not bare my teeth as I felt the silver and looked down. A fucking mail opener. The human had more spunk than I had given her credit for.

"I'm Jacky Leon. Heath Everson will know who I am, and it's not an enemy. Or an ally. I'm impartial at best, completely neutral at worst." Half-truths. I was supposed to be. I wasn't anymore.

"Are you...are you a werewolf? Security just said someone from the Werewolf Council was coming..."

"That was me, but no, I'm not a werewolf." I debated on how much I trusted the human and went in deep. It wasn't about trusting her in the end. She needed to see, and she could tell someone a strange woman came up looking for them.

I focused my stare on her more, focused on seeing her as prey for just a moment. My eyes shifted into a nearly colorless world, which proved to me my cat eyes were on full display.

What was more memorable than a cat-eyed woman named Jacky Leon?

"They might also know me by Jacqueline, though I wouldn't count on it." I smiled politely.

"What are you?" She was shaking now.

"Nothing you should ever have to worry about. Humans aren't something I generally play with." I released her, letting her keep her letter opener. "Please, all I ask is that you pass on that message, if you don't want to tell me where I can find one of them."

"Okay." She was nodding vigorously. She obviously hadn't believed me when I had tried to make her feel safe. I was one of the monsters that went bump in the night.

Well, no, I'm not. A good werecat doesn't go bump. It's completely silent before it kills. I'm here, though, so I must not be a very good werecat.

I stepped back slowly and didn't turn to the door until I knew it was within reach. I didn't want to take a silver letter opener to the back. I didn't go to the elevator, heading instead to the stairs and climbing up to the seventeenth floor for a similar game. This business was an accountant's firm. Good idea for any immortal supernatural species, since money was needed if living comfortably was the goal. Secrecy also took money, which was one of the reasons I let Hasan give me a lot of it when I had walked away. Well, also because he wouldn't let me leave until I took it. There was werecat tradition of giving away a quarter to half their wealth when their 'young' decided to branch out on their own.

The front desk here didn't have a woman. A man was standing behind it, frowning at something. As I walked in and closer to him, I could smell werewolf, but he wasn't it. Again, just the scent of a recent one, but not one I felt I could track. It led deeper into the offices, someplace I couldn't go with all the eyes on me. Or maybe the werewolf was gone, having worked all night, then headed home. It was possible that the scent in the center lobby of the building was just too covered by all the humans and I had missed it.

"Hello, sir. I'm looking for a werewolf."

He glared up at me then looked back down. It felt like he saw through me, not really taking in anything about me, dismissing me in the very second he'd glanced. "So? You one of those kinky fan girls?"

That took me aback, sending a rush of revolted shock through me. "How about fuck no, asshole? Now, before I come over this desk, how about you either tell me where I can find a werewolf to talk to or take a message for me?"

"No, lady, I don't think so." He didn't look back up. Wow, this one was an incredible specimen of a prick high on power. He didn't look like he belonged at the desk. I sniffed, curious, and realized I knew him.

I reached out and grabbed his tie, yanking him closer. It had him falling over the desk, trying to brace himself. Before he could call security, I covered his mouth. I bared my teeth, letting the feline in me come out a bit. It made my canines longer and sharper, curving them wickedly. When they were nearly half an inch long, and my cat eyes were glowing, I knew I had his attention.

"Jacky Leon. Not a werewolf, but looking for one. You and I had a run-in this morning, actually. I remember apologizing to you and getting called a street trash whore. Very good. Now, next time a little lady bumps into you on accident, you maybe should be a little kinder, because you never know when that might come back to haunt you. I'm stronger and scarier than your bosses. I'm not a danger to them, though. Or I shouldn't be. I just need to talk to them. So, will you take the message for me or let me know what I need to hear?" I ended that quite sweetly, giving him an innocent smile. I let him go slowly, releasing each finger individually. "Are we good?"

"Good," he agreed softly. "I can't tell you where any of them are. The few coming in right now are coming in at night, and for good reason. They can defend themselves better if they're not worried about humans getting in the mix and getting hurt. I can't call any of them either. They're all dark. I will keep your message in mind, though, ma'am. Jacky Leon, looking to speak to the werewolves of Dallas. Not a danger if you're not provoked, correct?"

He was a lot better at this than the woman with the construction company, that was clear.

"That's right, good sir. And about the other thing?" I crossed my arms.

"I'm sorry. You caught me on a bad morning." He lowered his head. "Will that be all?"

"Yes, and no need to call security. I'll see myself out." I turned on a heel and left the firm.

It was a short elevator ride down and I left the building quickly, out into the rapidly warming morning.

I spent all morning walking around Dallas, confronting different human employees, asking them to spread my name. All the while, I made sure to get my scent on damn near everything I could think of without going full cat and just rubbing the walls. I touched casually during polite conversations, keeping the contact appropriate, like hands and shoulders. I leaned on walls, signs, and posts when I was tired, especially around corners and intersections. I hit up everything I could find in and around downtown Dallas, opting not to go over into Fort Worth, which was technically a big city all its own a very short drive away. If the wolves wanted me, they would have to come to the area of the city I was slowly but surely putting a claim on.

Because that was the last part of my plan. I was letting my magic and my scent soak in and become part of the land. Normally, a werecat would go out in their feline form and mark a border, and a special connection would be created from the act. After that, the magic soaked in towards the center, where a cat would always be. It filled the region and gave me all my niftier abilities, like being able to track a supernatural creature on my land without needing to actually go find them. I could focus on them like a hot spot in my mind's eye and know where they were on my territory.

I was doing it differently here. Each person I touched was marked subtly with my scent, and that sent a message. They were mine. The more I walked, the more I was connected with the land. It would never be mine until I made a perimeter run, but I was throwing a challenge out there, just to get attention. The werewolves, if they met my trail somewhere, would notice it.

At lunch, I looked up a small deli a few blocks away, on a street I hadn't hit yet. I started walking, taking in the sights. Being mission-oriented was keeping me focused, and that helped me enjoy the city more than a casual visit, scared for my life. I didn't much care for my life at that moment, so that was a *big* worry off my plate.

I was a block away from the deli when the scent of wolf hit me, the first time all day I'd gotten it out in the open. I inhaled harder, trying to find the source, but couldn't. For all I knew, it was from a passing car. Shaking my head, I kept walking and found the deli. I slipped in and went to the counter, ordering two simple turkey sandwiches with triple meat and no vegetables at all. I didn't need anything but the dairy and protein for the moment.

I could still eat vegetables, even though felines were obligate carnivores, because my human body still needed them. My cat just needed to do a few things to my diet that would make many humans very concerned, like steaks were served to me blue now. It was the step below rare, and most restaurants didn't even offer it due to health concerns. I needed a lot more protein in my diet, and even if I accounted for the increase in that, I had to triple my calorie intake when I was active. I had been very active and very bad at eating enough in the last week, which was going to make me crash due to lack of energy soon if I didn't start keeping an eye on it.

While I didn't care about my life too much, because Carey remained mine and my cat's number one priority, eating was very important. I couldn't save her if I was passed out from malnutrition.

I sat down with my order and took a large bite of the first one, frowning as a blonde teenage girl walked in. The reason I frowned at her was because she smelled like she had just been cuddling a werewolf, an idea that made me want to spit my food up. It wasn't because werewolves smelled bad, but because of her age. Teenage werewolves were unpredictable and dangerous, unfit to be making out with some high school human girl.

I watched her, able to swallow my food and go for another bite as I realized she wasn't injured. She ordered something and turned my way when they handed her the order.

I raised an eyebrow as she walked directly to me, sitting down quietly and without asking.

"I know you aren't human," she said quietly, leaning over as she unwrapped her sandwich. "Um...We're going to eat lunch, then leave together, okay? Like we're friends." She was speaking quietly enough that none of the other humans in the room would have been able to hear. "You've...you've gotten people's attention, which is something it seems like you wanted."

"How do you know?" I asked softly, keeping my eyebrow raised. "You're human."

"My dad," she whispered. "He's Everson's fourth. Inner circle."

"Is he who I smell on you?" I asked, going back to my sandwich. "And what's your name?"

"Oh, um...my name is Stacy, and yeah, he hugged me and told me to stay safe before I came in. He's going to take you where he thinks you want to go." She took a tentative bite of her own lunch. "Look, I've never done this. I'm nineteen and the pack is in shambles, which...I never thought was possible. I don't even know what or who you are. They won't tell me. They just said I'm safe around you. They don't think you'll hurt me."

"Why did they send you?" Another girl sent by the wolves. Either they were very smart or cowards. I couldn't decide which.

"They don't want a scene. Heath didn't think my younger brother would work because he's...well, he's human, too, but he's also a seventeen-year-old boy." She gave a wary smile that I returned. That was kind of cute, really. The wolves were smart, then. They sent a very good little message. 'Look, we don't want problems. To show you that, here's the most non-threatening thing we have. A seemingly kind nineteen-year-old human girl. She'll be completely at your mercy.' Amazing. It was a risk. I could easily kill her, but they knew my kind well enough to know that wouldn't happen.

"I won't hurt you," I promised gently. "I don't plan on hurting Heath or your dad either, if he's loyal to Heath."

"Oh, good. Thanks." She giggled, nodding. A faint pink blush covered her face. "So...what are you?"

"A werecat," I answered. She was going to find out soon enough. There was no way things were going to stay quiet once I was in the middle of a bunch of werewolves and in front of Heath. "Rarer, different. Solitary creature."

"Heath started acting really weird when he found out some Jacky Leon was leaving messages for the wolves in the city. That's you. So..."

"I need to keep my information to myself until I see

him. What gave me away first? Was it the roughing up of the guy at the accounting firm?"

"Yeah. He'd left my dad a message, that my dad didn't get until an hour ago. Said you scared the shit out of him. Why did you do it?" Now she was interested. Still wary, but curious.

"He dismissed me for a pack-bitch," I answered. "A human who fucks werewolves for kicks. Even insinuated I...uh..." *Well, damn. How do I tell a nineteen-year-old that he said I screwed werewolves in their animal forms?* It was just a disgusting thought—and a total myth. Even I knew that. No self-respecting were, cat or wolf, would *ever* do that. The wolves even had a Law against it.

"Oh, gross!" She choked on her own tongue for a minute, probably trying not to gag. I didn't say anything as she took a large swallow of her drink, shaking her head. "Wow, that's awful. Someone should talk to him about that. He likes werewolves, but he's one of those who doesn't understand what all the fanfare is about. I get it. My dad is one. Has been since I was 3, but that's no reason to be rude about people who find werewolves impressive."

"I don't find werewolves impressive," I said, smirking. "Maybe because I'm higher on the food chain, but that's neither here nor there."

"Are you really?"

"Well, your dad might have a different response, but yeah, I am. It's long been a point of contention between my kind and theirs." I smirked. "One I'm not going to bring up when I'm around them, promise. Not here looking for that kind of fight."

"But you are here looking for a fight."

I stayed silent this time, letting her follow her own train of thought. I wouldn't answer her. It was good that they had sent someone to me, which meant I had done what I intended, but I wasn't going to tell her too much, not anything that she really didn't need to know.

Like how I'm planning on killing any wolf between me and Carey. Or that Carey is with the wrong wolves. Heath is the first person I'm saying it to. He's probably already figured it out. I honestly hope he has.

"Let's finish eating, then get out of here. I really need this meal." I held up my sandwich, getting a nod in response. I ate faster than her, finishing the first sandwich and bagging the other. I could eat it in a moment. At least something was in my stomach again that wasn't junk food or coffee, which had been all I had for nearly the last fourty-eight hours.

I held the door open for her and followed her as she pointed to an SUV. "That's our ride. There're two werewolves in the car. My dad is driving and I'll be sitting up front. You'll be sitting in the back with the other."

"Okay." I followed her there, keeping behind her instinctually. I knew the reason, but it made me uncomfortable to acknowledge. If they tried to shoot me, I could grab her as a hostage. It left a bitter taste on my tongue to think I was even considering it. I would never hurt an innocent human girl, but I would hold her until the wolves listened if I had to. Of course, they would probably shoot me for just considering it, so I stepped out, letting the idea go and putting it to rest. *I'm not a hostage-taker, damn it. I won't sink that low.*

I waited for her to load in, then went to the back door, keeping my eyes down respectfully. I couldn't pose a threat to them now, not if they were taking me to the wolf I needed to see.

"You were prettier in the pictures, Jacky. Less... battered." His voice was like a smooth brandy, somewhat chilled, and very secure, brimming with an arrogant element of confidence. I looked up to see the wolf next to me and found myself looking into the grey-blue eyes I already knew well.

Heath Everson was right next to me, and he didn't look pleased to see me.

"Where's my daughter?" he demanded.

14

CHAPTER FOURTEEN

I sat stunned for a moment. There were a couple of problems that kept me from getting my brain to function properly.

One, I wasn't used to the power that filled the air around me. This wolf was powerful. It was in his scent. It was in his posture, leaning back half against the seat and half on the far door, with one arm stretched out over the back, which he could use to grab the back of my neck if I wasn't careful. He'd positioned himself carefully, with his long legs stretched out into my leg space, an obvious play that I had no personal space he cared to respect.

Two, he was disarmingly good-looking. He hadn't seemed like that in the pictures I had seen of him, quietly sitting in the back. His smiles in those had been soft. The one I was confronted with was sharp. He wasn't a rugged man like most werewolves I'd seen. He was classically beautiful, with a sharpness that made me uncomfortable. The only thing about him that wasn't styled to perfection was his hair, which looked like he'd run his hand through it too many times. It fell over his face, framing his dastardly grey-blue eyes. And that was all before I got to his broad shoulders, encased in a crisp black suit. He didn't look like a man who was fighting for his life. Not in the slightest.

Three...well, it was time for me to tell him that his daughter was taken from me, and I was pretty certain he would try to kill me after that.

"Start talking, Jacky." He didn't remove his eyes from me as the SUV got moving.

"Twenty-four hours or so ago, a hunting party showed up at the location I was hiding her at. We'd already been chased out of my territory by a small group that had silver on them. The next one was twice the size and put four silver bullets in me, leaving me for dead, and taking her with them." I hoped he understood that I had done everything I could have thought of.

His eyes darkened with rage and for once, I was genuinely scared of a werewolf. Not because he was stronger than me. Not because he was faster.

He was a father who had a little girl, and now that little girl was in danger. Very real danger. *Makes him the most dangerous monster in the city, to be honest.*

"And you're here," he whispered.

"I made a choice to come and save her. I wasn't going to give up and fail my Duty, no matter what Laws told me I probably should." *Let that be enough. Please.*

"What about the silver wounds?" he asked, looking over me with disdain now. "You don't look very injured."

I didn't have a way to say anything without whining, so I pulled my shirt up enough that he could see my gut, with the scabbed hole from one of silver bullets. The bruising around it was only going to get worse before it got better. I lifted higher to show him more.

"I have another hole in my thigh. There were some bystanders who kindly took the bullets out and did CPR on me."

Someone coughed in the front. I glanced quickly, not wanting to take my eyes off the dangerous wolf next to me for too long. Stacy was staring into the back, her eyes wide. Her father was looking over at her.

"Stacy, stop staring."

"Dad, they shot her!" she cried out. "Heath, you have to put a stop to this! Why is this about Carey? What happened?"

"Stacy, stay out of it," her father snapped. "*Now*."

She looked back to the front and I knew the teenage attitude when I saw it. I was a nineteen-year-old girl once and pulled the exact same move more times than I'm certain was necessary. Her arms crossed and she thumped back into her seat, creating the same effect as slamming a door.

"CPR? You died?" Heath lifted his chin and looked down his nose now, but I could see a tiny amount of lightening of his eyes. That boded well for me.

"For two minutes, they said." I wasn't going to tell him about Brin and his family. It wasn't the wolf's business. Brin had never exposed what he was to Carey, therefore it wasn't much of consequence. "There had to have been thirteen wolves in that hunting party. I'm not an old or experienced werecat. I did what I could." I felt shitty for it since it hadn't been enough, but it had been my best.

"I know," he said softly. "So, you think my daughter is now somewhere in Dallas."

"The first group...They said they wanted her to flush you out. I expect you'll be getting some hint or message soon to meet or something. Trade her safety for your defeat. Not very honorable, but from my understanding, nothing about this has been." I shrugged. I didn't really want to talk wolf politics with wolves. I was suddenly worried about being out of my territory, the anxiety making my chest tighten. I was in an SUV, an enclosed space, with two wolves, one of them very angry at me—and he had the power to destroy my life. Even kill me. He could invade my territory, even if I did make it back there. "I'm sorry, Alpha Everson."

"It's not your fault," he whispered. "I knew you would fight hard if it was needed. I didn't think they would attack you so blatantly."

"How..." I stopped and considered a different approach. I couldn't just question this guy. I needed to know he would be receptive. Hasan was the same way in that regard. "May I ask you a few questions?"

"I'm here, aren't I?" He raised an eyebrow.

"How did you even know about me?"

"Oh." He snorted, a small smile finally overcoming the angry stone expression. "I thought you had something difficult to ask. It's simple, really. Someone came to me, wondering why a werewolf opened a bar in Jacksonville. It must have been right after you showed up. I got curious and drove out, but stopped when I realized that I was about to cross the border of your territory. Started digging into you after that, but I didn't want to out you to your humans, so I told them that you were private and that if anything happened, they could let me know and I would deal with it."

"Fucking hell. Do you know a guy named Joey?" I asked, eyeballing him hard now.

"I do," he murmured, the small smile turning into a predatory grin.

"What all do you know about me?" I demanded, crossing my arms. I even tapped a foot as I waited for an answer. "I think I deserve to know, because I was living a very quiet and happy life before you decided I should be a part of your daughter's protection detail."

"Everything I could find. It's decent intel. I know your full name is Jacqueline Leon, not Jacky. I know you have a lawyer in New York and an accountant up there. Through the accountant, I found a few of your aliases. I like to know who and what is living in my state, and since you were fairly close, I figured you could come in handy. You have, even if it wasn't exactly the outcome I wanted."

"Really? Your daughter was taken from me—"

"You died for her, which means a lot to me," he snapped. "I'm angry she was taken, but I'm not foolish enough to think it was your fault. It's the wolves who took her and they're going to pay for that."

"Even though you failed, you bought us some damn

valuable time," the wolf driving said casually. Stacy stayed quiet, which was probably for the best. A nineteen year old didn't need to wade into this serious of a conversation.

"Exactly. You were able to keep my daughter out of the line of fire, which meant I could focus on finding out who is and isn't loyal to me here in Dallas without worrying about her as much. Harrison told me she made it to you, since you had called him. Did you tell him that the wolves grabbed her back?"

I nodded. "Last night."

"He hasn't contacted me yet..." Heath shook his head, growling. "Damn. He probably doesn't want me to make this a bigger bloodbath than it already is. Still, stupid of him to keep that kind of a secret from me."

"Yeah." I didn't say what I was agreeing with, opting for letting everyone believe what they wanted to believe. "So, where are you taking me?"

"Your hotel. I looked it up when I realized you were here," the Alpha answered. "You're going to get your things and come with us. Don't make it hard, please."

"No, of course not," I said, my throat tight and my mouth dry. "And where are we going?"

"You're terrified," he said, shaking his head. "There's no reason for you to be."

"What do you know about werecats? I'm out of my territory. I'm in the same city as a werewolf war that should have nothing to do with me. I was attacked twice and a little human girl, *your daughter*, was taken from my protection, which was never a place I ever thought to have a girl. In my protection, that is." I leaned over for a moment. "Of course I'm terrified. If I really believed you weren't going to kill me for losing her, then that's just one problem off the list of them. I'm breaking the Law by even fucking being here, and that's a big fucking problem, too. A bigger one than what you're dealing with."

He watched me as I leaned back into my spot, away from him. Far from him.

"You're right. You do have a lot of reasons to be worried." He inclined his head. "So...what side do you choose?"

"While I was protecting Carey, I was trying to remain impartial," I explained. "While I tried not to be totally fatalistic to her, I was ready for an outcome in which she would go to a legal guardian and not a parent or other family." I swallowed. "Now, even though they've taken her and tried to kill me, I am still trying to remain impartial. I'm not going to help you win this. I'm going to get your daughter back and keep her safe from all harm. That means once I have her again, I'm leaving with her until this settles." I was lying to his face, but politically, it was the only thing I could have possibly said. I fully wanted him to win. I wanted to rip his opponents to pieces and feed on their corpses. I wanted to roll around their dead bodies like a fucking rabid animal. It wasn't a feeling I was accustomed with, but I was growing more used to everything it flared in my chest.

But I had to watch my own back as best as I could.

He didn't call out my lie. "And you recognize that

working with me is probably the fastest way to finding her."

"Sort of. I caught one of the other wolves last night. I didn't hold him, but I had him deliver a message to the wolf he reported to. They failed to kill me and I was here to pick a fight for her again."

"Why are you doing this?" He propped his elbow on the window and door, leaning on it. He was now watching me with an intensity that made me want to squirm.

"You're the third person I've explained this to, but the others were werecats..." I huffed. "It could be considered a failure of my Duty that I let Carey get taken from me, but I like to think that's only the case if I give up. I'm not giving up. There's been a lot of Law-breaking around here. They started it. I'm going to continue to do what I swore I would do, even though the Laws will hang me for it." I wanted to snarl about how they took something that belonged to me, but I wasn't foolish enough to say that in front of her father. I wasn't her mother or her sister, or even a friend. I was a werecat who promised to try and be all of those things and a body shield, and it would end when I gave her back to this man. It was still a bone I was choking on, but I would abide by it.

"That's...honorable of you," he said softly, nodding. "Very honorable, to put your Duty over your self-preservation."

"If I was worried about self-preservation, I would have given her up to the first hunting party. Not get shot five times in less than a week," I snapped, baring my teeth. "Older and wiser werecats have told me this is foolish. I made it clear to them...that I didn't think so and there's no other option in my mind."

"I'm glad I sent her to you, then." He extended a hand. "I haven't properly introduced myself. I'm Heath Everson."

"Jacky Leon. I prefer Jacky, by the way. Don't call me Jacqueline."

"Why not? It's a pretty name," he countered.

"Fine. Call me whatever you want." I pulled my hand back, shaking my head.

"I will. I tend to do whatever I want without needing someone's permission." He smirked. "So, do you know anything else about what's happening here in Dallas?"

"Um...Council Alpha Harrison of Atlanta gave me some small details," I answered. "Things he thought could help me protect Carey and understand the situation and how dangerous it is. You really have wolves out there fighting over loyalty?"

"It was my idea, actually. Good way to weed out the weak traitors. My top twenty or so wolves are mostly on my side. We have a couple unaccounted for, but I'm certain they're lying low, keeping their heads down until they think it's safe to reach out. Even if they're traitors, I overpower them."

"How did this start?" I went back to crossing my arms, not wanting to think about how warm and calloused his hand had been. Reminded me of my late fiancé.

"I was working late. Sniper took a shot and hit me in

the back, which is why we've been quiet, hiding. So I can heal and deal with the challenger properly, while figuring out who belongs to who. Shamus here found me and took me underground and into hiding while also scrambling to find out about my family. My sons protected Carey long enough for her to get out, and somehow she made it to you. She's a smart kid..." He trailed off, showing just a peek at the worried father I knew was underneath.

"She is," I agreed. "I enjoyed spending time with her. She's a sweetheart with a big heart."

"Yes, she is." He nodded. "Well, I think my sons were taken, but we haven't had word. That alone has given me a little hope about this. No word means they might not have been grabbed and they're also hiding out. They're adults, and intelligent. I trust their judgement in staying safe and helping me from afar, if that's what they're doing."

"Oh! Then I do have some news for you." Finally, something good I had to offer for him. "Carey, at one point and against my wishes, checked her cellphone. I say against my wishes because of GPS tracking, but—"

"Carey's phone couldn't be tracked. I swear to you on that." He waved that off. "Now, what were you—"

"Then how the hell did the wolves find us outside of my territory?"

He sighed. "They could have at least one person who knew about you, or more likely, stole my file on you from my office. Either way, I think they used the information I had on you. For that, I am sorry."

"That makes a lot of sense, considering what you

knew. Okay, so back to the important thing. Carey got a text from Richard that said he and Landon were okay."

I heard him stop breathing, even if I couldn't see any change in his posture or outward appearance.

"Thank God," he exhaled. "Richard and Landon are my..." He rubbed his face. "Nothing. Between those two and Carey, I'm glad to hear that. That's the best news I've had in days."

"Good," I murmured, lowering my eyes.

"We're here," Shamus said softly.

Heath straightened and fixed himself. I didn't think he looked rumpled at all, but apparently he did. "Stacy, go in with Ms. Leon and help her retrieve her things. Jacky, I recommend staying checked in with the hotel and leaving your vehicle here. It'll distract the wolves until they get access to security and see Stacy with you."

"How are you keeping Stacy safe?" I asked, flicking my eyes to the girl. "She shouldn't..."

"She's opted for the Change. She's to be treated like a wolf until that time," Heath answered.

I nodded respectfully. Fine, then. Stacy hadn't told me that, but then, no human wanted to admit to a stranger that they were willing to give up their humanity.

She and I jumped out and walked inside together. I ignored the front counter for the most part, just making sure it wasn't the woman from the night before, and it wasn't. Stacy was silent beside me until we reached my room. I was aching by the time we reached it. Between the walking I'd done all morning, the running the night before, and, you know, being shot until I died, every part of my body fucking hurt.

"You were protecting her..." Stacy looked over my things, frowning. "They shot you for it."

"Have those two taught you the Law?" I asked softly, putting my things back into my suitcase.

"Yeah. I never read more than the general rules and the part about the werewolves, though."

"There's a werecat section that deals with all Laws for my kind and for others dealing with mine. We're the reason the Laws exist, you and I. Did you know that?"

She shook her head, and I rolled my eyes.

"Ask your father or Heath for a better history lesson, then." I zipped up the suitcase. "Do you know Carey?"

"I babysit her," she said with a bite. "Of course I know her. My father is Heath's fourth."

"Ah. I'm sorry, then." The guilt ate into my soul a little more the longer Carey was missing. I failed all of them by losing her. Being dead just didn't seem like a good enough excuse to me, even if it was for them.

"So, you were really injured...we have someone who can help with that. A half-witch who can heal."

"Really?" That perked me up. I knew about the half-witch, but I didn't want to reveal that. They might not have liked Carey talking about pack secrets with me, and that should be a secret. I definitely did *not* know she could heal.

"Yeah. We can ask Heath if she can patch you up. No offense, but you walk funny and you're favoring your right arm."

I hadn't even noticed, and while I hurt, I wasn't going to bitch about it or let it slow me down. "Yeah. If you feel comfortable with that, sure. I'm fine, though. Really." *Not really, but again, not letting it slow me down.*

"Good." She nodded wisely and took the suitcase from me. She carefully laid my gym bag on top of it.

"So, you want to be a werewolf," I said casually.

"I want to try. I know the Change might kill me, but it's my decision." She raised her chin, ready for me to try and convince her not to, I bet.

"Who's mad at you?" I asked softly.

"My mom, who divorced my dad ten years ago. She doesn't get a say, in my opinion. My dad and Heath are going to walk me through it, so my odds are pretty good. There's something about genetics, that if one person in the direct line successfully Changed, then the others have a good chance. I want to research it when I'm in college and beyond. I can help further humans and wolves, if we can discover what that little...something is that determines it."

"You can," I agreed. "Though the chance of it being successful is higher when someone is born to the werewolf and not to the human before the Change."

"Yeah, but still, my odds aren't one out of ten or worse, like they are for most humans. There's more like a sixty-six percent chance of me surviving, which is why I think my dad relented and let me go through with it. Those are good odds." She shrugged.

Fuck. I hope I'm never that comfortable facing my possible doom.

Wait.

I shrugged with her. "Fair point."

"How did you choose?" she asked as we left the room.

"I didn't," I answered. "I was dying."

She didn't say anything else, just giving me a wide-eyed stare as the doors closed. Finally, she broke out of the shock. I knew it would puzzle her.

"Is that a werecat thing?"

"Not at all." I shoved my hands into my pockets. "Ask Heath. He seems to know a lot about my kind."

"Yeah, but you're one of your kind. So why don't you tell me?"

"Not out here in public. My kind isn't out to the humans, kid." I scoffed as the doors opened and walked ahead of her, ignoring my pain. The curiosity of the young. I was only thirty-six and that meant in the eyes of many, I was a child too, but I wasn't *that* nosy. Or rather, I knew how to be nosy without...being overtly nosy, or so I believed.

We got back into the SUV and I sat quietly next to Heath as we started driving off.

"You haven't told Stacy how the Laws came to be," I said, loudly enough that I knew they would all hear me and the small bite of 'what the fuck' in it.

Heath bared his teeth. "You mean the war with your kind we had and practically won, before we were forced to sit down and play for peace?"

"Woah!" Stacy heard that too, looking back at us. "Really? We had a war? With her kind? And yet you let her protect Carey?" The end was angry at Heath, disbelieving.

"Jacky here is too young to have been a part of the war."

"How do you know?" I demanded, glaring at him.

"You act too modern. If it helps, I wasn't around for it either, but I'm much older than you." He kept his teeth bared, but it turned into a predatory smile. "You brought it up."

"I just figured that's something you should teach people. She's also never read all of the Laws."

"Have you?"

No, but I wasn't going to tell him that. I read the ones that really mattered. "She should have at least read the section about werewolves and werecats."

"Don't tell me how to teach my pack," he snapped.

"Do you make all your wolves prove that they have read and understand them? It might have kept the others from blatantly breaking them and coming after Carey and me." I wasn't dropping it now.

He snarled, reaching out for me. I grabbed his wrist, holding him off. I was weak, I was tired, and I was in pain, but I was still a damn werecat. Two werewolves and a human teenager were no match, especially if I fought each of them one on one. My confidence soared in my chest again, less afraid than I had been, as I pushed his hand further away from me.

"Forgive me," I said softly. "But I think I have a point."

"Yes, I make sure they all know, but do you know

when the last real Tribunal concerning a broken Law was? A very long time ago. A lot of wolves barely make it to fifty, which means they weren't alive for it. To them, the Law and being in front of the Tribunal is a horror story, not something that actually happens." He yanked his hand away, looking down at it. "I didn't know you had it in you."

"Did you forget I'm the stronger species?" I asked, raising an eyebrow.

"No. I actually never believed it. I've only met one werecat, and it was in passing. I couldn't believe that she would be able to beat me, and I didn't think you could stop my strike. Consider me educated."

"Same. You have a point." I crossed my arms again as I realized he wasn't going to try again. I couldn't really be mad at him. If I had been challenged like that, I would have gone for a control hold too. I knew he had wanted ownership over my throat to make his point and his position in the ranking clear, but this was exactly what I had been telling Carey.

I had to prove I was the top predator, and it made the Alpha very insecure. He didn't like that he couldn't take me, still staring at his hand and flexing it.

"How old are you exactly?" he asked, giving me a curious look. "If you're like my kind, you get stronger with age. Call me curious."

"I'm thirty-six and I've been a werecat for ten years," I answered, looking away from him. I was a baby compared to the other werecats. "I'm the youngest werecat I know of by...ninety-two years." I looked back over at him, watching him absorb that information.

"Interesting," he murmured.

"You?" I was curious, probably too curious, and the adage about cats' curiosity came to mind. I smirked. "Call me curious."

"I was Changed during the American Revolution, at the age of thirty. I'm two hundred and seventy-eight." He didn't like his answer.

I overpowered a nearly three hundred-year-old werewolf. I knew my kind was stronger than his, but he was old in their terms. Not by werecats terms, but for his kind, he was a survivor. With werewolves and their dominance struggles, they died easier, faster, than my own.

"Wait," Stacy cut in. "Can I ask more?"

"Stacy," Heath chastised softly, giving her a look.

"It's fine." I shrugged. I figured if there was nothing to do about Carey until we got with the rest of the wolves, I might as well help educate the wily youth about other supernaturals, especially if she planned on joining the ranks.

"Fine," he relented.

"Why are there no other young werecats? I mean, there's young wolves all the time. Lots of them. Everywhere."

"I know the answer to this one," Heath said before I could open my mouth. "It's a cultural difference."

"Yeah." I nodded in agreement. "We're solitary. We don't go out looking for companionship most of the time.

To Change someone is putting someone in our care, probably for a long time. Like...if and when Heath or whoever Changes you, they're going to be responsible for you until you can handle things on your own. That's a bit of a turn-off to werecats." I sighed. "Also, we practically never Change someone without consent and years-long education about it and our world beforehand. Then you have to account for failures. So a werecat can invest thirty years in adopting a baby, raising it as their child, offering the Change, doing it, and..."

Well, I had heard from Hasan how heartbreaking those cases were. He hadn't done something like that in two hundred years, and he'd told me about two failures he had ages ago. I could still remember the shadows I saw in his eyes when he talked about the two young men that it happened to.

"Oh. So...there's no process like there is with us?" She frowned. "Why? There must not be many of you."

"There never will be. We're not community-oriented. We're territorial and stand-offish. We don't want too many werecats. There's not enough land to go around between us, you werewolves, the fae, the vampires, and so on. Our numbers are healthy right now, though." I yawned, suddenly tired. "You done? Any more?"

"You said that werecats practically never Change someone without their consent...but you were. Did anyone get into trouble for it, or is it just rare?"

Heath's eyebrows went up. That was something I really shouldn't have shared, I realized belatedly. He hadn't known that. Hell, Lani didn't even know that.

"Yes, well, I was dying after a storm made the roads slick and I went over a cliff," I said quietly, shifting my body to face away from Heath, an obvious sign I wasn't up to giving away any more of my life story. "It's just rare," I finally said. "And avoided."

It was because some people didn't accept the Change. For the werewolves, Hasan had told me they were laxer about it because they were easier to put down. For werecats, because of the bonds we made and the strength we had, it was too risky. He'd said if I didn't have control of my werecat within a year, he would have put me down before I got too strong for him to potentially stop.

Luckily, I gained control.

"I think we're done interrogating the local werecat, Stacy," Heath said gently. "Why don't you call the safe house and let them know we're on our way back?"

"Okay...Sorry, Jacky, if I offended you."

I shrugged. "Not offended. Just a sore topic," I told her. "You didn't know. Don't feel bad." Couldn't have kids feeling bad for their curiosity.

The rest of the ride was quiet for me, as everyone else talked softly about who was where and doing what. When we arrived at the warehouse, lost somewhere in Dallas, I was ready to face the next challenge.

I had to work with a wolf pack to get Carey back.

15

CHAPTER FIFTEEN

The warehouse was completely nondescript. Boring, plain, it blended in with several other warehouses. Heath walked in the front of our group with Stacy next to him. I wish I could say it was a place of respect, but I knew it wasn't. It was a place of safety. He was showing the pack that Stacy mattered and he would die for even their future wolves, probably because the future was important, or something idealistic like that. Shamus was behind him, a few feet back. Casually protecting his Alpha's back without crowding or being overprotective. A sign that he trusted his Alpha to protect his still-human daughter.

I was tailing the entire group, just behind Shamus, who smartly kept me more to his back right and not directly behind him. A sign that he knew I could make trouble and wasn't going to let me get the drop on him. Smart wolf. Not that I was planning on trying, but I had nowhere else to walk. They didn't really leave me any other options.

There were no werewolves outside the warehouse, giving even more of a normal, 'nothing weird going on here' look, but I could smell them. There were so many that the scents blended together until it just smelled like werewolf and I couldn't pull them apart.

It was disconcerting, and I was about to walk into the middle of them. The idea made me feel fidgety and anxious, something that must have become obvious as Shamus looked back at me when we got close to the building, frowning.

"We're not bringing you back here to eat you," he said quietly.

"Sure," I replied, crossing my arms to cover the important bits, like my lungs and heart.

"I thought werecats were supposed to be a werewolf's boogie man." There was something light about Heath's tone from the front.

I hissed. In the presence of other animals, I knew I could relax on one thing, and that was showing the more animalistic parts of my personality. Any humans in this building would probably know about the werewolves, and that meant there was a chance they knew about me or my kind.

"What big eyes you have," Shamus teased, a toothy grin appearing on his face. "We've got her right where we want her, boss."

I snarled, snapping at the closer wolf. He jumped away, laughing.

"Kidding. We've got more important things to do than trying to kill you."

"He's right," Heath said loudly, looking back at us now. "Killing you only gets rid of one more layer of protection my daughter could use. I'm not going to do that. And I'll swear it here: no wolves of mine will attempt to hurt you while you're here or in our territory, as long as you prove to be dedicated to the task of rescuing my daughter from those that would do her harm."

I inclined my head as my anxiety eased. If any of his wolves broke that, he would be required to step in on my behalf if he wanted to keep his honor, and for Alpha werewolves, honor was everything. "Thank you."

He nodded back and continued walking. Stacy ran off ahead. We didn't enter through either of the large shipping bay doors, but rather a small side door for employees. I was, of course, last to enter.

I felt paralyzed for just a second as the scent of wolf covered me, filling my nose until I could smell nothing else. I was also in front of five wolves I hadn't met yet, which didn't help anything. A couple of them snarled, baring their teeth. Their eye colors shifted from their human colors to their wolves', much like my hazel turned gold.

"She's here by my will and in my good graces," Heath snapped, staring down the wolves. "Meet Jacky Leon, a werecat that lives a couple hours southeast of us near Jacksonville. She's oath-sworn to my daughter, a werecat called to Duty. You'll treat her with respect."

"And where's Carey?" one asked, his anger fading quickly, replaced with worry.

My heart clenched. Carey was a human princess among wolves. They would all probably die for her, I realized.

"A hunting party incapacitated our feline cousin here and took her. Jacky is here to help us get her back. Or we're going to help her."

"We're going to work together as equals in the effort to get Carey out of their hands," I said, fixing the problem Heath had walked into. On principle, a werecat would never bow and take orders from a werewolf Alpha, and he couldn't let me be above him, since it would jeopardize his position of power. Equals, however tentative, was the only solution.

"That works," he replied, nodding. He turned back to his wolves and waved. "I need everyone for a pack meeting so we can discuss our next move."

"Yes sir," the speaker said, jumping up and running out of the room. The others followed, slower, but no less purposeful.

"Is that one a youngin'?" I asked, raising an eyebrow. I threw on a bit of a southern accent to soften the question into something humorous.

"He is, but he's got a good head on his shoulders and a decently dominant streak. He'll climb into someone's inner circle one day, if he's trained right and has the chance to grow. Right now he's all about pleasing and doing his part." Heath gestured for me to keep following him. As I did, he said something else. "Shamus, I want you there as well, but I think it's time for Stacy to help with the kids."

"Of course, Heath."

As I left the office with him, I heard Stacy whining about being put back on babysitting duty, something that made me smirk.

The warehouse before me was full of werewolves, many lying on cots, talking to their neighbors. Some were sitting on boxes, probably taken from the warehouse. Some were lying on large crates, others were playing on computers.

"Nice war camp," I said, trying to be polite and probably failing at it.

"Yeah. It was the best we could do with the short amount of time we had when this all started. We have a couple of injured, but nothing too bad." He gave me a sideways look.

I ignored it, opting to instead meet the eyes of the wolves now watching me intently. My comment had drawn their attention, and now probably two dozen or more wolves were looking at me, expressions ranging from shocked to confused to downright angry.

"Hi." I waved. "Do I look funny?"

Heath snorted. More than a few of the wolves snarled, while others had the opposite reaction and laughed.

"They're all here. Time to get this out of the way and move the pack to open discussion on what to do," he said softly to me. "Everyone, meet Jacky Leon. If you don't recognize her scent, she's a werecat, and one oath-sworn to my daughter, Carey, who has been taken by the traitors. She's our ally, but we must attempt to let her maintain an air of impartiality. She's already lost her life once in service to my daughter, and let's try not to let that happen again. I don't want the other werecats thinking we callously throw away their kind as if they're chattel. Two minutes, was it? How long you were dead?"

"Yeah, so I was told," I answered, shrugging. He really knew how to put the spotlight on a girl.

"Now, she's not here to help us defeat the traitors, so don't expect her to. However, all efforts about saving my daughter? She's going to be a part of those. You'll respect that, am I clear?"

"Yes sir!"

"Good. Now I want two teams. A small team will be on the mission of reclaiming my daughter so she can be returned to safety. You'll work with Jacky, so put whatever problems you have with werecats aside. My daughter is more important. The second team, a larger force, will continue to flush out the traitors and bring their numbers down. However, I want some captured and brought in alive for interrogation now. They must be feeling their losses, and that will weaken their resolve to continue down the path they're on."

I stood uncomfortably next to him, listening to the orders being handed down. After a few more lines of similar rhetoric, I tuned him out. There was still a lot I didn't know, but now wasn't the time to find out.

When Heath was done, everyone started talking amongst themselves of their own accord. He leaned closer to me, and spoke quietly. "I'm going to stick close to you. I love and trust my wolves, but you're an unknown factor. I have two who were alive during the war. One's a Beta, and not very aggressive, but he might hold a grudge. Lost his parents and a sibling back in those days. He also loves Carey, so he's going to join the team with you. The other will hopefully avoid you, but he's… he's got a few screws loose, which is why he isn't in my inner circle, no matter how powerful he is. I don't want you alone where he can find you. Understand?"

"I don't need your protection," I said softly, narrowing my eyes on him. "Not from two wolves, anyway."

"You're also working to get my daughter back. I'm never going to be far just because of that."

"Fair point," I conceded. "You should keep a line of communication open. Your traitors might call."

"I've already considered that. It'll be your team's job to manage the phone I'm going to have you set up."

"My team?" I said that probably louder than I should have. I laughed, shaking my head. "Oh no. I'll work with a team. I haven't been a werecat long enough to give up that bit of humanity, but I'm not a leader. I don't do in charge very well. Please tell me that's not your intention."

He smirked. "Not fully, no. I want you working with whatever leader they're going to put up on the pedestal."

"Thank God," I mumbled, shaking my head. I caught a glance at a group already walking up to us. "Looks like we have our team." I nodded to the four wolves headed our way.

"Looks like it," he agreed, turning away as well. "Teagan, Laurent, Chrissy, and Sheila. Some of my smarter wolves. They're good. Teagan is the one I was mentioning. The Beta wolf." He pointed out each respectively, giving me a chance to know their faces and names before the work truly began. He nodded to the one in the front, but I didn't need him to.

Years with Hasan and the few times I had met with Lani in person taught me to see the walk of one of the older supernaturals. For werewolves and werecats, age meant power, a slow, steady growth in strength as the world continued to knock us down. Teagan had the air of being powerful, much like Heath next to me.

"What makes a Beta wolf?" I asked.

"Slower growth in strength. A calmer disposition that lends them less power in the pack. They aren't the bottom of the pack, still able to fight for a place that suits them, but they make others protective, and they're less likely to resort to violence."

"You know, since we're on this topic. Why do you wolves use Alpha and Beta and that nonsense? Wasn't it disproved that wolves do it?"

Heath chuckled. "You say that like we should care. The scientist knew werewolves and thought the same rules applied to real wolves, so he saw what he wanted to see while doing his research. No, real wolves don't have such a strict rank structure as we do, but then, they aren't part human. Humans need leaders and control in their lives. Routine. The Alpha and pack structure is to appease that need, but remain as wild as we're able to be."

"Interesting," I murmured, nodding. "Like all things in our lives, a blend of animal and man."

"Exactly," he agreed.

We waited for a few more moments while the group made their way through the large warehouse. They had started a fair distance away and now they were nearly upon us.

Teagan was stiffer with each step closer, and was the first one to speak. "A werecat, Heath? Really?"

"Hm. An oath-sworn werecat, but yes, a werecat." Heath didn't seem perturbed by Teagan's obvious aggression, and therefore, I didn't let it bother me. "Teagan, she's not old enough to have been a part of the war. She's innocent in all of it."

Teagan looked me over, calculating and severe. I wasn't sure what he saw, but after several heartbeats, he visibly relaxed. "You are a young thing, aren't you? What are you doing in this mess?"

I gestured to his Alpha. "Someone here thought it was a good idea to send Carey to a werecat for protection without telling the werecat it was part of his plan. I was called to Duty before I even knew how bad things really were here."

"Huh. Heath, that's a bit rude of you, don't you think?" Teagan frowned. "I was there when the Laws were signed. If Hasan was still walking around in the world, he'd have your head for not giving the cat fair warning."

"It's not against the Law to keep my security plans a secret," Heath replied, shrugging.

"You know Hasan?" I perked up slightly. *A wolf that knows my...father? I never thought I would see the day.*

"Not really. I was just there, and so was he. Big, powerful son of a bitch, even back then. I swear, I think he's the first of your kind because of how old he is." Teagan smirked. "From my understanding, you werecats still worship the ground he walks on."

"Kind of," I said, shrugging. "It's just rare to hear anyone outside our own kind mention him."

"Are we going to get to work?" Sheila asked, tapping her foot, her hands on her hips. "I'm sure after this is all said and done, we can play friends with the werecat, but Carey is more important than this."

"Yes." The Alpha nodded, gesturing to the Beta wolf. "Teagan, I'm going to need someone in charge of this group—"

"We're all going to vote for Fenris," he answered. "You've brought a werecat in. You can't expect him to take it as well as I might." The Beta wolf eyed me again. "He's going to make her life hard, you know that, right? He's not going to let her out of his sight."

Oh, well that's pleasant. The angry, crazy one is going to join in on the fun, is he?

"No. I'm not going to accept that. Either you or me. I'm not letting Fenris lead the team to save my daughter just because he's going to want a piece of the werecat. It's not going to happen."

"You might have to fight him on it. He's not here right

Oath Sworn

now, but when he gets back and finds out about this?" Teagan snorted. "Alpha..."

Heath growled, a sound that made my bones vibrate thanks to how close he was. I stepped away slowly, trying not to draw the eye. I didn't want pack fights over me, so I cleared my throat until the Alpha looked in my direction.

"What?" he snapped.

"I'll be fine," I promised.

"Teagan, you're going to be in charge of this team. You might not be a violent wolf, but I trust you to keep the others directed in the right ways. Chrissy, Laurent, Sheila? Any problem with that?"

"No sir," they answered back in unison.

He never took his eyes off me, searching my face for something. "You're a foolhardy feline if you think Fenris is someone you can handle. My daughter's life is in your hands right now, along with these wolves beside me, and that means you're an honored guest of my house. I would protect any of my wolves from each other if I felt the reason for their pain was unjust. I don't let my wolves get bullied for circumstances beyond their control. I'm not going to let a guest of my house be treated that way either."

I raised my hands in mock defeat. "Then hover, but don't fight my battles for me. Some of your wolves might need a hard lesson in what it means to pick a fight with a werecat. You should let them learn that lesson."

"Foolhardy," he repeated.

Probably, but I couldn't risk the reputation of the werecats as a species by hiding behind the coattails of an

Alpha werewolf. I had to take his word that he would protect me, but I also had to stand up for myself. As long as I wasn't jumped by a group too large for me to handle, I was going to be fine.

Hopefully.

He exhaled a long breath in exasperation and looked back to the werewolves I was going to be working with. "I'm going to check on the others. Keep an eye on her, and god damn it, if Fenris shows up, come get me."

"Yes sir," they responded, once again in unison like dutiful little soldiers.

16

CHAPTER SIXTEEN

Suddenly, I was alone with four werewolves that I had just met. I lifted a hand and waved. "Hi."

"Hello," Chrissy said, looking like she smelled something awful. "So. A werecat in a werewolf war."

"Yeah. I would rather not repeat that conversation, so let's just get to work, shall we?" I tried for a smile and knew it failed by the eyeroll Chrissy gave me.

Sheila started to laugh, leaning on the other female. "Certainly. We can take this into the offices and set up a phone in case we get contacted. Laurent, you know how to monitor cell phones, right?"

"Yup. I can hook something up where we get calls and texts on my laptop. Can only do one number, though."

They started walking, letting me trail behind them. I was out of place, listening to them discuss technologies I knew little about or had only heard of in movies. We went to a different part of the warehouse, entering into an 'office' filled with cubicles for the most part. On one side of the room, however, there was a meeting table with several chairs and a whiteboard.

Without talking to them, I wrote what I knew about the situation.

"What is she doing?" Laurent asked softly behind me.

"Ask her," Teagan snapped, seeming annoyed by the question.

I wrote everything from Carey's name to the timeline of my time with her from the moment she showed up to the moment she was taken. Then I wrote even further, my own timeline to finding the pack.

Carey was missing now for over twenty-four hours and time was everything. At least in the human cases of missing children. She wasn't taken by sick humans, though, who would try to dispose of her. She was taken by werewolves who needed her, and if she died, none of them would have a chance in Hell of surviving the wrath that would come down on them. The circumstances were different.

The thing that had me worried was that I wasn't an expert on any of this. As I wrote what I remembered about the wolves that attacked me, I kept coming back to that. I was running off instinct and whatever I picked up from television, movies, and books. Hell, even video games. I was so far out of my damn depth that I felt like an imposter.

"It's everything I know," I finally informed them,

stepping back when I was done. "Carey got to me on Saturday morning, very early. Probably around one in the morning. On Saturday evening, we were attacked for the first time. Five wolves. I didn't check their bodies or their vehicles for information. At the time, I was playing defensively, so I'm sorry about that."

"It's your job," Teagan said, not unkindly. "A werecat isn't meant to go into the offensive with these types of situations."

I nodded in agreement. Things were different now, though. "Yeah, well...We left my place and went to a small motel, somewhere out in the middle of nowhere. The information your Alpha had previously collected on me made it easy for the traitors to track me, though, something I never knew to expect. More than thirteen of them that time."

"Wait...how did you get away from the first five?" Sheila asked, stepping closer. "Five werewolves are no joke."

"I killed them," I answered, raising an eyebrow. "Five werewolves for a werecat? That's...well, it's not child's play, but it's not even footing either. I had the upper hand, especially since one was in human form and more focused on grabbing Carey."

"Jacky is right," Teagan cut in. "Normally, we wolves need a hunting party of ten or more if we're hunting big game like a werecat. Those wolves learned that the hard way when their first group failed, so they sent a bigger group the second time. In werecat form, though, you should have been able to take out most of them before dying."

"I wasn't in werecat form. I was in human form. They had planned their attack well. Getting to Carey was the only thing I was worried about, and I didn't think I could spare the time to Change." I sighed, closing my eyes for a second, remembering the action. "I jumped in, human and stupid, and killed a few before they were able to put me down. They're carrying silver, by the way, so when we do find Carey, be mindful of that."

"Shit," Chrissy growled. "That's low of them."

"Right?" I chuckled darkly. "In the last week, they've put five silver bullets in me." I started to laugh, a bit too high-pitched. "Oh, this is a fucking disaster." I was laughing harder now, bending over.

The wolves stepped away from me as I laughed until I cried. I was in the middle of a werewolf pack having what was probably a nervous breakdown. Carey needed me, but my brain was refusing to function properly as the severity of what was going on once again pressured me into freaking out.

Warm arms wrapped around me. "Woah there, cat," Heath whispered. "Hey, it's going to be okay. None of this was supposed to happen." A hand rubbed over my hair, and I was led to a seat. "Jacky...are you going to be okay? Do I need to put you in a safe house?"

"No. No safe houses," I finally managed. "Ah, shit, Heath, you brought this down on me and I wasn't ready for it." I rubbed my face, trying to wipe the tears away.

"I know," he whispered. "I know."

"How?" I looked up, finding him kneeling in front of me. He gave me a sad smile. The other wolves were behind him, looking various degrees of concerned and freaked out.

"I did a *lot* of research on you, Jacqueline. I know you have two living human parents and a twin sister who is a successful doctor. You didn't make it through med school, though, opting to become an EMT instead. You're not a soldier. You aren't a killer. You saved things once, and it was that reason I picked you over the other werecats to protect Carey." He sighed. "I'm sorry my actions have changed that for you."

"You know too much," I said softly. "My *family*... They could have been at risk because of you."

"I'll see all the information burned and deleted myself, the moment this is all handled," he promised. "You don't have to keep going, Jacky. You can stay here and let us handle the rest. You can go home right now and I won't begrudge you for it at all."

I shook my head. "Too late for that. I'm fine now. Thanks." I pushed him away a little, standing back up to get some air. "God. Sorry about that. I've been running on fumes."

"You look like it, too. I take it the wolves put those bruises on your face?" Laurent pointed, gesturing to my entire face.

"Yeah."

"Huh. I thought werecats were cold-blooded killers," Chrissy said thoughtfully. "You don't seem like that. You definitely don't seem like someone who's killed...over ten werewolves in the last week."

I crossed my arms protectively again. "I did what I had to do," I said softly. "I'm fine. Let's continue. They're armed with silver. Does your pack keep a supply of it?"

"Yes, but it's more for self-preservation. Rogue wolves causing trouble and the like. We've never authorized its use on your kind or anyone in the pack proper." Heath was watching me curiously. I *knew* he was probably thinking about my breakdown, everything he knew about me, and everything that had happened. He probably thought I was weak now, because I was suffering from a moment of massive panic and insecurity about it all.

That was why I had pushed the topic back onto the job at hand, and I was going to force it to stay there. "Where did you keep the supply?"

He shook his head. "Everywhere. Everyone had a small supply for self-protection from other wolves, though the rule was to use it only as a last resort. There's no secret stash I can point at and say 'the guns are right there.' That's going to have to change. I won't feel comfortable letting my wolves keep silver after this."

"Sir, they're not going to be your wolves soon," Teagan said softly.

"What?" I raised an eyebrow, intrigued by that new revelation. Heath's glare at Teagan made it apparent that he hadn't wanted that to come out. "Heath, I'm in the middle of this now. I need to know what the fuck is going on."

For what it was worth, he looked back over at me and

finally nodded, gesturing for me to sit down. "This goes into how this all started, I think. You're right. You do need to know what possibly set this off." I sat down and he picked the seat across from me. "I've been planning on retiring," he started, clasping his hands in front of him, resting them on the table. "It's for my daughter and myself. I've been an Alpha consistently for the last hundred years, and a Council Alpha for fifty."

"Okay..."

"When Carey was born and I got custody over her, I knew there would come a moment when she needed a father. I started planning for passing on the reins to another wolf once the time was right. He's my third, Tywin. Good wolf, and a very old friend of mine. My second is Landon, and he's never had any aspirations for leading his own pack. Tywin, however, once was an Alpha to a smaller pack that I absorbed. He's well-suited for the role. He wouldn't become the Council Alpha without the other Alphas in the region agreeing, but he would take this pack from me."

"Where's Tywin?" I asked.

"No one's seen him since this started," Heath said softly. "I'm worried for him. We've been planning for my retirement to be next year. Word was beginning to spread so the transition could start now."

"And?"

"And some weren't happy it was going to be him, but it wasn't their call. They weren't happy I skipped other options, probably. Some wanted Fenris, but Fenris...no, he'll never be an Alpha. He can't. Some wanted it for themselves, and to them, I said they should challenge Tywin when he's Alpha, but since they couldn't beat me, they would have to wait to make their point known."

"Oh..." I leaned back, rubbing my face. "This is so the next guy doesn't take the throne. Dispose of you before you hand over the reins, because they don't think you have the pack's interest at heart. Isn't it?"

"That's my best suspicion," he confirmed. "With Tywin missing, and possibly dead, it's the best idea I have."

"Who else wanted power?"

"I could give you ten names and not know which ones are actually the problem," Heath answered. The other wolves stayed silent, probably letting their Alpha take the reins on this because they might have been ones to preach for other possible options. In the end, they fell in line behind the Alpha they trusted and respected, even if they didn't like his successor.

"Any close to you?" I asked, curious.

"Some preached for Dean, who refused. Emma being a half-witch removes her from the equation. She's not allowed to hold real power in the pack, living somewhat outside of it. She and Dean would share my fifth spot of my inner circle if it was allowed."

"Meaning you treat her like one of the inner circle without making it obvious enough to cause trouble." I pursed my lips, daring him to say any different.

"For a young, reclusive cat, you know a lot."

"I had a good education. Plus you make it obvious in the way you talk about her. You respect the hell out of her. You want her to be able to hold some power, half-witch or not. Maybe not Alpha, but something."

"Good ear," he complimented.

I shrugged. "So some wanted Dean, and in turn, his half-witch wife that he would probably share power with. Some wanted this Fenris, a very old, somewhat crazy wolf."

"There's also..." Heath frowned. "Teagan, people talk to you. Tell Jacky here."

Teagan jumped in there, rattling off names of people who were suggested to the Alpha and those who presented themselves as options. Most were middle of the pack males who had all the balls but none of the strength. A couple were females, recommended by their mates or lovers as potentially kind leaders who could help the pack look better to humans. They would also give their male mates power in turn, helping them get boosted through the ranks.

"You have to understand. This is pretty normal when an Alpha decides to step down to a peer instead of dying in action," Teagan said. "It's not the most common way for an Alpha to go and it leaves all sorts of openings and ideas of democracy and the like. The 'maybe we can just vote on our next Alpha' sort of things. The thing is, wolves? We don't work that way. Until Heath leaves, he's still in charge, and he'll train who he sees fit. His successor can deal with the rest when he's in power."

"So everything was 'normal' until a sniper tried to kill you," I said to Heath, considering everything they had just told me. "So someone decided to take matters into their own hands, rules and Laws be damned. Which isn't something new to be learned. I mean, I figured that out when I had wolves enter my territory. They don't care about anything but the power at the end. There might even be a bit of a grudge against you for not giving them the position."

"Exactly."

"And that's why they wanted Carey. Because if they get you to surrender to them, Tywin's place goes out the window, even though he's the third of the pack and there's no other better options above him. Tywin would have to fight and kill the new Alpha, who gained his position from blackmail and war."

"Exactly," he repeated softly.

"So we're dealing with someone who doesn't know that every supernatural race is going to come down on his head for breaking the Law, whether he wins or not. Someone arrogant and possibly uneducated. Someone young enough to think the Law is a boogieman and not the very real foundations by which we can live our lives." I was rambling a little now, but it was helping me put things together. "Who fits the description? When was the last time someone was executed for breaking the Law?" I couldn't remember off the top of my head.

"Probably the case a century ago. A fae who killed a werewolf without grounds. He was attempting to steal the wolf's skin, much like Selkies use seal skins for transformation. Before that..." Teagan took a deep breath. "The werewolves who killed Hasan's daughter, only a couple years before the fae."

I froze for a second. I had no idea that wolves had killed her, only that she was killed. It took me a moment to convince myself to think on that later and get back on topic.

"So we're dealing, probably, with a wolf or wolves under a century old, probably even younger, since most closer to a century would remember the aftermath of those Tribunal executions."

"Good. Most of the traitors are quite young so far," Heath agreed. "That means Fenris is off the table completely, which I already figured. He's too old to think he can break the Law and get away with it. He's crazy, but he's also not going to get an entire pack killed for himself."

"Who else?" I asked.

Teagan began writing in a notebook, crossing out names as he spoke. I didn't absorb all of it. I really didn't want to leave Dallas knowing the name of every werewolf who wanted power.

"None of these wolves have proven to be traitors yet, though a couple are missing. Our security plans actually have Dean and Emma hiding alone, protecting their son. Magic and wolves pisses some on both sides off. They won't contact us until everything is over, which is what I ordered them to do." Heath ran a hand through his hair and I realized the problem.

Wolves were normally very straightforward. They didn't do betrayal and plots and blackmail. It wasn't in them, so Heath, no matter how smart he was, wasn't very good at thinking like those who did those things.

"What if we're looking at the wrong angle?" I cut in, against my better judgement. I really shouldn't have been helping them find the traitor just for the sake of it. "Some of these names were recommended by other people, for a variety of reasons. Best friends, lovers, siblings. They would have gotten power by proxy if their suggestion was used."

"That's..." He smiled at me. "Huh. A week hoping we can just beat the answers out of the traitors, and you walk in with the obvious. Teagan, do we remember who recommended everyone?"

"You aren't used to this sort of thing," I reminded him, shrugging. "Werecats...we don't have politics, but we're cats. Cats are fucked up."

"True that," Chrissy muttered.

"I don't, sir. The mated males putting their wives forward? That's easy to see coming, but some of these? It was random wolves. I had no idea there was any connection. They could have just liked a wolf they reported to. I don't..." Teagan shrugged. "I don't know."

"I'll get someone looking into it. We've gotten off track here." He nodded back to the whiteboard. "We should be focused on Carey."

"Figuring out our traitor is one of the fastest ways of finding her," Laurent said from his seat.

"Yeah, but I'm walking a tightrope." I couldn't let anyone forget that I was in a place I wasn't supposed to be.

"What you do or say in this room will remain with those of us here," Heath told me. "Right, wolves? We're not going to betray her to the Tribunal if we are called to the stand when this is over."

"Yes sir," they answered, *again* in that annoyingly perfect unison.

"What places do the wolves own as safe houses? Places where it's feasible to stash Carey."

"We've cleared all the safe houses since this started," Heath answered. "For other reasons, but we've done it."

"Okay...you know what. Tell me what you can. You obviously know more about Dallas and your wolves than I do." I threw my hands up.

"And what? You'll just be the muscle when we find out where she is?" Chrissy raised an eyebrow.

I bared my teeth. "If that's what I need to do," I answered.

"After the breakdown we just witnessed?" She shook her head. "I think you should take Heath up on his offer and go home."

"Too late for that," I whispered, looking down at my hands. "It's just too late for that."

"Werecats have an obsession with those they feel are theirs," Teagan told everyone at the table. "Jacky won't be able to stop until she's dead, especially young as she is, fighting against instincts that are stronger than her."

I pointed at Teagan, an indication he was right. Instincts I wasn't fighting again. Nope. I fully embraced them.

"Really? Even if you're on the verge of a breakdown?" Sheila snorted. "Foolish."

"I can break down after, and I probably will, but I'm going to see this through," I snapped.

"Stop," Heath ordered. "Wolves, collect everything we know."

"I guess I get phone duty then," I muttered.

"Whatever works, feline." He walked out then, leaving us to our own devices.

Laurent jumped up and put his laptop down on a desk. "Come here, Jacky. I'm going to set this up for you. To answer calls, just hit the green button on the screen. To see texts, look at this window." He pointed everything out when I walked over to stare over his shoulder. "You'll be monitoring Heath's phone number. I can only do the one, and he seems like the most important."

"Okay. I'll keep an eye on it."

"Cool. And I know we haven't said it yet, but thanks for coming to us and helping us find Carey."

"Of course." I sat down when he vacated the chair and proceeded to stare at the screen.

17

CHAPTER SEVENTEEN

Hours passed. No one called or texted Heath's phone, leaving me bored as the 'team' I was with walked around and played on other computers. They were constantly coming and going from the room, too.

Which was how I didn't notice a new wolf walk in. Everything smelled like wolf, and even after a few hours, I still wasn't able to figure out their individual scents.

So when one of them growled behind me, I froze, both worried and confused. I looked over my shoulder slowly to find a grizzled thing, three scars running across his face. His teeth were bared, already showing signs that he was losing control along with his glowing green eyes.

I stood up slowly and raised a hand. "I'm Jacky." I greeted him carefully. I was pinned in the cubicle, and the last thing I wanted was another fight, especially one that wasn't needed.

"I knew I caught wind of a murderer," he snarled out, stepping closer.

"Now, didn't anyone tell you I was here? I'm helping your pack. The traitors have Carey—"

"Oh, I heard. Why should I believe anything that's come out of your mouth, *cat*?" He spat the word, taking another step closer. "You walk in here and hide behind us and my own damn Alpha. You have other wolves running around, doing your bidding."

"You must be Fenris," I guessed, moving slowly to try and edge away out of the cubicle.

He sidestepped and stopped me, ending up even closer than he already was. "I'm glad someone told you my name. Remember it as the name of the wolf who killed you when you go to whatever Hell you belong in."

He lunged for me. I was thankfully faster, and my healing was going well. Every hour that passed gave me more of my original strength and speed, with less of the painful repercussions. I ducked under his grab and made it around behind him. I kicked his ass, sending him into the chair and desk I had been using before doing the smart thing.

Running.

I hauled ass, heading for the door of the office. I didn't want this fight. Hell, I didn't even know where it came from. They had said Fenris was crazy, but I hadn't figured he was 'attack on sight' kind of crazy.

I got the door open before he reached me. I dodged his grab and tried to slam the door in his face. There was a problem, though. He was too old and too far gone into the partial shift and animal craze for me to be very effective against him. He pushed the door into me and sent me into the far wall, which cracked as my back slammed into it.

It knocked the air from my lungs, leaving me gasping for air, but other than a bruise, I didn't think it would cause too much of a problem. Nothing felt broken.

I scrambled to stand up as I realized he was closing the distance again. He reached out for me, and before I could stop him from grabbing me, a blurred grey-blue shape took him out of my line of sight.

"Oh shit, Jacky!" Chrissy. "Fuck. We had no idea Fenris was back from his mission. Sorry."

"Who?" I pointed to the blurry, furred object wrestling Fenris to the ground, biting painfully into his shoulders, arms, and legs.

"Heath. He's got a quicker shift than most of us," she answered.

I looked up to her, frowning. "How much faster?" I asked.

"About five minutes," she informed me, holding a hand out. "You think you can stand?"

"Yeah." I grabbed the offered hand, grateful for it. "How did he know..." I nodded to the wolf still putting the feral old one in his place. Fenris was snarling and trying to protect anything vital, but from the rage in his eyes, Heath still had some work to do if he wanted Fenris to leave me alone.

"We were about to go out on a hunt. Heath shifted first, to guide some of the slower ones through easier. We heard Fenris across the damn warehouse. He wasn't exactly quiet. Heath and I came running. Teagan, Laurent, and Sheila will be here any minute." She gave me an embarrassed look. "One of us was supposed to stay with you at all times while Heath was dealing with the other wolves."

"It's fine," I said, flexing and rotating my shoulder. "Nothing's broken."

"Good. That's good."

A yelp and whimper suddenly replaced the snarls and growls.

"I cede, Alpha!" Fenris called out. "I cede! She's yours!"

I looked back to the fight, not ready for what I saw. Heath's jaws were dripping with blood and Fenris' left leg was so mangled I wasn't sure it could ever heal. I watched the painful beginning of Heath's shift back into his human form as Teagan, Laurent, and Sheila ran up. Teagan continued to move, heading for the two further down the hallway. He bowed low to his Alpha, who looked like a freak mashup of man and wolf, then kneeled to tend to Fenris.

"Will Fenris be okay?" I asked softly.

"Yeah. Old wolves like him and Teagan have seen worse damage. He'll be out of commission for a few months, but it's really his fault. He should have submitted faster instead of trying to tumble with Heath," Laurent answered. "Idiot. We need strong wolves right now, and he's gone and done that to himself."

What the hell have I gotten myself into? They don't

even have an ounce of sympathy. Even I do, after he definitely tried to kill me. I wrapped my arms around myself, shaking a little. Not from fear. It had been a sudden rush of adrenaline I hadn't been expecting, and now I needed to come down from it. "Why can't I catch a damn break?"

"You're a werecat. What do you mean?" Chrissy was frowning at me now, obviously confused by my state.

"I own a bar!" I growled. "I don't fight wars or kill werewolves all the time! The only reason I've been doing it recently is because of Carey, and once she's safe, I'm fucking getting out of this business." I turned back to the Alpha. "Heath, you better hope this doesn't happen once everything is said and done. When Carey is safe, I'm fucking done with you wolves."

I stomped back into the office, breathing hard. A few minutes later, the door opened and slammed shut again. I was already back in my chair, slumped and tired. As Heath came into view, I sighed. "Well. That was interesting." I tried for a weak smile, but it refused to come.

"I'm sorry. It was the very thing I was trying to avoid. You're not hurt, right? Chrissy—"

"I'm fine," I interrupted. "I'm just fine."

"Jacky, what you said—"

"I was serious. When this is over, I never want to hear from another wolf, especially not one from this fucking pack. Is that clear? I've been shot at. I've been clawed and bitten. I've been harassed, and oh, the best one, fucking killed. I should apologize for my attitude to you right now, but I won't because all of this is your fault!" I was standing and never even remembered making the move. "I'm in here, just monitoring your damn phone, and some fucking rabid animal comes for me! Now, I'm sure that Fenris has a *great* reason for hating my kind, much like Teagan probably does, but god damn, I'm trying to help here!"

"I know." He clasped his hands and let them hang in front of him. "Fenris is a one-off case. He's more traumatized by the old war than Teagan. I'm sorry. I really was trying to keep an eye out for him, but then I got busy with everything else and—"

"I'm not one of your wolves, so you forgot about me." I jerkily nodded, understanding. "Yeah. Well, leave. I'm going to get back to work."

"I'll stay here," he said softly, pulling up a chair.

"What?" I couldn't have sounded more *not okay* with that than I already did. I curled a lip, trying to understand why he was sticking around. I didn't want him breathing down my neck all damn night.

"I promised to keep you out of harm's way, that my pack wouldn't attack you. I failed due to my own distraction. I'll be sitting right here until we find you a place to sleep that I feel is safe and secure." He pulled over a chair from the meeting table and sat down. "So, no one has tried to contact me today?"

"No. No one," I answered, breathing hard. "Have the others talked to you?"

"They brought me what they've put together so far. I don't think we're going to find my daughter the old-fashioned way." He sounded distant for a moment. "We have to hope they call."

"They will," I promised. "Could be tonight. Could be tomorrow, but they will. There's a chance your wolves capture a traitor and we get the information that way. You never know."

"You said earlier that you found a wolf and sent him with a message."

"Yeah, to his superior, Little Tim. Apparently a nickname for a guy called Timothy. Want to tell me about him?"

"He's seventy-three and something of a slime ball. I never thought it was in a bad way. He's good at business and leading people in the direction he wants them. He has a fascination with magic. He helped with the accounting firm. Middle of the pack."

"Never considered he would betray you, being 'somewhat of a slime ball'?" I raised an eyebrow in question.

"No, but then, no Alpha thinks half his pack is going to betray him." He chuckled darkly. "Arrogant, I know, but it's unheard of. Hostile takeovers are normally one wolf who takes on and takes out the Alpha. The rest of the pack falls into place. We don't do political parties or any of the human nonsense. We just lead and follow. We survive, knowing that the strength of the community is more important than the wealth and power of the individual."

"Ah. Confident in how your people think, are you?"

"I'm nearly three hundred. I've known a lot of wolves," he said, giving me a bitter smile.

"Do you think your sons will contact you?" I asked softly. "Do you think they're safe from the machinations of the traitors?"

"I hope so. They're not young, my boys. Richard is only twenty-two years younger than I am. I had him while I was still human and Changed him myself. Landon was born during the Civil War. They're good men with good heads on their shoulders." He leaned back, shifting around in the seat. "What about you, Jacky? Like I said earlier, I have a lot of research on you. I know about your human life. I know about a lot since you moved to Jacksonville. What happened in between?"

"I was Changed and I lived with my werecat parent," I answered, shutting down any and all emotion on my face. Wolves were the last species I could say Hasan was my father to, not if their kind killed his daughter before me. "I flew the nest younger than most do, but said werecat parent supported me in it."

"Who?" He sounded blandly curious.

I just stared at him, refusing to speak.

"It's really interesting that you refuse to answer that. I thought werecats looked back on their 'line' as if it was something to be proud of. Like that one werecat I met. She introduced herself that night as Lani, daughter of Arobi, son of Lesna, or something." He tilted his head much like a dog would. "But I never found out who your werecat parent was. It's elusive. A mystery."

"That sucks. For you." I turned my chair, looking

back at the laptop. I knew other werecats were all about that, but for a thousand reasons, I couldn't be. I just couldn't.

The minutes ticked by, becoming an hour, then two. The door opened with a squeak and closed just as quietly. Heath growled, standing up slowly.

"Fenris..."

"I came to apologize to the miss," the gruff old male said. I couldn't see him yet, but I could pick out his scent now. He was like a wild forest touched with darkness. It contrasted with Heath's summer sun and fields. "Others have imparted on me the importance of her presence, and I was foolish to think she was doing this and not taking her own risks. I was...lost in a moment of madness."

"Let him," I ordered softly, standing up.

Heath nodded and slid to stand at my side, a protective gesture I knew was rooted in his vow to protect me from his own. It was also the closest I had been to a man in years without it being a fight or a drunk dude who needed to be shoved into his car. He even put his hand on my lower back, a silent offering of support.

Fenris grew closer. Now that he wasn't dipping his toes into madness, his eyes weren't glowing forest green, but an earthy brown. He offered a small bow. "I am Fenris, a wolf granted shelter by Alpha Everson when I found myself without a home thanks to my madness. Because of my regard for him and his trust in you, I offer my apologies for my behavior. I was hasty, only thinking of my own past with your kind and not the current peace we have." He looked up from his bow to his Alpha and continued. "I'm sure I speak for everyone when I say thank you for your assistance with saving little Carey."

"Jacky Leon. Apology accepted." I inclined my head, remembering all the training and lessons Hasan had given me, especially when it came to dealing with the old ones of any species. *Hasan, you better be fucking proud of me right now. I'm here and I'm not starting a war with the werewolves. Look at that.*

"Move along, Fenris," Heath finally said. "Thank you for coming."

Fenris didn't waste any time getting out of my presence, leaving me alone with Heath's hand on my back. It was a casual touch, and for the werewolves, probably a natural one, but I stepped away, breaking it. It wasn't what I was used to and it reminded me just how damn lonely my life was before Carey stumbled into it.

How lonely it still is. *I should be honest with myself.*

He looked down at his hand for a moment, then up to my eyes. "Don't like being touched?"

"It's not normal for me, no," I answered, finding my seat again. I looked back at the screen of the laptop, settling in for more long hours of waiting. Eventually, I was going to need someone to take over so I could get some sleep, but I knew I could last until midnight if I needed to.

Thankfully, within thirty minutes of my deciding to go back to silence, someone ran in, spooking both Heath and I.

"We got one!" the wolf announced. "We captured a

traitor. He was snooping around one of the other safe houses."

"Perfect. Let's hope he knows something." Heath grinned, standing up. "Jacky, are you going to come?"

I nodded, standing up.

Damn right I was going to help with the interrogation. I would have loved to see any of the wolves try and stop me.

18

CHAPTER EIGHTEEN

I followed Heath and the young wolf to the center of the warehouse. Someone had tied the traitor to a chair. Not the best way to hold one of them down, but I figured the traitor wasn't going to be stupid enough to fight or run when he was surrounded by two dozen angry loyalists now also searching for a little human girl.

"Jeffrey," Heath breathed out. "I had hoped for better from you."

The wolf sniffled and glared across the room at him. I was standing right behind him and the heat of the anger felt like it burned even me.

"There's better options for the pack, and I'm supporting them," Jeffrey answered, the glare not abating.

"See, I was willing to forgive the idea that you're fighting for a better pack future. I was okay with that. After winning the pack back, I was going to have a long conversation with each of you about that." Heath sounded like he was amused, but I couldn't see his face. He began to walk closer to Jeffrey, the other wolves in the room backing off.

I followed behind him, only by a few steps, pondering Heath's next move until he spoke again.

"I could have forgiven it," he murmured as we got closer. "What I can't forgive is the kidnapping of my daughter from her oath-sworn protector, the werecat called to Duty." He gestured to me, having never lost track of my movement.

As the wolf paled in fear, I chose to circle, feeling my predatory instincts flare up, driven high thanks to the smell. It was basic, really. Fear and running drove a predator to react, to be a predator. I was thriving thanks to it.

"My daughter, Jeffrey. She had run out of this city, somehow able to make it two hours away, at only eleven-years-old, and called a werecat to Duty for protection. Can you believe that? My human daughter can't fight. She's not a threat to anyone, really. She must have walked to the werecat." Heath leaned over, putting his hands on the wolf's wrist to prop himself up in Jeffrey's space. "A werecat who takes her Duty so seriously that she's killed over ten wolves, all traitors. What that must have done to your numbers...I've had another ten killed. What does that leave you with? A possible twenty? Maybe more, if you got the rogues to join you?"

"Such a weak Alpha, you got a werecat involved," Jeffrey said, his voice shaking.

I sniffed loudly, soaking in the fear.

"Where's my daughter, Jeffrey?" Heath asked softly. "Answer me, and I'll find a way not to execute you. Don't answer me and I'll let Jacky here interrogate you. Or let Fenris release his aggression at her existence on you. Take your pick."

"I don't know where they're keeping her."

"Who's they?" I asked in a purr. It was so wildly not me, not the me I thought I was. Meeting Carey, coming to Dallas, I was noticing some remarkably different sides of myself.

His mouth closed up so I reached out from behind him, wrapping my hand around and yanking his head back. I looked down at him now, studying his face.

"Are you another idiot who follows Little Tim without really understanding what you've gotten yourself into?" I asked softly.

"Little Tim tells us that our leaders' identities are important to keep secret. I know who I follow. We're going to become a powerful pack, no longer beholden to the rules of other species. We're fucking wolves. We're better than that. I'll die before I tell some fucking cat our business."

I released him, looking up at Heath with a raised eyebrow, who sighed sadly.

"Okay, Jeffrey. Tell your leaders I'm ready to trade my life for the life of my daughter," Heath said softly, backing up. "I'm tired of playing this game. She's too important."

I reached down and untied one of his wrists slowly, holding it in place when he tried to raise it.

"You don't move until I tell you to," I hissed. I let Heath hold the wrist while I untied the second, then his ankles. Heath and I backed away in unison.

Jeffrey stood up and looked around, grinning. "Weak enough to work with the very kind that supposedly is such a problem to us," he spat. "This is why we can't trust any Alpha you want to train."

Some of the wolves around them shifted uncomfortably.

Heath pulled out his cellphone and held it out to Jeffrey. "Call your little leaders and tell them I'm willing to meet without violence. A simple trade. My life for my daughter's freedom."

Jeffrey nodded, dialing in the number. "Tim! I've brought news..." They all listened to him relay the news, offering Heath's suggestion, telling the traitors that the werecat was now with Heath and so on.

I wasn't sure of Heath's game, not really, but it was his, not mine. I couldn't see him as a man who would give up his own life without a fight, but I also didn't see him as a man who would endanger his daughter.

It left me with an odd, conflicting viewpoint of the man and no conclusions.

Jeffrey finally hung up and tossed the phone back. "They'll call you back with a time and place," he said, still smiling.

Heath smiled back. Then, in a lightning-fast move, he pulled a gun out and fired.

Jeffrey fell, the silver and heat burning skin, the bullet in his brain killing him.

"Traitor," Heath said softly. "They want to play dirty? I've been trying to avoid it, but fine, I can play dirty." He was angry.

No, furious. I could smell it boiling the air around him, adding an acidic note to the room.

He looked over his wolves, ignoring me completely. "My daughter is *not* a fucking pawn!" he roared. He began to pace, touching the cellphone to his chin. "When they give us the information, we are going in with a small force. It'll be me, Jacky—who will take custody of Carey —and a few others. Once Carey is in your care, Jacky, you're going to get her out of there. My group will take down anyone who wants to fight."

"I can fight," I said softly. "I would really even the odds, actually."

"It would destroy your attempt at an impartial image."

"I'm sure at some point one of them is going to threaten her or something. I'll play it by ear." I was feeling a little bloodthirsty, to be honest. Getting Carey back and safe was close, and the wolves who took her? They were going to submit or die soon enough. *And I'll get to pay them back for fucking killing me. Assholes.*

"Fine." Heath waved at me, dismissive. I took it as my sign to start walking away, done with the entire conversation until they needed me, but he grabbed me before I could get away. "Stay. I want you to hear everything."

"I feel the need to remind you that I don't take orders

from you," I said softly, leaning over. "And it would do my kind a disservice to stay on your order."

"I would very much appreciate if you stayed and helped make the basic plans to rescue my daughter and end the civil war gripping Dallas," he said, a small smile forming.

"Much better. I can do that." I turned back to the wolves and crossed my arms. "We *are* going to remember that I'm not some military commander, *right*?"

"But you are a predator," he pointed out. "And predators know how to hunt."

I couldn't disagree with him, but I was still growing accustomed to being that predator. It was one thing to acknowledge that I was. It was another to use it.

They talked for what felt like hours, until I sat on the floor even while they all remained standing. I didn't move or talk, just listened to them argue out who might be the best in a small team that would be for 'protecting Carey,' when we all knew I would be the one with that job.

They also made theories about things we couldn't possibly know. Would we learn who the leaders of the traitors were? How many wolves would they bring to this to potentially see Heath die?

No one had any idea what the answers were.

Finally, I yawned too loud for any of them to miss. I checked the time and noticed it was damn near midnight and stood back up.

"Hey, where can I sleep?" I asked. "There's nothing else to be done until they contact us. Even I'm smart enough to figure that out, and you've all started talking about things I have truly no business in, like what to do after the traitors have been squashed." I was tired, and being dismissive was the only way I could think of getting out of there. I was plagued with worry, had been for what felt like days, even if I had only met the Alpha that afternoon. I needed a break from it all. Just one night.

He offered an arm. I eyeballed it, curling a lip.

"I'm from a vastly different time than the one you are," I said, pushing his arm back to him. "I'm sure it's polite to offer to walk women around and hold them, but I'll pass this time around."

"Fine," he said, chuckling. "I'll show you, come on."

I followed him out of the main room and back to the office section. He opened a door near the large office space I had used all day and showed me in. I saw a few cots laid out and nodded.

"Thanks, but I could have managed with the floor, too."

"No. You're an honored guest, remember? This is where Shamus, Stacy, and I sleep. Shamus and I because we're in charge. Stacy because she's a human playing as a wolf until her Change. Still a little too vulnerable to be left out in the general area." He walked across the room to the fourth empty cot, gesturing to it. "This work? I can have your stuff brought in from the Explorer soon."

"Thanks." I fell on it, leaning on the wall that the cot was placed against. "So. Progress made on day one. This is good."

"This is very good," he agreed. "I feel this should be said again. Thank you for coming to Dallas, Jacky. Thank you for helping me with Carey—and even though she was taken from you and you were injured, you're here. I'm sad our half-witch isn't here. She could have patched you up."

"It's easy to ignore the pain," I said casually, waving off his words. "I'll be fine." *I hope.* "She talked a lot about you," I finally said when he didn't leave immediately.

"Did she? I'm blessed to have her." He sighed and sat on his own cot, staring at me. "Would you forgive me for being a little weak for a moment? I have to present a strong front for everyone, but...Well, I don't often get much of a chance to really think about anything anymore."

"I'm not going to judge you. I've had a nervous breakdown or four in the last few days." I shrugged.

"I was so worried about her when I was getting reports that no one could find her." He sighed. "I had no idea if she made it out of the city. I had no idea if she was safe. She's a tough kid, and my sons taught her to use a knife, but..."

"She's eleven. You had the right to worry," I finished for him.

"Exactly. She's a baby. I should have stepped down years ago, honestly. Once I realized I had a human child. Look at what I've done to her now." He leaned over, putting his face in his hands. For a moment, I saw the despairing father that hid under the shell of the Alpha. "And while my pack loves her...they would hate me if I put her before them completely. They need me too."

"The good of the many versus the good of the few," I

said softly. "Yeah, this is why I'm glad I'm a werecat." I went with honesty when he looked over. "I don't give a shit about your wolves. They're fighters, everyone here is built to fight. This is in our blood, especially wolves. You fight over power with each other all the time. Werecats, we fight over territory, which doesn't happen that often. Roamers are uncommon."

"Roamers...you mean rogues."

"Sort of the same," I agreed, nodding. "Werecats who haven't found the spot they want to put roots down yet. Sometimes they see what other cats have and try to take it."

"Like what's going on here."

"Except we don't put a lot of people in the middle of our problems. When we hire someone, we're one of many clients. Accountants, lawyers. They have lives and businesses outside us. And we don't have human children because...we're not allowed to. No one gets hurt when two werecats scrap over land."

"Good point."

"I'm not a wolf, and I'm a young werecat, Heath. I'm just here because I refuse to fail Carey."

"I know. I think that's what I like about you. Your intentions are the clearest of any here, even the wolves who are loyal to me. Even clearer than mine." He rubbed his face. "I want her back and safe, but I can't screw my wolves while I do it."

"I know." I crossed my arms. *He likes something about me. I Iow...interesting.*

"I'll get your things," he said finally, standing up. He

walked to the door, then stopped to look back. "Good night, Jacky."

"You too, Heath." I yawned as he left, falling onto the cot. The scent of wolf should have kept me up, but my injuries were hurting and the exhaustion was too severe. I was asleep within moments.

19

CHAPTER NINETEEN

When I woke up, I wasn't alone in the room. Stacy was snoring softly on her cot, something that wasn't normal for me, but oddly comforting. They trusted me to stay alone in the room with a human teenager. It was an honor, and also made sense, considering I was there because I wanted to save a human girl.

Sitting up, I rubbed my face and considered my last twenty-four hours. I went from dead werecat who lost her charge to honored guest of a werewolf pack. I was embroiled in a civil war, trying to get said charge out of it.

I was a long way from the simple bar owner life I had moved to Texas for. I wanted to get away from the supernatural nonsense that I had woken up to ten years ago, not get deeper into it.

I got up and found my bags in the room, pulling out clean clothes. I had no hope for a shower, but I grabbed my first aid kit from my gym bag next so I could, at the very least, clean my wounds. Pulling my old shirt off, I looked over the different holes in my body. My muscles were knitting back together nicely, and the stitches Brin had given me were well done.

I was halfway done when the door opened behind me.

"Oh shit," someone said in a hushed whisper.

I looked over my shoulder to find Heath and Shamus. Heath stepped around his advisor and frowned. "You showed me a few of those in the Explorer, but I didn't…" He was still frowning as he stepped closer. As his hand came up, I turned around fully, letting him see the damage in all its glory.

I wasn't one to worry about nudity, but I was happy I had kept on my sports bra while changing. His fingers grazed over one of the gunshots in my shoulder, then gently pushed me to show him my back again.

"There's some faint pinkness back here. Claws?"

"I had a wolf or two jump on my back during the first attack," I explained. "They should be pretty healed by now. I received an unexpected gift from a bystander." I shrugged aimlessly. "It is what it is."

"All of this to protect my daughter," he whispered. "I don't think I can truly say it enough. Thank you."

"It's fine." It wasn't, but neither was it really his fault. It was the system and the traitors. The system demanded I lay my life down at the feet of the one who called me to Duty. The traitors were the ones who broke the Law, challenged my protection, and did the damage. It wasn't a place I thought I would ever find myself, but it was a position I was willing to live with.

And see through to the end.

"Any news?" I asked, trying to change the topic.

"Were you cleaning these?" he asked. "Let me help."

"I've got it. Tell me if there's been any change," I demanded, stepping away from him.

"Feline, it's in your best interest to let an Alpha help. You've done a great service to the pack, and as a father..." Shamus looked over to Stacy. "Just let him."

I narrowed my eyes at the advisor, but sat down on my cot without any more argument. Heath grabbed my kit as the other wolf left the room. I could hear him distantly calling for hot water and clean bandages.

"I don't need to be wrapped up," I said. "I can't Change if I'm covered like a mummy."

"Your thigh should be wrapped. That will fall away naturally when you Change. I would never wrap your abdomen," he said softly. "One of these is already scarred." His fingers grazed my shoulder blade where the first silver bullet had hit me.

"Like I said, I received an unexpected gift from a bystander. Someone who understands the importance of werecats succeeding." I pursed my lips, trying not to say any more.

"You didn't appreciate the gift. I'm going to make a guess and say some fae shoved his or her nose where it didn't belong."

"He has a human wife. He felt it was his personal duty to make sure the reputation that werecats can protect humans is protected." I rolled my eyes, trying to smirk. I needed to lighten the mood, because Heath's grey-blue eyes were too severe for me. They were intense and I didn't want to buckle under the weight of the power in his gaze.

"Yeah, that's fae," he said, his voice betraying a humor that his face didn't. "So, he healed you."

"Yeah. It's a tale, but Carey never knew what he was and none of us told her, so I didn't think to mention it to you." *I didn't want to mention it to you.* I changed the subject back to the scar. "That one I got in my bar, not even twenty-four hours after she showed up. I was in werecat form and she...ended up having to pull the bullet out of me."

He froze, his eyes going wide. "My daughter...had to treat your wounds?"

"It was silver. I couldn't Change back and there was no one I could call," I explained.

"God damn it." That made him lean over, groaning. Again, I saw the immensely worried father and not the steel-spined Alpha. "How did she do?"

"Well enough for an eleven-year-old digging around in my shoulder with tongs." I was able to summon a weak smile. "You remind me of each other."

"She got my eyes," he said, going back to cleaning the stitched gun shot on my gut.

"More than that. You both have steel in you that the

world can see, but then you have these...flashes of vulnerability. Well, maybe that's not the right word for it. You cope and hide things until something reminds you of it, and then it shows up for just a second, whatever you're feeling underneath those defenses." I sighed. "There were moments where I could get her to smile and laugh, playing video games and keeping her busy, unable to dwell on everything going on. Then something...we would get talking and the tears would come. They would end soon enough, but I had to always remember that a fragile, scared girl was hiding underneath a veneer of strength. Her daddy taught her to be strong, and she knew how wolf packs worked. It didn't make it hurt less."

He blatantly stared at me, sorrowful eyes boring into my damn soul. "I couldn't let her grow up ignorant to the world her brothers and I are a part of."

"Of course not," I agreed. "Tell me about your sons while we're here, if you refuse to give me an update on what's going on. I want to hear about the brothers who always cheated to beat her in video games."

Heath laughed roughly, nodding. "They're both old wolves as well, so modern technology...we don't always get along. She's got great hand-eye coordination on top of it. She beats all of us. The boys tickle her to cheat."

"Oh, I heard. I finally gave up trying to beat her and did the same thing."

He continued to laugh. "Ah...Richard. He's my oldest, I think I've told you. My son from when I was still human. He's been a constant companion and family since the day he was born. Except for when I was fighting for America's freedom."

"A real patriot, aren't you?" I chuckled.

"I like to think I was one of the first," he said, the smile sticking now. I was grateful, because I didn't want any more of that damn intense stare. "Landon was born during the Civil War. Here's a picture of us all together, actually." He pulled out his cellphone and flicked his finger and tapped until he turned it for me to see. He pointed to the man who looked damn near exactly like him. "That's Richard." He pointed to a mixed young man who looked very little like the rest of the family. "That's Landon. Landon's mother was an escaped werewolf slave. Oh yeah, supernaturals had a problem with slavery too, especially being enslaved to humans, and she was a person of color so she got it from all sides. She and I met while I was fighting with the Union, knowing if we could end it, then wolves and humans like her would be able to walk free." He trailed off for a moment and sighed. "She died helping others escape about three years after Landon was born. Richard didn't fight, opting to take care of his new baby brother for me."

"I'm sorry for your loss." Then I couldn't resist just a touch of humor. "Three children with three different mothers," I noted, raising an eyebrow. "Woah there, stud."

"You think I'm a stud?" He looked as shocked as I felt.

"You're...an attractive man," I finally said as my face heated. "I was trying to make fun of you."

"Of course you were, but you called me a stud, and there's nothing insulting about that. Honestly, thank God someone finds me a catch. Three children and all of this? Ha. I can't get a date to save my life."

"I can't help you with that," I said blandly, trying to play off my own embarrassment. "And I never said you were a *catch*. A stud, for most animals, is just very good at getting others pregnant."

"Hm, but certain things are required to get women pregnant, and isn't a stud considered the cream of the crop, therefore everyone wants its children? And isn't he normally very good at those things?" The sly smirk that appeared on his face did nothing for my pulse.

Oh shit, he's actually flirting now? "I'm sure. We should put you on the market. Is there a Tinder for werewolves, or do you all just howl at the moon then roll in the dirt until both of you are ready to go home? And when we finally get you a date, just remember not to hump her leg. You didn't grow up in the modern era, but women don't really appreciate it."

"Are you sure? Have you seen how modern humans dance?" He kept smirking. "I'm sure I'll fit right in."

That broke me. I started laughing, and he joined in. "Ok, you have a point," I said, unable to stop laughing. I turned away, covering my face. "Is that how you picked up Carey's mom?"

He stopped and groaned. "Carey's mother was a mistake. I was tired, lonely, and she was pretty. She knew what I was, who I was. Nine months later, she brought me a gift and left, saying she couldn't be the wife of a werewolf, no matter how...fun I was in private. She wouldn't be seen in public with me."

"Oh, I'm sorry. That's rough."

"It's life as one of my kind. She gave me Carey thinking our little girl would end up a werewolf, but she's human. I'm always looking over my shoulder in case her mother comes back for her, but so far we've been in the clear."

"This isn't going to help if her mother finds out," I said gently. "You know that, right?"

"I do," he agreed. "She didn't give up her parental rights either, and I've been...too kind to have the lawyers take them away from her. I want Carey to have a chance at a relationship with her mother." He dropped what he was holding. "I'm done here. You can get a shirt on."

"Thanks." I had stopped noticing the sting thanks to the conversation and grabbed my new clean shirt, throwing it on just as Shamus walked in, finally, with a bowl of hot water and bandages.

"Took you long enough," Heath said with a bite.

"You two were having a conversation that I didn't want to interrupt," Shamus said quickly. "The cat gets fidgety when there's a lot of werewolves around."

"I thought I stopped being so obvious," I mumbled. Damn right I was fidgety with multiple wolves around. Any werecat with even a shred of self-preservation was fidgety around a lot of wolves. A shred was really all I had left, but it was enough.

"All right..." Heath looked between Shamus and I, then sighed. "Pants. Off."

"*Excuse me?* Change that please."

"Please remove your jeans so that I can bandage your thigh," he rephrased.

"Better," I muttered, unbuttoning my jeans. "This really isn't necessary."

"It is," he said softly. "You can go, Shamus."

I stood up for Heath so he could work easier, and hopefully faster. What I hadn't considered with that was the fact that he was kneeling in front of me, with my pants down.

Modern woman sensibilities and all, I was uncomfortable. He didn't seem worried at all and I couldn't catch anything in his scent that would betray him. My scent, however, was probably giving him all sorts of wonderful information.

He's a wolf. I barely know him. He's only down there for medical reasons. I've done it to other people. There's nothing attractive or sexual about this.

"Done," he announced, standing back up.

I swiftly pulled up my jeans and grabbed a jacket. As I started walking for the door, he chuckled again. "You know, I didn't understand how a woman like you lived so alone for all these years, but it's pretty clear now. You aren't good with people."

"I used to be," I said quickly, turning back to him. "But no one has seen me without pants since I was Changed." And that person had been Hasan, so there was nothing sexual about it, or even potentially sexual.

"I can tell," he murmured, still doing that annoying thing called chuckling. Who ever thought chuckling men were sexy? They weren't. I wanted to strangle the one in the room with me.

"Are you always like this with women, or am I just a shiny new toy you can tease?" I crossed my arms, not going through the door and blocking his way out.

"I find myself enjoying this," he admitted. "You're so skittish because I'm a wolf, but really, there's a lot I owe you for. For Carey. For the pack. I'm just trying to help you as an honored guest in my house, and you're making it really easy to bother you. The skittishness...amuses me, though."

"The worst," I muttered, leaving the room. I was ten feet away when I realized I really had nowhere to go except to another confined space to monitor his damn phone. I stomped into the office and found a wolf in my seat. "Hey, I'm here to take over," I told the little female.

"Oh, I just got here. Alpha doesn't want our guest working too hard. Says you'll need to take time to heal before the trade."

I ground my teeth as I heard the chuckling behind me. I looked over my shoulder and glared.

"I'm right and you know it. Why don't you relax and enjoy my hospitality until we receive word from the traitors?"

"I think I hate you." I wanted to stay busy. I needed to stay busy. Sitting around felt like I was doing nothing to save Carey. *And that's not acceptable. I have to save Carey.*

"That's okay, but really, after what I just saw, you do need to get some rest. You need to stop moving around and pulling the scars and stitches. Kick back and watch TV all day. Something. There's nothing to be done until we get a call." He leaned on the wall, crossing his arms. It was now a stare-down.

"You can't keep me here doing nothing," I warned softly.

"I can, and I will if I have to," he retorted. "I have over twenty-five wolves here. More than enough to handle an injured werecat, and I don't think you're going to kill any of the wolves helping get my daughter back."

He was right, but I hated it. I didn't want to be useless. Sure, I had no idea what I was doing, but I needed a task, any task and he even took my little job away from me.

"Let me man the phone, please," I asked, nearly begging. "I can't do useless."

"I'm not asking you to be useless. I'm asking you to heal so you can be the most useful at the right time."

Well, when you put it that way... "Fine. I'll...find somewhere to sit down. Anyone have a deck of cards or something?"

"I'm sure we can find one. No money, though. I don't let my wolves gamble. Terrible vice."

"Taking all the fun out of it then," I muttered, shaking my head. One of the reasons I made my bar into a billiard bar was for the light gambling done at the pool table. It added a bit of spice and I always made sure it was friendly. I didn't let pool sharks screw with my customers, because I could smell their intent from a mile away.

I let him lead me out of the office, feeling a little lost,

very out of place, and insecure as we walked into the main area of the warehouse. It was still packed with wolves, all doing their own things in little groups. A few looked up at Heath and me as we walked, only adding to my belief that I had a sign over me that screamed 'WERECAT' in big red letters. Maybe they thought I would be gone after a day, because something told me they were still as uncomfortable with me as I was with them. It was like everything was back at square one, the same as it was when I had arrived yesterday with their Alpha.

"Sit," he ordered. Before I could correct him, he rephrased. "Would you have a seat?" He indicated the chair at a table near the middle of the room. "Anyone have a deck of cards? I'm trying to keep our guest busy."

"Here, boss." One ran up and handed over exactly what he asked for.

Heath, in turn, handed them to me and sat across the table. "Would you like to sit down and play with us?" he asked the wolf.

I started shuffling, showing I had some skill in it. I played on the bar sometimes, and more than a few times, I'd hosted small poker nights at Kick Shot. I absolutely knew what I was doing.

"Sure..." The wolf fell into a seat as if his Alpha's words had been an order and not a question. The remaining three seats were taken slowly as I shuffled, waiting to see if anyone else dared to come play with the werecat. Once they were all full, I announced the game.

"Texas Hold 'Em. We're in the right state for it and

it's in vogue," I said, smirking. "I'll deal, and then pass counterclockwise."

"All right then." Heath waved a hand, welcoming the cards.

The game kicked off. None of the wolves really spoke to me, but it wasn't cold or rude either. Heath continued to strike up conversation, talking to others to put everyone off his own actions. I knew the strategy, keeping others distracted and hiding tells easier. I'd seen some blustery men try it more times than I could count.

About an hour in, I had won every other hand, grinning as I won another.

"Well, another game for me," I purred.

"I think one of us should shuffle the deck," a wolf muttered.

"I'm not cheating. Just practiced," I said softly.

"Sure." He took the deck anyway and began to shuffle. I shrugged when Heath stiffened up. It was rude to accuse a guest of cheating, but I wasn't going to take it seriously. I was a cat. For all they knew, I could very well cheat and have no problem with it because most of them had never met one of my kind.

So when I won the next hand, especially since four of them folded, it was no surprise when the wolf who had taken the deck from me jumped up. "This is ridiculous. Are we really going to let her play us like this, Heath?"

"She's not cheating. I've been watching her. Don't be a sore loser." The Alpha pointed the wolf to sit back down before settling those grey-blue eyes on me. "Professional?"

"No. Just a lot of practice against amateurs at my bar," I answered. "Everyone here except you has really obvious tells. If there was money involved, you would be the person with the most money because you play safe and keep everyone distracted. I would just clean out the fools."

"Fools?" the wolf snapped.

"You. The customers at my bar. Most people who get mad at poker with no money..." I raised an eyebrow, daring him to question my logic. "Don't make this a big deal. Just trying to kill time."

"Maybe, you should walk away," Heath warned his wolf.

"No! She's cheating, I know it."

"Let him," I ordered the Alpha, who tried to stand up to stop his wolf. I rose out of my chair, sighing. It would have annoyed me, but I had dealt with drunk men, angry men, and confused men. Kick Shot was quiet until the cards came out.

I spread my hands, let him check my seat—which was absurd— and even my pockets. When he touched my ass, probably an accident, I grabbed his wrist, spun him and pinned his arm behind his back.

"Happy now?" I asked softly. "I'm not cheating. Werecats are quite honorable. We know we have advantages. We don't need to cheat. My sense of smell isn't as good as yours, but it's still *very* good. You get upset over a bad hand, and it comes through in how you smell. Learn to control your reactions more and take the game less seriously." I released him, letting him step away from me.

"That was fast," he noted.

"I'm faster than your kind," I informed him, smiling.

"All right. Everyone sit back down or leave the table if you can't play nice." Heath sounded like he was done with the antics. I retook my seat politely and so did the other wolf, who was nodding to himself, mumbling about his scent. Heath leaned over to me. "We normally don't use our supernatural gifts for card games."

"I use every legal advantage I have," I told him. "How do you think my kind stays alive when we're loners?"

"Fair point."

We went back to the cards, and no one tried to accuse me of cheating anymore. Instead, when a guy lost to me, he leaned over. "How did you catch my bluff?"

"You tap the table once, softly, when you have a good hand. It's hard when you have a bad hand. A small act of aggression." I grinned as he groaned, leaning back. "I can hear the subtle difference."

"Don't turn my pack into professional poker players, please," Heath pleaded from his seat.

"I make no promises. If you got a pool table—"

"BOSS!" someone yelled. "Boss, they've contacted you!"

The cards were forgotten in an instant. Heath and I were both out of our seats at the same time. It was a race I won to the back office, and I leaned over the werewolf at the laptop, who made a disgusted noise as my scent must have hit her nose.

They had contacted. With a time and a location. It was in twelve hours, putting it after sunset.

Heath was behind me now, reading over it as well. "They don't want me bringing anyone except you, Jacky. You must have pissed them off."

"Or they know this will fail if you can't put Carey into someone's care," I said. "They might not want any of the wolves loyal to you, but I'm supposed to be impartial. Carey is my only concern."

"If I'm dead, the turmoil ends and whoever takes the pack has the right to challenge my will and claim my daughter as their own, 'for her own protection' and as a 'sign of good will,'" he said harshly. "They might think you'll hand her back over."

"Oh, that's really something I should have known before now," I muttered, shaking my head. "I'm not going to give her to anyone but you or one of your sons. I swear to it now."

"Even if one of them forced their way in as her new legal guardian?" He straightened up, looking down at me. I realized in that moment how much taller than me he was, just over six feet tall. For a second I felt very small.

Not all of it was thanks to his physical display.

I puffed my chest, all bravado and confidence even if I didn't feel it. "She deserves her family, and while under my protection...she is my family. I don't see any reason to believe she might be safe with the wolves who killed her father. I'll find anyone else or keep her before I let them have her."

"Thank you." He stepped away, beginning to shout

orders, telling everyone in the pack the news as he walked out.

I realized I had just signed up to possibly care for a little girl for the rest of her life. It sank in. When Lani had said something about it, it seemed like a far off possibility. Now it seemed like a reasonable outcome.

Shit.

20

CHAPTER TWENTY

I was sitting in a large circle as everyone argued about how this should play out.

"I'm sorry, sir, but you can't go in with just the werecat as back up!" Shamus snapped. Then he glanced at me. "Sorry."

"Oh, no. I agree. I'm not a warrior. I am not, and never was, prepared to be the sole defense of anyone. I would love to take all of you and crush them with overwhelming force, but that might just get Carey killed."

"Exactly. I think we follow their rules, to a point." Heath was pacing in a circle. "Jacky and I will be driven in by a small group. A couple of guards and a driver, who will wait outside for us—"

"So you aren't planning on actually sacrificing yourself? That's good." I couldn't resist making the comment. Should have, but couldn't.

"No, of course not!" Heath furrowed his brow and I found it kind of cute.

Bad Jacky. "Good. I just figured since it hadn't been explicitly said yet, it might be good for the class to hear that."

"You have a mean little attitude over there right now," he said softly, narrowing his eyes on me.

"I'm stressed out and possibly going to die tonight. It's the only way I can deal with it. If it helps: no, I never acted this way in front of Carey. For her I was a stoic, strong source of support and only cried and freaked out by myself in the shower while she was sleeping." Well, not exactly that way, but close enough.

"That's reassuring," someone said darkly. "Our so-called trump card is an anxiety-ridden mess who has no real experience. Heath, you sent your daughter to her to be protected."

"Well, it wasn't a bad idea of his. I did kill over ten werewolves in something like three days," I retorted. "I've just never walked into a wolf's den with the specific purpose of killing one of the wolves before. On top of that, even being a werecat should have deterred them. Obviously it didn't...but don't think your Alpha's plan wasn't sound."

"Jacky, do you want to be in werecat form or human?"

"Werecat," I answered immediately. "I have training in self-defense and hand-to-hand techniques, but I'm more comfortable in a fight when I'm in werecat form and less likely to die from a stray bullet."

"Communication wouldn't be possible, though."

"Let me worry about that," I said. Brin had fixed that

problem, and while I would never be comfortable with the gift, it was handy. I didn't *want* to use it, by any means. It would make me a target of the werewolves if it got out that their major advantage was suddenly being used by a werecat, but if push came to shove...I had the ability now and would use it.

A few of the wolves gave me odd looks and I shrugged. "I'm good at pantomiming," I explained. *I mean, I am.*

"Fine. That gives us a very powerful combatant in the fight."

"Wait. Her? Powerful?" A wolf snorted.

"I'm four feet tall at the shoulder in werecat form and over four hundred pounds, and none of that is fat," I informed him, yawning. "You really need to start educating your wolves better on werecats. I can tell you all sorts of things about werewolves."

"We don't run into your kind much anymore, so it's fallen to the wayside. The vampires are more of a problem these days." Heath seemed patient, but I could tell he was tired of everyone interrupting him. "Jacky brings up a good point, though, you do all need to start respecting her a bit more."

"That's not my point..."

"Werecats are larger, stronger, and faster than our kind. If you ever encounter one, make sure you have friends. Not a few. More like ten and even then, you'll probably lose a few wolves in the fight. That's what I'm counting on with bringing Jacky." He smirked my way. "While she's a bit of a hot mess, she is a werecat. She knows how to fight wolves. It's in her bones. She just needs to listen to them."

"I've fought before in my werecat form. This isn't new to me. Well. This particular case is, but I've fought other werecats. I'm not a pushover when I'm in my werecat form."

"Good," he said softly. "And you've had quite a learning experience with wolves recently. When do we need to let you Change? Before the trip, or…"

"I can Change when we get there. Doesn't take very long."

"Okay." He stopped staring at me now and turned to his advisor. "I want you to stay here, Shamus. Just in case."

"Heath…You think I'm going to let you—"

"You don't have to let me. I'm ordering you to stay here in case I die," Heath snapped. "Don't try to put our long friendship over the pack. Everyone left here will need a leader if I don't make it out."

Shamus lowered his head, displeased but respectful.

There were moments I was glad werecats were loners. There was really no one I had to worry about if I died. Carey was the exception, but if I died and her father lived…well, I didn't have to worry about her either. I didn't have to think about how this would leave Hasan without anything because he had other children, more family. He would lose another daughter, one who didn't like him all that much. *Oh no*. Lani would lose a friend who was off breaking the Law anyway.

No one would miss me. Not really. And my being gone wouldn't ruin anyone's life.

Not that I want to die, but hey, at least no one will be bereft of anything important if I'm gone!

Can I get any more pathetic?

"I'm going to pick who is guarding us next," he said loudly. "As honor dictates, I'll ask first. Are there any volunteers?"

Every wolf in the room stepped up.

I sighed. Wouldn't it be nice to have so many people willing to jump in front of a bullet for you? Scary, but nice.

I left the room after that, not needing to know who was chosen or be involved with the process. I shoved my hands into my hoodie pocket and left through the back of the building, enjoying the warm sun on my face.

Someone followed me, I could smell them, but I couldn't see them. I sighed. I wished I was home for a moment. At least on my own territory I would be able to pinpoint the exact location of my mysterious companion.

Then I caught the scent of human on the air, one I knew now.

"Stacy, come out," I ordered. "I don't like people sneaking up on me, and I would have hated it if I'd accidentally hurt you." And it was a real possibility. If I hadn't smelled her humanity first, I would have roughed her up like a werewolf, and it might have killed her.

"Sorry…" She stepped around the corner. "I got tired of being there, useless."

"Me too," I said, exasperated. "Now we just wait for

the wolves to make their plans and follow along. You just have to wait out the storm."

"I can help, but..."

"You can't," I said softly. "Don't get any foolish ideas."

"But—"

"People could die. Accept the lesson the easy way. Please don't risk learning it the hard way." I rubbed my face as she stepped up next to me. "You're human and your body is fragile. You'll be Changed when it's time, whenever the pack has a chance, and then you can get into the bloody mess with all of them, but you're not a wolf yet."

"Yeah..." She stared out over the terrible view with me. Other warehouses. So majestic.

"It sucks, I get it." *And soon it won't be my problem.*

"How? You're a werecat."

"I was once human, remember? I was an EMT. I saw...humans break all the time. I know exactly how fragile they are. Let's not give Heath or your father any reason to worry about you breaking, please? I'm not sure I can protect two human girls." *Hell, I've already failed at protecting one.*

"Good point. I just want..."

"What are you ladies doing out here?" Shamus said from the door.

"I was enjoying the sun for a minute. Stacy was keeping me company," I answered. "Any decisions made?"

"He's got a top five to choose between, which is

where I step back. He likes making final decisions by himself."

"Of course he does."

"Stacy, come inside. It's not safe wandering outside as a member of the pack right now." It was a tone I knew from Hasan and my human father. Chiding, soft, loving. A father who wanted his daughter to do as he asked without an argument.

"The door is right there!"

I resisted a snicker. "She's fine, Shamus."

"No. *You're* safe out here, but they've come through this place before and we barely stayed hidden. I don't want to see if they might have plans to try and find us right before we're done with this mess. If they catch you out, they might just assume you're squatting without us." Shamus stepped out further and motioned to the door. "Please, Stacy."

"Fine! Be safe out here in the dangerous world, Jacky." The amount of sarcasm in those words made me grin.

"I will." Shamus didn't follow his daughter inside, stepping to stand next to me. I leaned over and whispered, "Hypocrite."

"I wanted to talk to you alone, actually, and my daughter beat me to it," he said. "Are you sure you can handle tonight?"

"No, but I'll do my best," I answered, becoming as serious as he was, my humor dying.

"If you have to shift back to human, do you know how to use any weapons?"

"I can shoot a gun and I'm trained for self-defense with a silver knife." I threw my hands up as I remembered one thing I should have told the wolves about already. "Damn it. I'm sorry for not telling you this soon, but I stole a couple of sidearms from the wolves that attacked me. They're in my gym bag. You might be able to track—"

"None of the pack's firearms are registered. Thank you for finally telling me, but don't worry. They would be useless." He smiled kindly. "A silver knife, huh? Not what I'd expect."

"A gift from the werecat who Changed me before I moved out," I explained. "So yeah, I should be handy around a weapon if I get my hands on one. If I need to have hands."

"Good. I'm trusting you with my Alpha's life. It's not an easy thing for me to do, but you came here, got our attention, and offered help. When this is all said and done, he's probably going to rush into retirement so there's no chance of it interfering with his daughter's life again." Shamus took a deep breath. "Please make sure he has the chance to enjoy it."

"I'll do my best," I promised again, swallowing. "Let's get back inside." The sun didn't feel warm anymore.

He held the door for me and as we walked inside, I noticed it was much quieter than when I had left. Heath was standing with five wolves in the middle of the room, having a quiet conversation. I didn't interrupt, taking a seat nearby and watching. Whoever he picked were wolves I was going to have to rely on tonight. An odd place for a werecat to be. I couldn't forget that, no matter how hard I tried. I was a werecat in a warehouse full of werewolves in the middle of a werewolf war.

I'm an idiot and I'm going to pay for this. The Tribunal I'm going to face once it's all over...

"I have a question," I interrupted. Heath turned to me and waved a hand, beckoning me to say more. "When does the Alpha Council step in?"

He froze, letting his hand drop. "You're worried about the Tribunal, and which one of the Alphas here in North America sits on it."

"I didn't know that, but yeah, I'm worried about the Tribunal," I conceded. "Who sits?"

"The Los Angeles Alpha. He's incredibly old. You know, we could try to minimize your involvement in this—"

"I was already in contact with the Alpha Council before arriving in Dallas. He will have told someone with the Tribunal that I've broken the Law, if I'm still alive when this is all over," I said, rubbing my face. "Too late, Heath. It's too late."

"I'll speak on your behalf," he said carefully.

"Just answer my question. When is the Council going to step in? It's going to be their responsibility to take me into custody."

"You could run," he offered, then shook his head, dismissing it before I could. Running was psychotic. "I was going to call one of my trusted friends on the Council after this. They should be ready to come in at dawn, to help rebuild the pack and to help me finish transitioning into retirement—which I'm going to make effective as soon as the traitors are dealt with and I have Tywin back."

"I'll stick around then, until they show up. No reason to make this hard."

"I'm sorry. If it's any consolation, I'm grateful for you coming here."

"You've made that clear." I huffed. "I'll quit interrupting," I promised, waving at the wolves who were standing ready for him.

"Cats," he mumbled to them. "Everything is on their good graces."

"My niece wants a cat," one of them replied. "I'm trying my best to convince her it's a terrible idea."

"Good luck," the Alpha said, chuckling sadly. "Get her the cat, though. You never know when she might be gone and you've lost the opportunity."

Oomph. My chest tightened.

"Ranger, Keith, and Sheila. You'll all be with Jacky and me tonight." Heath made the decision quickly, pointing to the wolves he named. "Sheila, you'll be the driver. Keith, passenger's seat. Ranger, you'll be in the back with us." He looked over me next. "Tonight we're getting Carey back."

"I know." There was really nothing else to be done.

21
CHAPTER TWENTY-ONE

We left to no cheering or acclaim. I was patted on the shoulder a couple of times, which was nice, I guess. Maybe they were trying to offer some reassurance that this would end just fine.

For Carey's sake, I hoped it did.

I sat on Ranger's left in the Explorer, with Heath on his other side. I didn't know Ranger or Keith, and my interactions with Sheila were minimal. I hadn't spent much time since they were chosen to get to know them, and maybe I should have. I didn't want to get too attached to any of the wolves. I had to remember how this was going to end for me.

The drive started silent, until Sheila spoke up. "Think this is going to work, boss?" she asked softly.

"Yes." Heath was stoic. I had a feeling he was focused on all the parts of the plan that didn't have to do with those of us in the Explorer.

I knew the rest of the plan now, and it worried me just as much as my own part. While we were starting the meeting, half of Heath's loyal wolves were Changing and going on hunts of their own. They were making their way to us, and handling any wolves they saw along the way. The rest of his wolves were staying at the warehouse, just in case it was attacked. It held the children of several pack members, and as everyone had learned with Carey, children were the most vulnerable group. They had to be protected at all costs.

So while we played pretend, trying to secure Carey's safety and take out the leaders of the traitors, the rest of the pack was going to be fighting a war, hopefully out of the human eye. The last thing any of us needed was more videos of wolves killing each other to get onto the internet.

"Now's the worst time to start questioning the plan," I said quietly, rubbing my face. "Or so I think."

"You're right," Ranger agreed, nodding in my direction. "We have to stay focused, believe in our backup, the wolves watching the kids, and hope we've judged the situation correctly."

"Fingers crossed," I said, even holding up a hand doing just that.

"Jacky, you just need to worry about Carey. I don't care what happens to me, but I need you to make sure Carey is safe," Heath said, his voice rough. "Okay?"

"It's what I'm sworn to do," I replied. "I don't back out of promises."

"Thank—"

"Stop saying thank you," I demanded, covering my face. "Stop. I'm just...this is what good people do, right? We show up, even when we're not ready and we're totally out of our depth. I made a promise to her and I'm going to see it through. Stop...thanking me for that."

Silence fell on them again. Eventually, Sheila stopped the Explorer down the street from a construction site about twenty minutes north of Dallas.

"This is still pack land, right?" I asked, forgetting if one of them had answered earlier.

"Yes and no. Many of the pack don't live directly in the city, preferring the quieter fringes of the city," Heath answered as the doors unlocked. I stepped out, continuing to listen while he continued to talk. "So, we claim that any place our pack owns is part of the territory, even if it might not be in the city. This is near a few homes, actually."

"Cool," I said softly, swallowing my fear. Ranger, Heath, Keith, and Sheila circled me as I pulled my shirt off. I wasn't used to stripping and shifting with an audience, but it was security. This had already been planned. They didn't want me wandering off and possibly shot. I didn't want that either.

I handed my clothing to Ranger and nodded to Heath. "If I need to tell you something, you'll know," I told him one last time. Then I triggered the Change.

It burned through me. None of the wolves around me seemed disturbed by the crunching and breaking of bones. They were shocked by how fast it ended, though. I extended my claws, letting them scratch the asphalt, then retracted them. I stretched my new legs and flicked my tail around.

"She wasn't kidding about her measurements, was she?" Keith said lightly, nodding down at me. "I didn't know they had saber fangs like that. No modern cats have those."

"I think werecats are reminiscent of cats that don't walk the earth anymore," Heath said. "Built like a lioness, but more muscular—and those *teeth*. You're like a blend of the ancient and the current. Completely unique. Will Carey recognize you?"

I nodded.

"Good. Let's go. You three, stay here. If someone starts shooting at you, shoot back. Leave when Jacky and Carey are secure."

I growled. I made my opinion very clear in that moment. Him too. Carey needed her damn father after all of this.

"She'll have her brothers if I fall," he reminded me. "They'll come for her when the heat settles, I bet."

"They'd better, or I'm going to hunt them down and eat their dumb asses."

His eyes went wide. Only for a second, because then they shifted to calculating. In the dark, I watched his grey-blue eyes shift into a piercing, cold ice blue. The eyes of his wolf.

"Oh shit. You weren't supposed to get that. Don't react. Don't tell the other wolves. They'll kill me." God damn, I needed more practice with that. *"The fae wanted*

to even the playing field for me to help protect Carey and any future humans I might help."

"We're going to head out," Heath announced. He turned and started walking. I walked after him, keeping low. Once we were out of earshot of the other wolves, he started talking again. "I won't expose your secret gift from the fae," he whispered. "Only because of this. You're breaking the Law to protect my daughter and help me. For that, I'll leave you with this secret. Wolves do this to kill your kind. To hunt better. It's the *one* thing we have on you, our pack magic. And this fae gave it to you." He sounded pretty pissed off. "You didn't ask?"

"He offered it purely as a gift. I know he'll come collecting the debt eventually. He tried telling me it wasn't like that, but he's fae. They always collect."

"They always stick their noses in places they don't belong," he muttered.

"I said the very same thing. I think he's worried about his wife's safety, now that I think about it. And then he learned there's a werecat that lives nearby and...well, yeah."

"Makes sense," Heath said, sighing. We stopped across the street, able to stare right at the front of the construction site. "Are you ready for this?"

"There's no such thing as being ready for this," I replied.

"Fair point again, werecat."

We walked closer and I took a good sniff. Metal. Lots of metal. This wasn't a house being built, but something that was bigger, that needed the steel support. I saw the walls were nearly finished and the windows were in. A new office building being built? I didn't know, but it wasn't a wooden house. I could have done some structural damage to one of those, maybe in a desperation move.

This was like a fortress, and we were walking directly into it.

Heath grabbed the door and held it for me. I obliged, going first and sniffing around.

"Magic. I smell magic," I told him. I couldn't get a response from him, leading him through the building to a large center room.

I froze midstep as I saw what and who was in the room.

Two cages, both holding adult male werewolves in their human forms. One I didn't recognize, but the other…

"Landon," Heath breathed out behind me.

"This isn't good," I said quickly. *"Richard contacted Carey and said they were okay. I swear it. I don't know how he ended up here."*

He touched my back lightly, walking around me. It was reassuring. I could feel a pulse of that feeling run through me, which confused me more, but also pleased me. Its source wasn't from me, that was certain. He'd *given me* that emotion.

"Father?" Landon looked up, his eyes going wide. "Father! It's Richard. He's working with Emma and Dean."

"What?" Heath stopped. "No. They've…they've…"

"The magic we smell," I reminded him. *"There's only one* real *magic user in play."*

"I'm surprised, Heath," a woman called out, stepping through a door in the back. "You're a smart man. You have to be, to live as long as you have, and yet you didn't figure it out when you walked through the door..."

Heath stiffened. "Let them go. And where's my daughter, Emma?"

"You're not going to ask why?" Emma stopped where the light could hit her. Behind her entered two more men and Carey.

I made some sort of noise. I was unable to resist it. I lowered to my belly, inching closer, and did it again, hoping to catch Carey's attention.

She was scared. So scared. The scent of her fear washed the room and turned my vision red, fueling a deep, unsettling rage.

"Daddy?" she said softly. "Daddy!" She tried to run for him, but Richard held her back, no matter how hard she struggled.

"Carey. Darling." Heath sounded a little broken there for a second too. "I brought someone to take you away from this." He gestured to me as I continued to inch closer.

"Jacky? Jacky, I thought you were *dead*! I thought they killed you!" She started to cry.

My heart broke a bit.

Yeah, kid. Me too. I didn't use my new ability to communicate, though. As much as I wanted to talk to her, I didn't want her to accidentally give it away.

"Stop, little sis," one of the wolves snapped. "We don't cry in front of our father."

"She can cry if she wants," Heath growled. "Maybe you should just let her and Jacky go. Then we can finish this."

"I'm amazed you refuse to ask why," Emma said, curious and unalarmed by anything going on. She was confident she was leaving this building with the win. "Heath."

"I can ask why after my daughter has left," he answered. "Tywin and Landon with her."

"You always did love them more than me," Richard snarled.

"That's a lie, and we both know it. How dare you accuse me of that? You're my oldest son. My closest friend—"

"And yet I've been passed over at every opportunity when you need someone! Every position of power in the pack has been given to everyone else. You couldn't even make me your replacement. I'm your son, and yet have gotten nothing but a middle-pack position and your errands." He held up Carey's arm. "And then I became your babysitter when Carey showed up."

I snarled, drawing his attention.

"You even got a werecat for that now," he sneered. "You want her, kitty? Take her." He shoved Carey, who cried out as she fell.

I jumped forward, but I couldn't catch her. She landed wrong and my sensitive ears heard her wrist break. She cried out louder, holding her hand close to her. When I was within range, I gingerly grabbed her pants and pulled her back towards Heath, my eyes never leaving the wolves or the half-witch. I stood over her, protecting her with my body as she sobbed over her broken wrist.

"I'll kill you for that," Heath whispered. "How *dare* you? You never got a position of power because you couldn't earn it. If you weren't happy, you could have come and spoken to me. I would have given you more. There's no reason to take this out on your younger siblings."

"My treasured younger siblings. Landon, born a werewolf and strong, stronger than most. Carey, born a perfect, precious little human. Daddy's girl."

I had a twin sister. I could seriously relate to Richard's pain. There had been a lot of moments in my life where I was convinced my parents loved her more than me. But I *never* took it out on her. She was who she was, and I loved her for it. I could never imagine turning against her.

"You're dead to me," he told his oldest son, then turned on Emma and Dean. "Do you two have some sort of accusation against my character before you release my wolves? They don't need to die for this. I'm willing to accept my fate to keep them safe." He glared at Emma. "You know the Tribunal will never let this stand, right? Cross-breeds aren't allowed to hold power."

"The Law isn't strong enough to stop me," she hissed, leaning against one of the cages. "You would know that if you ever listened to me. I told you that if you ever wanted to give me a real place in this pack, I would be able to defend it. But no, you hold tight to your little Laws. So tight, in fact, that it was easy to think you would send Carey to the werecat over there. You thought no one would ever dare go against a werecat's protection. Fuck the Law. I'm taking control. I have the strength for it." She tapped the cage holding Tywin. "I had people go to you and tell you that Dean and I would be better than Tywin. I gave you chances. Didn't I, Dean?"

"You did," he agreed softly. "We tried, so that we wouldn't have to escalate this, but you were moving fast towards retirement and leaving in the next six months. We had to act."

"I was never going to go against the Laws, Emma. You should have been wise enough not to either." Heath leaned on Landon's cage, and the younger wolf moved closer to his father. Not much. They didn't touch, but I could see it was a simple proclamation of loyalty. Landon, even caged and beaten, would fight for his father to the bitter fucking end.

"This is why I didn't challenge Tywin. Because you, of all people, deserve to die. Not go happily into retirement. You say the pack should fight for each other, but you never fought for me." Emma's voice cracked. "You never fought for me!"

"This is why everything has been so ridiculous. So un-wolflike. Emma is a half-witch, and that makes her more human than the rest of us." I hoped Heath heard me and understood, but I continued, just trying to get through to

him. *"She could try something dangerous and underhanded."*

"Dean didn't earn his position in my inner circle," Heath said softly. "Oh, he's a strong wolf, but others could have taken it if I allowed them. He was there by my choice, which was frowned upon by some. He had it because I knew the pair of you were worthy of the position. I did what I thought was right, Emma." Heath spread his hands. "Please. I tried. Let my son and Tywin leave with the werecat and Carey. We can fix this."

"It doesn't need fixing," she snarled. "They can go after you die."

"Love! That wasn't our plan. Carey doesn't need to watch her father die," Dean said, jumping between Emma and Heath. "We had a plan. Don't..."

"Get out of my way, Dean." Emma glared at him. "Don't betray me. I'm the most powerful being in this state, probably this country! I want him to die now, on his own accord. Then I'll release his precious wolves."

"Emma—"

Dean flew, hitting a wall and staying there. Emma had a hand outstretched, as if she was pinning him with an invisible force.

"Don't make me take Carey back," she hissed. "I will. The cat won't stop me."

That caused Carey to cry louder and I snarled, snapping over in the bitch's direction.

"Look at her, so well trained." Emma flicked her other wrist and it sent me flying, leaving Carey on the floor and undefended. I slid across the floor into the back wall, then jumped to my feet, running back to Carey. The half-witch was just trying to prove her point, laughing as I huddled over the human girl again. This time, Carey used her unbroken hand to grab me.

"Emma, this is madness," Heath beseeched. "Look at what you've done to your husband. Your mate." He pointed towards Dean, who was still pinned to the wall.

"Leave it, father," Richard said, humor lacing his words. "Emma is going to get what she wants."

"No, she won't," the Alpha countered. "At dawn, the Alpha Council is riding into town to help clean up this mess. That'll either be to help me rebuild and get into retirement or put down whoever started this mess. If they can't beat you, Emma, the Tribunal will come. That *won't* end well for any of the wolves in the city, including you."

"I'm not scared of the Tribunal. More Laws no one cares about anymore. If anyone here should, it would be her, and yet she's here, breaking them just like I am. Your werecat and I are two peas in a pod! Are you going to let the Tribunal have her?"

He glanced over at me.

I nodded my large head.

"Yes," he whispered. "Because she's willing to live and die for her beliefs and knows the Law is in place for a reason."

"See, cat? He never fights for anyone," Richard spat. "Once you're not strong enough, once you're useless, he casts you aside for a new face. Just like he did to my mother."

"Your mother didn't want to be a werewolf," Heath said, his voice like sandpaper. "She'll turn in her grave if you start blaming her death on me. She wanted one human life. She didn't want to become a monster against God's children like we are."

"She was my mother!" his son roared.

"Ask them how they can keep their word if you're dead already." I told Heath. He was caught up in arguing with them, trying to talk them down. He needed to find another way.

"How can I expect you to uphold your end of the bargain if I let you kill me right now?" he asked loudly.

"I could have already killed you if I wanted to," Emma informed him. "I figured I would finally challenge you the way wolves do. I'll meet you on that battlefield."

Heath nodded, and waved me to move further back. I nudged Carey gently, using my body to help the girl stay out of Emma's line of sight. Dean slowly sank to the floor now as Emma grinned.

"Yes. The wolves won't question me if I kill you in wolf form." She sounded half-insane at this point. Pondering a future she would never have. No one would ever let her run a wolf pack, and her takeover was evidence as to why. She didn't do it right. She employed human tactics, underhandedness that the wolves would never respect completely. They might like her now, but when she started using her magic on her loyal wolves when they upset her? They would turn and bite the hand that fed them.

And she will *turn against them. She just proved it by throwing her own damn mate around.*

Heath and Emma both began to strip. So did Dean and Richard. Heath didn't say anything, but I knew he could see them as well as I could.

They all shifted together as well, Heath being done first. He was a brilliant grey-blue, almost like his eyes, with more white to him than anything else. He was also a bit bigger than the others. I felt good to have him on my side.

"Finally, I can talk back. Emma can still use some of her magic in wolf form. Be careful, Jacky."

"I will," I promised.

CHAPTER TWENTY-TWO

I kept my body between Carey and the wolves as Emma and Heath began to circle one another. Carey clung to me with her good arm, holding me tightly. For a kid, she was strong, but it didn't cause me any discomfort. Honestly, I was just glad she was there and okay.

I should have left with her. I knew I should have, but I didn't want to leave Heath fighting alone for the lives of Landon and Tywin. I couldn't bring myself to move, really.

"Don't tell anyone you can hear me right now. Carey, you should run. Down the street, three wolves are waiting. It's Ranger, Sheila, and Keith," I told her softly. *"You can make it to them, I promise, but I can't leave your father here alone."*

"I'm not leaving him," she said against my shoulder. "I have a plan."

"No, sweetheart. No plans. You just need to get to safety. Please."

"Just keep me safe right here. I'm not moving," she said passionately, the tears still in her voice. I could feel them dampen my fur. This kid had a broken wrist. Her father was readying to fight for his life.

And yet she was going to watch her father win.

"I knew you were strong. You stay right next to me, am I clear? When Landon and Tywin are free, we're leaving."

"Okay, Jacky," she whispered.

I watched the two wolves continue to circle, also keeping track of where Richard and Dean were. They made a large external circle around the two wolves fighting for dominance.

Emma launched first, missing Heath, who jumped to the side. Dean snapped at his leg, causing Heath to snarl at the uninvolved wolf.

Dirty fucking cheaters.

The next time Emma jumped for Heath, he met her in a flash of fur and growls, the snapping of teeth being the loudest thing in the room. They tumbled around for a moment until they broke the circle being made by Richard and Dean again, who both ran for them.

I resisted the urge to run over myself and leave Carey alone as Dean grabbed Heath's scruff and yanked him off Emma, tossing him a few feet away.

"There can be no assistance in the fight for Alpha," he snarled. I bet everyone in an animal form heard that. *"You two know better!"*

"Stay out of it, boys," Emma snapped as well, standing up. *"I can handle him. Richard, go play with your toy."*

Richard's dark wolf form snapped the air towards his father, who was immediately distracted as Emma jumped for him again. Dean didn't back off far, watching the tumbling wolves intently.

As I watched, I noticed one important thing. No matter how fiercely Heath attacked her, she came out seemingly unscathed.

"Her magic," I said to him.

"No. Assistance," he barked back at me.

"Jacky..." Carey pointed and I turned to follow her finger.

Richard was walking slowly towards us, teeth bared, drool dripping down from his long yellow-white fangs.

"Carey, does Richard want to kill you?" I asked, using my body to push her towards a door, knowing she wasn't able to fight back.

"I thought my brothers loved me," she whispered, a whimper there in her voice. "Richard! Please! I'm Carey. I love you, big brother! Why are you doing this?"

He snarled.

"I'm so sorry, Carey." I snarled back at the wolf, my hair raising. To him, I said, *"I wouldn't, wolf. I can more than handle you."*

He was shocked by my words in his head for only a second, then the rage came back. *"I was promised that this entire fucking family wouldn't exist after tonight. That I would be the last and the most powerful. I don't need to fight you. I just need to kill her."*

"Same difference," I growled, lowering myself. *"Carey, stay underneath me."*

She ducked down, holding her broken wrist against her chest. I was more than big enough for her to lie out underneath. If she stayed there, Richard wouldn't be able to get to her.

He moved forward, fast, almost faster than I could see. I used my head, ducking it down, to stop his advance. He snapped at the top of my head, grabbing an ear and yanking hard. I roared and swatted at his underbelly, raking my claws across it, but not able to get a deep purchase as he tried to pull me away from Carey, moving towards my right side. One of his paws hit one of my gunshot wounds and reopened it.

I hissed, snapping for him.

"Carey, move. I've got him!"

The moment she was out from beneath me, which had stopped the initial charge from the wolf, I shook, knocking him off and onto the floor. I pounced for him, but he rolled out of the way.

He ignored me now though. He lunged for Carey. I grabbed his back leg before he made it to her and shook hard, listening to joints break or dislocate. He yelped.

In the background, someone else yelped at the same time, and a vicious snarl sent chills down my spine.

Richard turned and bit my muzzle, but my saber fangs were deep in his flesh now, puncturing all the way through. I pulled him further away from Carey, shaking as I went, snarling with vicious rage.

She's mine. *You don't deserve her.*

When I was certain Carey was safer, I swung my head, taking him along for the ride and into a wall. I heard ribs crack under the impact and released him, stepping back. *"Stay down. I don't want to kill Heath's son."*

"He's as dead to me as I am to him. I'm going to have my due, damn it," he answered, lunging for me again.

This time, I didn't go for a disabling bite. I met him in the air and used my weight against him, taking him to the ground. He couldn't fight free from under my weight as I aimed for his neck, sinking my fangs into it, tearing through all the vital things there. Windpipe, jugular. It didn't matter. If it was in my way, I broke it. Blood rushed into my mouth, rich and thick. I tried to ignore it. This wasn't a hunt. This was a war.

I didn't wait for him to bleed out or suffocate like a normal big cat might. I shook hard, listening to his neck snap.

I dropped him and stepped away, looking back to Carey, who stared wide eyed.

"I'm so sorry. I tried to tell him to quit."

"I know," she whispered as I moved near to her again. She hugged me, and if I was human, I would have cried. I had just killed her brother and she was hugging me, covered in his blood. Finally, she continued whispering to me, "I think we should free Landon and Tywin."

"No."

"But..."

"Carey, it's too dangerous."

"We need them!" she said urgently. "Look. Dean is

helping Emma. Landon and Tywin can stop him and you can keep protecting me!"

She was right. Emma and Heath were still fighting and it looked brutal, but Heath was beginning to bleed from several spots while Emma was fine. Dean had blood on his jaws. He was still cheating to help his mate win.

"Carey, we can get them after—"

She started running for Landon's cage before I could finish. I went after her, glad that Dean was so focused on his mate and Heath that he was ignoring us. Carey started untangling chains.

"Carey, what are you doing?" Landon whispered. He was glancing anxiously over to the fight. "Please, run with the werecat."

"No! Where's the key? It must be in one of their pockets!" Carey ran for those next, and again, I followed. I glanced at the fight, seeing Heath on the ground with Emma over him. It didn't last long as he regained the upper hand and used his body to shove her away. They circled for a second before meeting again in a clash of fang and claw.

"Jacky! I need your help!" Carey tugged on my fur, and I turned to the clothing left on the floor by the werewolves. I sniffed around it, not finding anything in Richard's clothing, nor Dean's. It was Emma who had been holding the key. Made sense, since she wanted to hold all the cards, the mighty half-witch and half-werewolf.

"Right here," I told Carey. *"Probably in her pants pocket."*

Carey dug with one hand and found it. I looked over to Landon and Tywin in their cages.

"*Change into your werewolf forms,*" I ordered quickly. "*She's going to let you out, then I'm going to try and get her out of here.*"

They both nodded, stripping down fast as I led Carey back over to them. Thank God for wolves being obsessive over their mates. Emma was too busy fighting Heath and Dean refused to leave that unattended.

Or so I thought.

"*They're releasing the prisoners!*" Dean snapped in our heads. I wondered if werewolves could talk privately or if their communication always went to everyone in the room. Could humans hear them? Or only animals?

Questions I really didn't need answers to.

"*Dean knows!*" I told Carey, Tywin, and Landon. "*Hurry, kiddo!*"

"I'm going!" She was fumbling with one hand and I knew I couldn't spare the entire minute to shift into human form.

"*Get the reinforcements, Dean!*" Emma roared.

"Dishonorable cow," Heath growled. "*You'll die tonight. I promise you that.*"

"You'll try," she hissed back.

Howls began to echo around the building. I couldn't tell how many. When Carey got Landon's cage open, he stumbled out, half shifted. She got Tywin's open much faster, but they were still in the middle of their shifts.

I could hear the pounding footsteps of wolves. There was a hunting party coming, and it was coming for us.

"Carey! Lock yourself in a cage!" I used my head to push her into one, not having the time to worry about her broken wrist. She turned back to me, her eyes wide. *"Keep the keys on you and only let yourself out when it's safe!"*

"Okay!" I helped her close the heavy door and watched her lock herself in with the chains and padlock. "Landon and Tywin are still Changing!"

"I've got them," I promised her.

By the time I turned around, wolves were running in from the back door.

I snarled as the first one jumped for me.

It's on.

I snapped, fangs tearing through flesh and muscle into the first wolf. A second wolf jumped on my back, then a third. I flung the first wolf and roared, shaking hard to dislodge the wolves over my back. I tried to keep Tywin and Landon behind me, but with so many wolves, I knew there was no chance I could protect them too.

Another two wolves slammed into my side, and knocked me down. I felt teeth sink into my abdomen. I kicked with my back legs, slicing one of them. Once it backed off, I was able to get to my feet, snarling. Around me, the wolves circled. There had to be over a dozen of them.

It felt endless, rolling around and trying to keep the wolves from exposing my vulnerable areas. When another jumped on my back, it was knocked off by another wolf.

"It's me, Ranger," the wolf announced. *"Sheila and Keith are on the way!"*

I didn't respond as I turned to sink my fangs into a wolf behind me who was holding my back leg in his jaws. It got him to let go, and I held on until I was sure the wolf was dead, backing away with its body. The rest were fighting against each other.

More wolves, I was hoping Sheila and Keith, ran into the room and slammed into others. In flurries of fur, I saw wolves hit each other. I couldn't tell anyone apart, and it meant I couldn't go after any wolves or help anyone without possibly getting it wrong. I looked over for Tywin and Landon, and they weren't behind me anymore. They had to be among all of the wolves in the fight.

"Jacky, help my father!" Landon roared in my head.

I turned to the other end of the room, where Heath and Emma were still brawling, Dean trying to take Heath from behind. I ran over into the fight and barreled into Dean, sending the simple grey wolf to the ground. He jumped up, snapping back at me. I roared, bracing for the fight as I put myself between him and the fight for dominance.

He tried to get around me and I sidestepped, continuing to block his path. He lunged and I met him, ramming my side into him, knocking him back again.

"No more of that," I told him.

"She won't lose. I'm just speeding up the process. There's no reason for all the wolves here to die," he replied.

"Maybe you shouldn't have called the reinforcements, then." I snarled, snapping towards him.

He tried to meet me in a fight again but I swatted him aside, then began to circle him.

"Stay down," I ordered.

"Never. She's going to be the best Alpha this world has ever seen. She's going to put werewolves at the top. For this, we're going to see that your kind are driven into the extinction you should have had centuries ago." Dean began to rise to his feet and I lunged, slamming him into a wall. He yelped and whined as bones broke under the force.

"No." I wasn't having that. I let off the pressure for a second, only to slam him into the wall with my side a second time. Ribs broke under the pressure and he yelped again, sinking to the floor. *"Stay down."*

He whimpered and did the canine equivalent to a cough. I leaned over, sniffing. I must have really screwed up his ribs. I left him there after that and turned to Emma and Heath.

"No more Dean to help you," I said to her. I looked over to the big fight, seeing that it was an even match now and hoping the winning wolves were the ones on my side. Carey was huddled in the middle of her cage, terrified but safe. *"Your reinforcements don't matter. Submit to Heath."*

The dominance fight paused for a split second as both of them looked over at me. I stepped forward.

"Let this go, Emma. You're losing."

"I won't lose," she growled back at me.

There was an invisible blast that felt like a concrete wall hitting me. I slammed into the wall over Dean and I was barely able to recover before falling on him and crushing him.

"You trying to kill your mate?" I asked.

"Emma, this doesn't need to go further," Heath said gently. He was panting, moving slowly between her and I.

"Heath, stop. I can defend myself," I hissed. *"Think of Carey."*

"I am," he growled, launching himself at Emma. They clashed and Heath flew away, sliding across the floor.

I took the chance, Wolf rules be damned. I wasn't a wolf. Emma was only half a wolf. I was going to put an end to this goddamn war.

Heath was up and running as well, faster than I figured he would be.

"Fight with me," he ordered. For once, I wasn't thinking of giving him a hard time for trying to order a cat around. Finishing this was too important.

We met Emma at the same time. He went for her head as I tried for her back legs. My teeth glanced off her, though, as something stopped them. Emma bit down on Heath, and I used my body weight to force both of them to the floor.

I was able to sink my claws into her side now, and Heath was able to get free, jumping to go for her throat. I bit down into her side, ignoring her mental scream.

A few seconds later, even that was over, and I backed

away, panting. The first place I looked was for Carey, finding her still in her cage with a wolf sitting at the door. She started using the keys to open it and I grumbled.

"Who's next to you?" I asked her.

"Landon," she answered loudly. "It's Landon, Jacky. Tywin is right there." She pointed. "Ranger is next to him, then Sheila."

"Where's Keith?" Heath asked.

"Gone," Tywin answered. *"He was overwhelmed."*

Heath threw his head back and howled.

It was over.

CHAPTER TWENTY-THREE

"Daddy!" The moment Carey was out of the cage, she was running, leaping at him as if she hadn't been hurt. He was still in wolf form and lay down as she threw her arms over him. The howl ended as he nuzzled into her and she held his big head.

I was glad to see the end of it. It felt worth it in that moment.

Everyone started shifting back in their human forms, and I was the first done, with nothing to wear. I sat down in the corner of the room, trying to keep to myself. Carey was walking between her father and her brother, making sure they were okay.

I was fine with that, too.

The wolves returned to their human forms after several minutes, Ranger and Sheila running out to the Explorer to get the first aid for everyone. I was too tired to think, too tired to talk. My body hurt, so I looked over everything. The wolves had gotten me a few good times, especially the bite on my stomach, but I wasn't bleeding too badly. I would be walking funny for a couple of weeks, and I definitely wasn't going to try any heavy lifting. That much was certain.

"Here," Heath said, tossing me something. I held it up after it landed in my lap, frowning. "It's a shirt. Put it on."

"Thanks," I murmured, pulling it on. I winced as the movement tugged at all the small injuries I had.

"And these," Ranger said, walking over to me. "We put a pair in the Explorer, just in case." He held out sweatpants for me. I grabbed them and pulled them on, but didn't leave the floor and the small spot I had found that didn't have blood on it.

"And we should look over everyone's injuries," Landon reminded them.

I stayed quiet, not finding the energy to get up. I wasn't bleeding out or anything. I was just tired. Nearly a week of wolves, being shot, and fights, I was done.

"Jacky?" Carey greeted me softly. "Are you okay?"

"I'm just tired," I answered her. "How are you?"

She lifted her left hand, showing me the purple, swollen wrist. "It hurts, but I've broken my wrist before playing, so..."

"Ah." I gave her a weak smile.

"You came for me," she said, sitting down on the clean spot of the floor with me. "You said you weren't allowed to come here and help Dad."

"They took you and I made a promise," I reminded

her, wrapping an arm over her shoulder. "I don't break my promises."

"That's good. You're going to be okay, right?" Her eyes fell to the blood spot slowly coming through the shirt.

"Yeah, I'll be fine," I said gently.

"Promise?"

I shouldn't. I can't promise her that. I'm probably going to be executed. "I promise," I said, throat tight.

"Good." She nodded as if that was enough. Then she looked away, her face paling at the sight before us. I knew the shock was wearing off, the adrenaline was leaving her just like it was leaving the rest of us. That meant her brain was going to start processing exactly what was in the room.

Carnage.

"Heath," I called out softly. He was with Landon and Tywin, talking quickly and quietly, probably making sure everything was ready for when the Alpha Council arrived with more wolves.

"What?" He looked back at Carey and me, confused. "Is something wrong? Ranger's tending Sheila, but—"

"I'm taking Carey outside," I explained, pointedly looking down at the floor and the dead wolves between him and me. His gaze followed mine, and he nodded. I didn't need to hear any more, standing up and helping Carey to her feet. "Let's go. You don't need to keep staring at all of this."

"Thank you," she whispered, taking one of my hands in her good one. I led her out, and once I saw that Ranger and Sheila had moved the Explorer closer, I opened it and sat her down in the back. I left the door open, leaning against it and sighing.

"I'm sorry they took you, Carey. I'm so sorry." The urge to say it was too strong. "You should never have had to see tonight. You should have been safe with me, and—"

She lunged at me and her little arms wrapped around my waist. I tentatively wrapped my own arms around her, holding her tightly for a long time.

"You came for me," she said into my shoulder. "You came for me with Dad. I'm so glad I met you, Jacky."

"I'm really glad I met you, too," I whispered into her hair. It might have ruined my life, but damn, I was glad to have met her. I wanted to promise her that I would always come for her, protect her, but I knew at dawn, I wasn't going to stay. I was going to be carted off. At least I would be taken for something worthwhile. At least Carey was going to be with her family again.

"Jacky? Carey?" Ranger spoke behind me. "I need to look over your injuries."

"Carey first," I ordered him, letting go of her and stepping back. I stumbled a little and sat down on the ground. My ass was one of the few things that didn't hurt.

"Jacky first," Carey said, pointing down at me. "She's bleeding. All I have is a broken wrist. I'll need a hospital, right? With the x-rays?"

"That's right," Ranger said, ruffling her hair. "I have no ice packs, but once I get everyone patched up, we'll head out for you. Take these. They'll help." He held up a hand and Carey took whatever he offered.

"Thank you." I had never seen a kid take pills without water, but Carey could. Impressive kid.

Ranger turned on me again and frowned. "They got you pretty good. Let me see." He knelt and pointed at my stomach. "Let's go."

I pulled it up and let him work. It was nice being able to lie back and let someone else do all the hard work for a minute. It stung when he cleaned the wounds off, then it hurt as he stitched them up.

"I should be ashamed. Carey's tougher than me," I noted, smiling. I was getting a tad lightheaded.

"She's a tough kid and she's used to breaking bones. In the last two years, she's fallen off a rock and broken a wrist, broken her leg while trying to climb something we told her not to, and broke four fingers when she tried to push around some rocks to make a fort. Her building plans weren't...weren't secure." Ranger was smirking when he was done. "It's why her family isn't hovering. She hates it when they do that and so they leave her be unless she's crying."

"Oh, that's cute," I murmured, looking over at her. She was cradling the wrist pretty well, even trying to move her fingers. When I saw her wince, I sighed. "Don't play around with it. Just wait until we get to a hospital."

"Okay...Ranger, are Dad and Landon going to come out soon?"

"Any minute now," he answered.

Sure enough, he was working on my last stitch when they walked out. Heath, Tywin, and Landon, a solid line of wolf and power. Top three ranking wolves in the region. I could feel why, deep in my bones. Sheila trailed behind them, limping but stable.

They all passed over me and went to the Explorer. Heath looked over his daughter's wrist, then kissed her forehead. "Hospital," he said gently. "Let's move out. Landon, help Ranger get Jacky into the back."

"I can get up," I said, a little grumpy he would think I couldn't. I pushed up slowly, and stumbled to the Explorer.

"Back seat." He pointed to the spot next to Carey. "Ranger, is she going to be okay?"

"No internal damage," the wolf answered patiently. "A bit of blood loss might be making her lightheaded, but nothing life-threatening. Sheila's hip was worse. How are all of you?"

"Tywin and Landon need to eat and rest. I'm fine. Minor flesh wounds." He grabbed me around my waist and lifted. "Get in there. You're moving too slow for me."

"I can walk," I snapped. I slapped his hands away as he reached for the seat belt. "I can definitely put on my seat belt!" I grabbed it and buckled in. "Are we leaving all of this?"

"Tywin and I are staying. Landon is taking you ladies to the hospital." He pointed at Sheila. "I meant all three of you. Get in."

She bared her teeth. At least I wasn't the only one being babied. Ranger took the back seat with Carey and me, looking over her wrist again.

The doors were shut and I made sure she was secure as Ranger wrapped her wrist in a quick splint.

Oath Sworn

We were at the hospital in twenty minutes. Carey was ushered in quickly for x-rays. Sheila and I were taken to a room, sat down, and waited.

It wasn't a doctor who walked in. It was another wolf. I tensed, but Sheila grabbed my arm. "He's a rogue, but he's a doctor. We let him stay and not join the pack if he treats us all equally. Neutral."

"Not that it matters anymore," he said with a sharp smile. Then he sniffed the air. "So you're the werecat. Well, let's see."

"Carey, Landon, and Ranger?" I asked, lying back on the bed.

"Are with a human doctor looking over her x-rays," he said after Sheila nodded. "Ranger did a good job cleaning you up. Give it some time to heal. You've got a lot of stitches in you. Had a rough week?"

"You have no idea," I mumbled, sitting back up and pointing at Sheila. "Your turn."

"Yup..."

It was quiet, everyone getting checked out. I met Ranger, Landon, and Carey back at the Explorer with Sheila. We didn't leave, just loitering around for a moment. Carey had a new bright blue cast and somehow already had her hands on a sharpie, which she held out to me.

"You have to sign it," she demanded, holding it out.

I chuckled, taking the sharpie and putting my name and 'get well soon' on her cast with a cat face next to it. "Happy?" I asked, holding the sharpie out for her.

"Yeah. So...you're going to be our friend now, right?"

I looked up to Landon and the other wolves. How was I supposed to tell her?

Landon frowned. "I don't see why not," he said. "Jacky, after all of this, you're more than welcome with our family."

Sheila began to cough and grabbed the old wolf. "We need to talk."

He seemed confused as Sheila pulled him away. Ranger only sighed, giving me a sad look.

"I'll be your friend for as long as I'm able," I promised Carey. It wouldn't be very long, but it would be as long as I damn well could. "Are we going to head out? Where do we go from here?"

"Heath and Tywin will meet us back at the safe house." Ranger thumped the hood of the Explorer. "We'll leave when those two are done." He nodded to Landon and Sheila. I winced as Landon looked my way, his eyes wide as Sheila explained.

Oh yeah. The werecat that helped save your family? Going to be arrested at dawn for it. You know, the Laws and all that. Don't tell Carey. She doesn't deserve that.

AT THE WAREHOUSE, Heath grabbed Carey and forced her to stay by his side.

"I've been really nice, letting you go to the hospital without me. You're not leaving my sight anymore," he explained, pointing to a seat.

"Okay, Dad. Is it over? Are we going to go back to normal? Are we safe?"

"We're safe," he promised softly, kissing the top of her head. "There's going to be a lot of changes coming. How do you feel about moving?"

"I would like that," she answered. "I don't want to go home where Richard..."

My heart hurt too much for one night. Heath looked up to me, his eyes betraying a deep sadness. "I'll leave you with Landon for a minute. I want to talk to Jacky."

"Yeah." Carey pulled her legs up to her chest, her brother sitting quietly beside her. Heath didn't need to say any more. I followed him out of the room, crossing my arms as I leaned on a wall out of sight from the other wolves. It hurt, but felt secure.

"They'll be here any minute," he told me. "I..."

"It's okay." I shrugged. "I did what I thought was right. I knew it was going to get me in trouble, but that's the decision people have to make sometimes."

"I'll speak for you," he promised again.

"I know." We stood in silence for a minute until I couldn't hold it back anymore. "I'm sorry about Richard. If he hadn't...He came after Carey."

"That's more my fault than it's yours. I don't think you should carry the blame. I should have realized he was unhappy. After so many years..." He propped himself on the wall next to me. "Thank you for protecting Carey. That's all that matters. That's all you had to do. Richard made his decision. It was envy and rage that were his downfall. I might have been able to be a better father, I'll never know, but it's over now. Carey's half in shock. She'll miss him tomorrow. Landon's been his captive since this started. He'll be over it quickly, though he'll have a hard time trusting anyone for a time. He was always stand-offish with everyone except the family."

"Then his family betrayed him," I finished.

"Exactly. But we'll heal."

"Emma and Dean?" I asked. "They have a son..."

"Dean was still alive when I sent all of you to the hospital. We got him into a holding cell before you got back. He'll stand for the crimes committed by his mate in front of the Alpha Council. Maybe the Tribunal. His son will be sent to some extended family, but that's going to take time to figure out." He was fiddling with his hands. "I'm having a hard time reconciling the Emma and Dean I knew with the ones from tonight. I had no idea they were so..."

"Power-hungry?" I filled in.

"Yes. I should have seen it coming."

"No." I shook my head. "I say that because...a week ago I could have never seen me going this far for anyone, and yet, the opportunity came and I took it. They might have been fine...Until they weren't."

He nodded, looking away from me, his eyes distant. We stayed there in silence for a long time until someone knocked on the door.

"Sir. The Council is here."

"Send them in," he called back. The door swung open and several wolves walked in. A few of them glanced at me. "Welcome to my safe house, Harrison."

An old-looking wolf inclined his head. I recognized his voice as the Harrison I had spoken to when he started talking. "It's good to see everything has been resolved. You have two prisoners for us?"

"I'm going to send wolves out tomorrow night to look for any stragglers from the coup. It's going to take a couple of weeks to stabilize. But yes, right now I have one prisoner and—"

"I'm turning myself in," I said, cutting him off. "Hi, Harrison."

"You knew it was going to end this way, Ms. Leon." Harrison pulled out a pair of handcuffs.

"I did." I put my wrists forward and let him cuff me. Another wolf grabbed my elbow and began to pull me out of the room. I looked back at Heath. "Tell her...That I'm fine with this."

Heath nodded.

As I was led out, some of Heath's wolves saluted me. Some wished me well.

Carey begged Landon to explain to her why I was being led away like the bad guy.

24

CHAPTER TWENTY-FOUR

They held me in a hotel in Dallas for over a week. Ten days, actually. My guards included several supernatural species, from vampires, werewolves, and witches, to fae, a rare kitsune, and more. I wasn't allowed to leave unless it was to be taken in front of the Tribunal, where I wasn't allowed to speak. Not until the last day.

There were procedures to Tribunals. Upon being taken into custody, they descended like riders of the damn apocalypse on whatever location they needed to be in. They came to Dallas to deal with me. It took a few days, since they came from everywhere, including the lands of the Fae.

After that, there was a week of trial. I was on the last day, but the previous days hadn't been so bad. The Tribunal put a call out for supernatural creatures to speak on my behalf. They didn't need anyone to speak against me because my crimes were clear. They were looking for people who might help make my punishment more lenient.

Not like they really wanted to do that, but they were required to try. There were no executions without exhausting all other options.

Lani showed up to speak for me as fast as she could, arriving on day two. Heath and the pack spoke on my behalf every day, filling up entire days with recounts of my actions and behavior through the entire event.

Brin showed up, and strangely enough, the fae were hushed for him, letting him speak about my time at his motel. That had been nice. His family showed up as well, including his human wife—unheard of. No one stopped him, though.

But it was now the last day. It was my day to speak for myself.

I washed my face, staring at my reflection. The bruises were gone and most of my stitches were removed already. I was healing better, which was a blessing. My body had taken a beating, but I wouldn't be limping into the chamber for the last day. My eyes were finally my human hazel again, too. I was finally able to pull back the werecat a couple of days after turning myself over to Harrison.

I got dressed, putting on the set outfit they left for me. There was a dress code for appearing in front of the Tribunal. My clothing was supplied to me before they showed up. It was a severe black suit, much like a lawyer would wear, but instead of pants, like any decent person would wear, they gave me a pencil skirt today.

How nice of them.

My guard was waiting for me in the little kitchenette of the hotel room, a sword strapped to his back. He was a vampire, one of the few I had met—all of them in the last week. "Time to go," he said, gesturing to the door. "Are you ready?"

"As ready as I'll ever be," I said softly, swallowing. Heath had promised me on day one that he wouldn't let Carey come to this, but on day six, I had asked him to bring her on the last day. Just so I could see her and say goodbye. Tell her that meeting her and helping her family made me feel like a hero for a minute. A good person. She made my world a little less lonely. She deserved to know that.

It was a trip to get to the Tribunal. They were in the hotel, but not in the hotel. They rented out a room, then made a pocket dimension in it, the cheaters. It was a fae trick. The Tribunal's meeting ground stood in the space between worlds, which was why the Tribunal members were willing to travel. They could have their special little room anywhere.

The vampire had to get a fae and a witch to open the door. I followed him in and was led to the front, to sit down where everyone could see me, like every day before. I sniffed the air, getting an idea for the crowd around me. There were a lot of species in attendance that I had never met before, but Hasan had taught me about. I was surprised to smell a naga, another rare species. Many of the smaller species didn't hold positions on the Tribunal, but they agreed with the Laws over the centuries, knowing they were only meant to keep the peace between all of them. The Laws were the very things that kept nagas and kitsunes alive, both hunted down in their home lands nearly to extinction, much like werecats once were.

I sat down, sitting stiffly in front of the Tribunal. The room was too quiet, so I stared at the men and women in front of me without greeting them. I didn't want to break the silence and draw any more attention than I already had.

The Tribunal itself was an amalgamation of the five species that grouped together to stop the war between werecats and werewolves. Two fae, two werewolves, two witches, two vampires...and there were supposed to be two werecats.

I knew there wouldn't be. One of those seats belonged to Hasan. He claimed the other seat was the one for his missing mate, and none of the werecats around wanted to step up and take it. So the seats remained empty for my entire Tribunal, no support or condemnation from my own kind except in the form of Lani, who sat as close to me as she could.

"Welcome to the last day of Jacqueline Leon's trial, everyone," a vampire called. "Today we're going to hear final arguments from anyone wishing to come forward and speak on her behalf and from the prisoner herself. Is there anyone wishing to step forward?"

No one answered. All of the wolves were done. A

smothered cry came from the back that made me turn around. Heath was whispering to his daughter, probably explaining to her that humans weren't allowed to speak on my behalf. She was only allowed to watch. I waved at her, hoping she would see me.

When she waved back, I knew I would do it all over again.

"No one?" a fae asked from his spot, standing up as well. "Really? Are we finally out of wolves that want to talk? Finally."

"Packs," one of the Tribunal werewolves said softly. "They're always like this. I never thought I would see a pack defend a werecat, but if one was going to, all of them were. Fenris surprised me. That must account for something."

Fenris had surprised me too.

"Doesn't matter. Jacqueline, please stand and begin your final argument."

I stood up, clasping my hands in front of me. I had over a week to think of all the things I had wanted to say, and they escaped me. I was blank for a moment.

"Well?" A witch sounded impatient.

"I wanted to do what I promised," I started, swallowing my fear. "I swore an oath to Carey Everson to defend her, to protect her as I would a child of my own. I only did what my Duty demanded—"

"Yes. The other werecat said this argument as well," a vampire yawned as he spoke. "And we're not inclined to excuse your involvement with werewolf politics, something explicitly against the Law for werecats. You entered their territory and joined something you had no part in."

"It's been eight hundred years since the war!" I snapped. That brought my words back. "Eight hundred years. And you know what? Yeah, Lani and I are in agreement. I did as my Duty commanded of me. I might have lost Carey, but I didn't give up on her. I wasn't the party who broke the Law first. Dean and Emma, and their lackeys, were. Would you have dragged them up here and put them under fire for a week?" I pointed a finger at the bored vampire. "And maybe you should think of the repercussions of executing me, like Brin pointed out. Werecats were put in the position we hold for a reason. What does it say to those with human families that you're willing to execute someone who is brave enough to go the distance to protect them? My kind, we can't afford to fail. We can't afford to be useless. We have to succeed. So I did. It was the right thing to do, not just for me or the werewolves, but for the supernaturals everywhere. So they can go home tonight with their human spouses or mates and feel like their local werecat is the right choice to make to defend them when things go sour."

"And it was the right thing to do for the humans," someone called from the back.

The voice made me gasp. I spun around so fast that I knocked the chair over.

"Hasan," Lani whispered near me.

"Forgive my tardiness," he called to the Tribunal. "I was in the middle of some family things." He was standing at the main door, which was just closing behind him. "Jacqueline has a point. You can't execute her. This entire situation has been a mess. The best way to let it lie is not by killing her, but by accepting that she did the right thing. The honorable thing." He began to walk slowly down the center aisle. "I've been on this Tribunal since before it was this big." He didn't look at me. He looked over the crowd, which was nearly every supernatural in the state of Texas and a few of the neighboring states. "It's grown in the last century, it seems..."

"Hasan. It's good to have you here," a fae said, grinning. "But tell me, how is it good for the humans, too? Werecats are still covered by secrecy."

"For now," he agreed. "But if you start killing my kind for being in the tough position of oath-sworn and honorable and following a ridiculously old Law, I'm going to change that."

"Excuse me?" The female Tribunal werewolf sat up, narrowing her eyes at Hasan. I was now completely forgotten. I didn't mind. I was still trying to process what Hasan had just said.

"Humans. That's who we werecats protect. Wouldn't it be a good PR move for my kind to come out right now with Jacqueline's story? To tell the world 'Look. One of the monsters in the night is on your side.'" He smiled. "'And the other monsters killed her for it.' I'll even tell them what killed her. I'm not afraid to expose us all."

I let my jaw drop finally. He was serious.

"You...you can't out your kind without—"

"I think I'm the only werecat that can do whatever I want without anyone telling me I can't. I brought my kind peace. I saved us from extinction. I'm much older than most, and while I've been away..." He shook Lani's hand as he passed her, patting the back of it once. "They have remained respectful of me. I can tell the world about my kind. If you push me to it, that is."

I still wasn't moving when he stopped at my side, looking down at the chair I knocked over. He righted it for me and patted the back.

"Sit, please, Jacky," he said gently. He even used the name I liked more. He never did that. "You're not dying tonight."

"Thank you." I fell into the chair, still finding it hard to breathe. He'd come to help me.

"You can't promise her that. You can't hold the Tribunal hostage with the threat that the humans will be on your side!" The male wolf pushed out of his seat, fury turning his face red. "Damn you, Hasan, you don't get to walk in here—"

"I can, I will, I just did," he growled. "Don't test me, Callahan. I'm leaving here with her tonight and no one is going to stop me. My children are prepared to send the evidence the human media needs about the existence of the werecats right now."

He got my older siblings involved. I looked up to him, wide-eyed. My 'siblings' and I hadn't spoken since I walked out on the family when I found out Hasan let my fiancé die in that car.

"Why are you doing this for a no-name werecat?

She's not anyone special among your kind. We've checked. Even Lani, the other werecat here, doesn't know where she came from. She had no lineage to back up her strength, something your kind finds important. She has no allies but the ones she's met in the last week." The female vampire seemed confused. "Hasan, certainly—"

"I won't let another of my daughters die to werewolves," he said softly. "And sometimes it feels like all of the werecats are mine." He squeezed my shoulder. He claimed me as a daughter and still kept our relationship a secret.

I wanted to hate him, but in that moment, hating him was a hard thing to do. He was going above and beyond anything I ever expected from him, ever wanted from him.

And he doesn't have to. I've never been the best daughter—or werecat.

"I agree with Lani, Jacqueline, and the werewolves. She didn't enter the werewolf war over Dallas-Fort Worth without cause. She was oath-sworn, held by the very Laws you want to hang her with. She showed undeniable courage to risk herself for the safety of a human girl. She tried to remain impartial but knew there was only one good way to keep the girl safe. That was to help the Alpha, Mr. Heath Everson, defeat the traitors he was fighting against and rescue her from them." Hasan ruffled my hair next, one of his more fatherly actions. I had picked it up from him. "I'm honored to have this werecat among the rest of my kind. I hope we shall all live up to the example she's set." He took a deep breath. "And maybe it's time for us to rethink the Laws."

Gasps filled the room. Chaos erupted. People were clamoring to speak, some yelling at Hasan, some cheering for him. The Tribunal watched in silence, and so did I.

"SILENCE!" a witch screamed, magic flying through the room. It wasn't a graceful way to bring order, but it was an effective one. I looked out at the crowd. People were still yelling, but nothing could be heard. "It's not permanent, everyone, but we must stay on track. Hasan, how would you recommend to change the Laws?"

"Like all things, Laws must evolve to meet the needs of the world. We can discuss it over drinks, my old friends. After you acquit Jacqueline Leon of her supposed crimes."

The Tribunal looked between each other before one of the fae spoke up again. "Recess for one hour," he ordered everyone, standing up. "Hasan, please come with us."

He nodded, finally letting go of my shoulder and walking away. Lani was the first person to me once he was gone, grabbing my upper arms.

"He's here! Hasan is finally back with us!" She was grinning. "You have brought about interesting times for the werecats, Jacky. I hope you realize that."

"Yeah..." I watched his back as he left the room with the other Tribunal members. I pulled away from her and looked over to Carey, who was smiling as her dad explained what was happening. Landon waved at me this time, smiling broadly.

I didn't go visit them, knowing it was time to keep my distance. There was no place for me with that family, but I was glad to see them together.

The hour flew by, and Hasan came back out to me, finding Lani and I talking quietly.

"Lani, it's been so long," he greeted, taking her hands again. "I'm glad you and Jacky have become friends. She's young and needed some guidance these last few years."

"You..." Lani seemed confused for a moment. "You know her?"

"Oh...Hasan, please—"

"Let's keep this quiet, for her sake." He nodded towards me. "Jacqueline is my daughter. I Changed her a decade ago."

Lani's sharp intake of air made me worried. She didn't breathe again as she looked at me. "You...Every time I ever talked about Hasan and how I wished he was back helping lead our kind, and you..."

I looked away. Yeah. I figured this was coming.

"She's private, my Jacky, and we have our differences. She kept that from you, though, because she knew I didn't want to be found by most of the world, much like my other children pretended for the last century that I was nowhere to be found. They never lost me." He patted Lani's shoulder. "There's big changes coming for our kind."

"Oh, Hasan, what did you do?" I demanded, throwing my hands up.

"You'll see," he promised. "But you're going home tonight. That's all that matters."

"Oh, I don't believe you, but sure." I crossed my arms. He did something. Now I just had to hope that it wasn't terrible for my health.

The Tribunal walked back in and called everyone back to their seats. It was one of the fae who stood up and began to read from a scroll.

"In the matter of Jacqueline Leon, we have decided to acquit her of all charges. There shall be no punishment passed down based on the events here in Dallas-Fort Worth." He took a deep breath. "Going forward, werecats who are called to Duty will be protected from future charges if the events are similar, so long as they can adequately prove that their actions were in the best interests of the human or humans in their care."

People cheered. Well, howled. It was mostly the werewolves that were excited for me. I had saved Carey and helped them. Of course they would be happy to see me walking away alive.

I threw my arms around Hasan. "Thank you so much," I whispered.

"One day, I'll tell you the truth about Shane," he told me softly. "But smell the truth when I say it wasn't a decision I made thinking it wouldn't hurt you. Or one I made lightly." He pulled away, holding my shoulders. "What you said about Duty...I wasn't going to let them take away your life for finally finding something to fill the hole you have here." He pointed at my chest. "I would never let that happen."

I could smell the truth, just as he wanted me to. And tomorrow, I could pressure him for the rest of the truth about the day I was Changed.

He did say 'one day'.

Today, though, I was just going to be grateful for being alive.

CHAPTER TWENTY-FIVE

Two weeks later, I was completely healed aside from the scars, and at home again. I looked over my bar, knowing I wouldn't be able to open for another week, but I was getting back to my life. That was really all I could ask for.

Hasan and Lani had stuck around for a couple of days, talking about times before me and the future. With the announced changes to the Law and to the Duty of werecats, we could be a little more open about it.

I wanted no part in it. One time was enough for me.

When I had finally chased them off, Hasan made me promise to visit for the holidays, prompting me to glare at him until he finished loading his car and left. I texted him an hour later and promised to come home for Thanksgiving. I wasn't doing Christmas with that family under any circumstances. They always out-gifted me.

Things settled back down, and I was happy for it, for the most part. It was a return to the quiet life I had known, where no one knew I was a werecat and I had very little to fill my days except the bar and video games.

I was looking over my stock, knowing it was the last thing I needed to do before reopening, when someone knocked on the glass door.

"Closed!" I yelled. I didn't care who was out there, and I touched my magic, wondering if it was a supernatural. I had been too focused on my work, because it was—a werewolf. Idiotic of me, after everything that had happened, to ignore my bond with the land and miss one of those sneaking up on me.

"Even for me?" Heath called back.

I jumped up, running to the door. I swung it open and there he was, his grey-blue eyes lighter than I had ever seen them. He was happy.

"Come on in," I told him, holding the door open. "How have you been?" I had been hoping to see someone from the pack since the Tribunal, but none of them had visited me and I needed to put the time into getting my life back in order.

"Good. Officially retired from pack Alpha and the North American Werewolf Council," he said, sitting down next to my books. "Trying to reopen?"

"I am," I said, waving at them. "Have to get back to life as I know it, right?"

"Certainly," he agreed, looking down at what I was doing. "Stock. It's been years since I've managed a place like this, but I'd recognize stocking records anywhere."

"Yeah. It keeps me busy. Gives me something to do." I was nervous now. "So, how's retirement?"

"Quiet. I have two more weeks to move out of pack territory or there's going to be problems." He seemed okay with it, but I was just confused.

"Move out? Are they throwing you out?"

"No, no!" he said quickly, shaking his head. "I have to, for the good of the pack. If I stay, I inadvertently undermine Tywin's authority, which...is a little rocky. He's rounding up the rogues in the region, and establishing his inner circle...Landon and I needed to leave. Not far. We're going to stay nearby for our personal business, but we can't live in the city anymore."

"Wow, you wolves are ridiculous," I replied, laughing. "That's a lot for just wanting to retire."

"Isn't it? It's not a permanent retirement, though. They all know once Carey is an adult and there's an opening, I'll make a new pack."

"So, did you come just to catch up with me, or...? Not that I mind if you did, I just figured, after two weeks, that we were...well, done. You don't need me anymore and..."

"No, I'm here to ask a favor of you, actually," he admitted softly. "Your territory. How big is it?"

"I just expanded, actually. My territory now reaches forty miles in every direction from my house. I took over all of Tyler. Oops." I smirked. "Why?"

"I was hoping my family could move in," he answered, leaning back. My jaw dropped and he chuckled at my surprise. "A few nights ago, Carey had a nightmare. She didn't scream for me or Landon. She called for you. She wanted you to save her. She's fallen in love with you, Jacky, and now I'm a lone wolf. So is my son. We're not equipped to properly protect her—"

"Yes, you are," I retorted. "You just want an added layer of protection." It was a touch insulting. He was using me and I wasn't foolish enough to miss it or ignore it. It had to be called out.

"One that I trust, yes." He nodded, meeting my stare.

I thought about it, swallowing. "She really wanted me?" I asked, crossing my arms. I had to look away for a second.

"She did," he confirmed. "She's wanted to see you since you were taken by the Council. I took her to the Tribunal just to see you, because I thought it would be the last chance you both had. She adores you, Jacky, and I would be honored if you shared your space with us and helped me protect her."

"Where do you want to live?"

"We were thinking Tyler, but closer if we had to," he said, smiling. "Only an hour and a half from Dallas, it would be easy for Landon and me to commute when we need to. And yes, you'll be able to see her any time you want. It would be helpful, actually. I'm out of free babysitters. I have no teenage wolves to order around."

"Okay." I nodded. "Yeah, move in. You do know that I'll always be able to find you, right?"

"Even better. If you need Landon or I for anything dealing with Carey, that will come in handy."

"This is still my territory, wolf." I was firm, shoving a finger to my table. "That's clear, right? You're a guest. No moving other wolves in under my nose."

"Agreed," he promised, smiling. "Thank you for this, Jacky."

I grinned back, letting the tension in my posture go. "As long as we do game night. Carey can kick all our asses together."

"Deal." He extended his hand and I took it. "Friends?"

"Of course," I agreed. I made a split-second decision I probably shouldn't have. "I, Jacqueline Leon of the werecats, hereby do swear to protect Carey Everson from all harm that may befall her for as long as I shall live. I shall afford her the right to live in my territory with her family or legal guardians and to contact me when the need arises. I reserve the right to revoke this protection in exceptional cases."

"You cats and your oaths," Heath said softly, shaking his head. He couldn't hold back a smile, though. "You do me a great honor."

"You do me one." I meant every word of it.

An hour later, Carey and Landon walked in. I laughed as she hugged me, showing me her cast that now had dozens of names on it. We talked for hours and when they left, I felt better than I had in years. For the first time in a long time, I didn't feel lonely and didn't think I would for a long time.

Keep reading for more information about the next release, special news, and more.

DEAR READER,

Thank you for reading!

Jacky will be back for more adventures. I'm excited to begin this journey with her and you. She's exciting for me to write, and a refreshing change of page I hope you enjoyed as well.

If I still have you, head over to my website to get the latest updates on the next book in the series. Head over to my website and sign up for my mailing list! There are exclusive teasers for those who are signed up: Knbanet.com/newsletter

Also, I have a Patreon, where I write a monthly short story or novella. You can check that out here: Patreon.com/knbanet

And remember,

Reviews are always welcome, whether you loved or hated the book. Please consider taking a few moments to leave one and know I appreciate every second of your time and I'm thankful.

THE TRIBUNAL ARCHIVES

The Jacky Leon series is set in the world of The Tribunal. Every series and standalone novel is written so it can be read alone.

For more information about The Tribunal Archives and the different series in it, you can go here:

tribunalarchives.com

ACKNOWLEDGMENTS

I'm very bad at giving really public praise. I shower people in praise in private. But that's not everyone's love language and that's okay.

So this little page shall now be dedicated to everyone who helps me get these books from the concept to the release and beyond. From my PA, to my editor and my proofreader, to my wonderful friends helping me through the hardest moments. To my husband, who doesn't read my books, but loves that I write them and is willing to listen to me talk about them for hours.

And to you, the reader, for without you, I wouldn't have anyone to share these stories with. I'm a storyteller at heart and you have given me the greatest gift of listening.

I love all of you. Thank you for continuing to go on this journey with me.

ABOUT THE AUTHOR

KNBanet.com
Living in Arizona with her husband and 5 pets (2 dogs and 3 cats), K.N. Banet is a voracious... video game player. Actually, she spends most of her time writing, and when she's not writing she's either gaming or reading. She enjoys writing about the complexities of relationships, no matter the type. Familial, romantic, or even political. The connections between characters is what draws her into writing all of her work. The ideas of responsibility, passion, and forging one's own path all make appearances.

- facebook.com/KNBanet
- instagram.com/Knbanetauthor
- bookbub.com/authors/k-n-banet
- amazon.com/K.N.-Banet/e/B08412L9VV
- patreon.com/knbanet

ALSO BY K.N. BANET

The Jacky Leon Series

Oath Sworn

Family and Honor

Broken Loyalty

Echoed Defiance

Shades of Hate

Royal Pawn

Rogue Alpha

Bitter Discord

Volume One: Books 1-3

The Kaliya Sahni Series

Bounty

Snared

Monsters

Reborn

Legends

Destiny

Volume One: Books 1-3

The Everly Abbott Series

Servant of the Blood

Blood of the Wicked

Tribunal Archives Stories

Ancient and Immortal (Call of Magic Anthology)

Hearts at War

Full Moon Magic (Rituals and Runes Anthology)

Made in the USA
Las Vegas, NV
22 April 2024